W9-CEW-039

Alice-Miranda
in the Alps

MOTHER TERESA
Phone: 08 9591 7100
Fax: 08 9591 7105
731 Eighty Rd PO BOX 4200 BALDIVIS WA 6171
ABN: 75 518 849 663
Website: www.motherteresa.wa.edu.au

Books by Jacqueline Harvey

Alice-Miranda at School
Alice-Miranda on Holiday
Alice-Miranda Takes the Lead
Alice-Miranda at Sea
Alice-Miranda in New York
Alice-Miranda Shows the Way
Alice-Miranda in Paris
Alice-Miranda Shines Bright
Alice-Miranda in Japan
Alice-Miranda at Camp
Alice-Miranda at the Palace

Clementine Rose and the Surprise Visitor
Clementine Rose and the Pet Day Disaster
Clementine Rose and the Perfect Present
Clementine Rose and the Farm Fiasco
Clementine Rose and the Seaside Escape
Clementine Rose and the Treasure Box
Clementine Rose and the Famous Friend
Clementine Rose and the Ballet Break-In
Clementine Rose and the Movie Magic
Clementine Rose and the Birthday Emergency

Alice-Miranda in the Alps

Jacqueline Harvey

RANDOM HOUSE AUSTRALIA

A Random House book
Published by Random House Australia Pty Ltd
Level 3, 100 Pacific Highway, North Sydney NSW 2060
www.randomhouse.com.au

Penguin
Random House
Australia

First published by Random House Australia in 2015

Copyright © Jacqueline Harvey 2015

The moral right of the author and the illustrator has been asserted.

All rights reserved. No part of this book may be reproduced or transmitted by
any person or entity, including internet search engines or retailers, in any form
or by any means, electronic or mechanical, including photocopying (except
under the statutory exceptions provisions of the Australian *Copyright Act 1968*),
recording, scanning or by any information storage and retrieval system without
the prior written permission of Random House Australia.

Random House Books is part of the Penguin Random House group of
companies whose addresses can be found at global.penguinrandomhouse.com.

National Library of Australia
Cataloguing-in-Publication Entry

Creator: Harvey, Jacqueline
Title: Alice-Miranda in the Alps/Jacqueline Harvey
ISBN: 978 0 85798 274 2 (paperback)
Series: Harvey, Jacqueline. Alice-Miranda; 12
Target audience: For primary school age
Subjects: Skis and skiing – Juvenile fiction
            Vacations – Switzerland – Juvenile fiction
Dewey number: A823.4

Cover and internal illustrations by J.Yi
Cover design by Mathematics www.xy-1.com
Internal design by Midland Typesetters, Australia
Typeset in 13/18 pt Adobe Garamond by Midland Typesetters, Australia
Printed in Australia by Griffin Press, an accredited ISO AS/NZS 14001:2004
Environmental Management System printer

Random House Australia uses papers that are natural, renewable and recyclable
products and made from wood grown in sustainable forests. The logging
and manufacturing processes are expected to conform to the environmental
regulations of the country of origin.

For Ian, who took me to Switzerland,
for Mum and Dad, who introduced me to skiing,
and for Sandy, who loved to travel.

Prologue

The man tore off a chunk of bread from the loaf on the table and mopped up the remnants of the stew. He chewed slowly, under the weight of her silence. Once he finished eating, he wiped his mouth with a napkin and looked over at his daughter.

'Nina,' the man said calmly, 'I have no choice.'

'Please don't send Opa away,' the little girl begged. A tear escaped onto the top of her cheek. 'I can stay home and look after him.'

'No,' her father replied firmly. 'You must go to school, and he cannot be left on his own. You saw what happened last week and again yesterday. Would you have him burn down the house? Or shall we find him frozen on the mountain?'

'What about the museum?' the girl whispered. Her meal lay untouched in front of her.

Her father sighed, his eyes downcast. 'Your grandfather hasn't spent a day down there since . . .'

Nina could feel the heat rising to her cheeks. 'Say it, Papa. Say her name.'

The man buried his head in his hands. 'I cannot,' he breathed.

'You are not the only one who is hurting,' Nina said. She brushed her plait over her shoulder. 'I will look after things for now.'

'You're a *child*. I won't allow it,' the man said. 'Besides, Opa is the only person capable of running all those ridiculous contraptions.'

'You're wrong!' Nina shouted. She pushed her chair back and fled upstairs to the top floor.

Sebastien Ebersold stared at the doorway, wishing more than ever that he could rewind the clock and change that terrible day.

In a room just off the landing, Nina's grand-father lay in his bed. His eyes were closed but he had heard every word. It had always amazed him how the sound travelled in that big, old place. He couldn't remember how he had reached the peak. He could hear them shouting. It had seemed like hundreds of voices when in reality it was just two – two skiers urging him to come away from the edge; him standing there, feeling as if he might fly. There were days when he felt paralysed by his memories and others when it was as if he had fallen asleep and someone else was in charge of his ancient bones.

The door creaked open.

'Opa, are you awake?' Nina whispered.

'Yes, my dear.' He rolled over and looked at her, his weary eyes the colour of her favourite green marble.

The girl rushed to him and threw herself onto the man's chest. 'I won't let Papa send you away.' The tears she had been fighting flowed freely now.

'There, there, my Nina bear,' he said, touching her cheek lightly. 'Your father must do what he thinks best.'

'How can it be best for you to leave us?' Nina whispered, sitting up.

The old man reached across and opened the top drawer of his bedside table. He pulled out an exquisite silver box and cradled it in his palm. 'I want you to have this,' he said.

Nina gasped. 'But it's your favourite.'

He wound a tiny mechanism at the back of the box, and together they watched as its oval lid sprung open and a little bird began to trill, fluttering in a circle as if it were alive. When the creature finished its song, the lid shut once again. 'It is the most special, like you,' her grandfather said.

Nina stared at the case in wonder.

'Take it.' He pressed the box into her hand and smiled. 'Remember that whatever happens I love you from the mountain tops to the stars and all the way back again.'

Nina hugged him tightly. 'I love you too, Opa.'

Chapter 1

Hugh Kennington-Jones crept into the kitchen, where Alice-Miranda was standing on a stool beside her mother. The pair had their backs to him at the far bench, engrossed in their activity.

'Hello darlings,' he said loudly.

Startled, Alice-Miranda flicked the wooden spoon out of the batter she was stirring, sending splatters of gooey chocolate cake mix all over her mother's face.

Cecelia jumped in surprise and the pair spun around, bursting into laughter.

'Daddy, look what you made me do.' Alice-Miranda reached out and wiped a glob of mixture from her mother's nose, then popped her finger in her mouth. 'Yum, this is going to be a good cake.'

'Give me a taste.' Hugh wrapped an arm around his wife's waist and kissed her cheek. 'Mmm, that is good,' he said, grinning cheekily.

Cecelia rolled her eyes and tapped the ski goggles on his face. 'What on earth are you wearing?'

'Yes, why the balaclava, Daddy?' Alice-Miranda asked. 'Are you planning a heist?'

'I was just on the phone to Brigitte at the hotel in St Moritz. I wanted to make sure that we are all set for next week,' Hugh explained.

'And are we?' Cecelia giggled. 'You do know you look ridiculous.'

'I think Fanger's is going to be topnotch. They've given us an entire wing so everyone can be together,' Hugh said as he tried to dip his finger into the mixing bowl, only to have his daughter shoo him away.

Alice-Miranda's eyes twinkled. 'I can't wait.'

After cleaning up the mess, Cecelia picked up a large round cake tin and began to grease the inside of it. 'I think the White Turf racing is going to be spectacular.'

Alice-Miranda plunged the wooden spoon back into the batter. 'Are we going to see Uncle Florian and Aunt Giselle while we're there?' she asked.

Hugh shook his head. 'Each time I've tried Florian's cell it goes straight to one of those silly long-winded messages that end up telling you that you can't leave a message.'

Cecelia's brow puckered as she pushed up her sleeves. 'That's such a pity. It would have been lovely to have him and Giselle over for a few days. You know, last time we spoke I thought he seemed a little worried about the business.'

'But they're always so busy whenever we're there,' Alice-Miranda said.

'I wondered about that too, darling,' Hugh admitted, 'but their hotel was fully booked when I checked online. Otherwise, I would have suggested we spend another week and take the Glacier Express over to Zermatt. I much prefer skiing there than anywhere else and I think it's safer for the children, given there are no cars in the village.'

'I wish I could see Nina too,' Alice-Miranda said. 'We always have such fun together.'

Hugh nodded. 'I'll try again tomorrow. I think we should tell the ladies this afternoon – there's not enough time for Shilly to come up with any excuses now.'

Alice-Miranda and her mother grinned.

A mumble of voices grew louder as the family cook and the housekeeper walked in through the back door.

'Good heavens, are we being robbed?' Mrs Oliver cried in mock horror.

Hugh, Cecelia and Alice-Miranda laughed.

Mrs Shillingsworth shook her head. 'Sir, I know where your spare glasses are. There is no need to resort to those silly-looking things and, truly, it's not that cold out.'

'I thought I might spark a new trend.' Hugh took off the goggles and balaclava, plonking them onto the kitchen table. His hair was sticking up all over the place.

Dolly Oliver bustled over and picked up the teapot from the end of the bench. 'How's that cake coming along?'

'The mixture's delicious,' Alice-Miranda said as she helped her mother pour the batter evenly into the two tins. She gave them one final swirl, then licked the spatula.

'I hope you haven't pulled all the ski gear out

of the attic, Hugh Kennington-Jones,' Shilly said sternly. 'I knew exactly where everything was and I was planning to get it ready for you this afternoon.'

Hugh looked at her with his puppy-dog eyes. 'I was just trying to help and you know very well that you don't need to pack for me.'

'Yes, but this trip isn't just about you, sir. What sort of a mess am I going to find upstairs now?' the woman scolded.

'It's not a mess,' Hugh said. 'More of a mountain, really, and I was going to sort it out. Scout's honour.' He held up three fingers and gave a salute.

Shilly tutted, then walked to the sideboard and pulled down several teacups and saucers. Alice-Miranda turned and smiled at her father, who gave the child a wink.

'How are your ski legs, anyway, Shill?' Hugh asked.

'I haven't had any for longer than I care to remember,' the woman replied, 'and I don't suspect I'll be needing them again anytime soon.'

'I think you might,' Alice-Miranda said.

'What are you lot up to?' Dolly asked. She lifted the lid off the giant glass cake dome and began to cut several slices of date loaf for their morning tea.

'Well, we were thinking that you and Shilly might like a break,' Hugh began.

'We don't have time for a break,' Shilly said as she laid the table. 'I've got everyone booked in for the quarterly clean and then we've got the garden party planning and umpteen other things coming up.'

'Nonsense,' Cecelia said. 'We have plenty of time to get things done.'

'So, ladies, do you fancy a Swiss sojourn?' Hugh asked.

Shilly looked at Hugh and Dolly spun around.

Alice-Miranda jumped off her stool and clasped her hands together. 'Please say yes.'

'You don't need Shilly and I spoiling your fun,' Dolly said.

'You won't spoil anything,' Alice-Miranda insisted, her eyes wide.

'Plus, you could both do with a break,' Cecelia added. 'I promise, no looking after the children and you can do whatever takes your fancy.'

'I also heard that a certain someone has a birthday coming up,' Hugh weighed in.

Shilly rolled her eyes. 'Don't remind me. I feel like I'm a hundred.'

'You're only turning sixty-five, which is ages off one hundred,' Alice-Miranda said.

'And you're as fit as a fiddle,' Hugh added.

Cecelia nodded. 'Daisy collapsed in a heap last week after only half a day's work with you.'

Dolly opened her mouth to protest, but Hugh held up his palm like a policeman directing traffic. 'We won't hear another word from either of you. You're coming with us whether you like it or not.'

'Goodness me,' Shilly huffed, 'you two must be the bossiest bosses in the world.'

Alice-Miranda raced over and hugged the woman around her middle. Then she ran back to hug Mrs Oliver as well.

Dolly tried to suppress a grin. 'Yes, it's dreadful the way they insist on taking us on holidays to exotic locations.'

Shilly smiled too. 'Oh dear, Dolly, it looks like there's no getting out of this one.'

'Well, that solves that,' Hugh announced. 'Get your goggles, ladies. We're off to the Alps.'

Chapter 2

The doorbell buzzed sharply just as Delphine Doerflinger had climbed into bed.

'Otto, you nincompoop,' she grumbled, jamming her feet into her slippers. She grabbed the satin robe that was draped across the chaise lounge.

The bell buzzed again.

'I'm coming!' she shouted, scurrying down the wide corridor. 'Why didn't you get a spare key from reception? We live in a hotel, for heaven's sake!'

Delphine wrenched open the front door. 'You

will forget your brain one of these . . .' She stopped, realising that she was speaking to thin air. Delphine peered into the hallway at their private lift. 'Otto, I am not amused,' she called into the half-light. 'It is far too late in the evening for your silly games.'

But there was no reply.

Delphine huffed and turned to walk back inside when she kicked an envelope on the floor. She bent down to pick it up and saw her name written on it in floaty script. Delphine looked into the hallway again, her nerves jangled. She quickly closed the door and hurried to her study. She flicked on the lamp and reached across for the silver letter opener, slicing open the top and pulling out a single piece of paper.

You should not have made promises you cannot keep. You have two weeks.

Delphine began to shake. She could feel the fury rising within her like a dormant volcano shuddering back to life.

'How dare they?' she seethed. 'I am a woman of my word.'

'Delphine, my lovely, are you there?' Otto's voice echoed through the palatial suite, accompanied by the sound of claws tripping along the parquetry floor. 'Where are you, my little munchkin?'

A low, rumbling growl exploded into a series of high-pitched barks as Gertie, Otto's beloved Maltese terrier, nudged her way into the room and stood there yapping. The dog's perfectly coiffed hair skimmed the ground, and Delphine wondered if a more indulged animal had ever walked the earth. She only had her hair blow-dried once a week, while Gertie had a ten-o'clock appointment every other day.

'Get lost,' she hissed. But Delphine's words just served to further aggravate the animal. The creature rushed to her side and yapped ever more urgently.

Delphine hurriedly stuffed the letter under a pile of papers in the top drawer of her desk and quickly closed it.

'There you are, my dear. I thought you would be in bed by now.' Otto Fanger appeared in the doorway, his round silhouette taking up the width of its frame. As always, he was immaculately dressed in a three-piece suit. His wiry hair, despite an abundance of product, resembled a steel scouring pad sprouting from the front of his head. At least it gave him some much-needed height, Delphine supposed. 'Gertie, come to Papa,' he instructed.

The little dog danced around her master's legs before he scooped her into his arms, cooing and cuddling the creature as if she were a baby. Gertie's tongue shot out and licked Otto's rosy cheek.

Delphine rolled her eyes. 'Life does not stop just because you take the evening off to play silly card games.'

'You work much too hard, my petal,' Otto simpered.

'And one day you will thank me.' Delphine stood up and switched off the desk lamp, putting an end to the conversation. She knew what she had to do. Losing the hotel was never going to happen as long as there was still breath in her body.

Otto Fanger looked up from his newspaper. 'Good morning, my darling heart,' he said happily.

'Why is it so good?' Delphine asked as a waiter in a crisp black suit rushed to pull out the chair for her.

'Every morning is a good morning with you, my love,' Otto replied with a smile. He folded his newspaper and set it aside. Gertie lay on a plump velvet cushion on the chair to his right, her head resting on the arm.

'Stop that,' Delphine snapped as the waiter attempted to shake a starched napkin onto her lap. 'I can do it.'

The man gulped and scurried away.

Otto gazed out at the glistening white peaks and the frozen lake beyond the snow-covered roof of the building. 'The sun is shining, the lake is sparkling and the hotel is full,' he continued dreamily.

Delphine rolled her eyes.

The ornate dining room was indeed busy with families and couples, many of them dressed in their ski gear, ready to head up onto the mountain straight after breakfast. On a podium at the end of the room, a harpist with flowing blonde hair serenaded the diners with the melodious plunking of strings, the tune instantly recognisable as Pachelbel's Canon.

Another waiter walked up to their table and placed a large plate of bacon, fried eggs, hash browns, tomatoes and sausages in front of Otto.

The hotelier patted his stomach with glee. 'Thank you. This looks delicious.'

A dour woman with pinched cheeks and a nose like a needlefish, Delphine eyed the plate with disgust. 'You eat too much bacon, Otto. It is no wonder I am having to arrange for your suits to be let out again.'

Otto waved a hand in her direction and concentrated on his breakfast. Every now and then he passed a titbit to Gertie, who, despite her genteel appearance, wolfed it down like a starved hyena.

Yet another waiter descended upon the table, depositing a latte and a plate of buttered toast in front of Delphine. 'I took the liberty of having some toast made for you, Frau Doerflinger.' The young man smiled tightly.

'That toast is burned and you have overfilled my coffee,' Delphine spat, her tongue clearly as sharp as her nose. When the young man went to remove the offending items, she swatted his hand away. 'What do you think you are doing now?' she barked.

'Getting you some more toast and coffee?' The fellow's voice had risen from an alto to a soprano and he looked to be on the verge of tears.

'Leave them, you numbskull.' Delphine turned her attention to the red folder she had brought with her. She flipped it open and ran her finger down the list of names. It was a ritual she performed every morning, making sure that she was familiar with any

VIPs or celebrities. 'Interesting,' she said, taking a sip of her coffee.

Otto paused for a moment and picked up the salt shaker. 'What is interesting?'

'We have some very important guests about to arrive,' Delphine replied. 'They have unfortunately chosen to bring young ones too. Urgh, how ghastly.'

'*All* of our guests are important. That is why Fanger's Palace Hotel is the best in the whole of Switzerland,' Otto said. 'I do love having children in the hotel. It makes me feel young again, and Gertie just adores them.'

'Yes, yes,' Delphine muttered. Otto was a fool. She knew the value of ensuring that their very special guests were taken care of. The others, well, there would always be people with delusions of grandeur willing to part with their hard-earned money. But there were far weightier matters on her mind than the guest register. Delphine closed the file and looked at her husband. 'Otto, I have been thinking about expansion,' she said.

'Stop talking about my waistline, woman,' Otto huffed, shovelling another forkful of food into his mouth. 'I promise you I will go for a walk this afternoon.'

'I wasn't talking about your gut this time,' Delphine replied, arching a generously plucked eyebrow.

'Then you must have whatever you want, my dear. There is the plot of land to the side of the hotel. What are you thinking?' he asked. 'A helipad, perhaps?'

'Something a little more than that,' she began.

'I don't think we will be allowed to go up any higher,' Otto said, shaking his head. 'Besides, it would destroy the beautiful roofline of the building, and if we consider anything further down the hill we will have to supply our guests with canoes to get to their rooms.'

'I want to buy another hotel,' Delphine said impatiently.

'Another hotel?' Otto looked at her. 'But you have enough to do just running this one and the chocolate factory. And you know there is only one other hotel in Switzerland that I have ever coveted and he will never sell.'

A smug smile perched on Delphine's lips. 'What if I heard that he might?'

Otto almost spat out his food. 'Are you toying with me?'

'I am deadly serious,' Delphine replied. 'He is broke.'

'Then we must buy it at once. I will be the King of the Alps!' Otto puffed out his chest and sat up ramrod straight in his chair. 'Or perhaps just the Baron.'

Delphine smiled. 'I do not think the title comes with the hotel, but I am sure we could buy you one if your heart so desires.'

Otto put his cutlery down on the plate and reached over to take Delphine's hand into his own. He raised it to his lips and kissed it gently. 'You are so clever, my love,' he gushed.

'And you are clever to know it,' Delphine replied. 'I take it that I have your blessing?'

'My beautiful wife, you have my blessing to do whatever makes you happy.' Otto released her hand and resumed eating.

Delphine rolled her eyes. She was a lot of things but beautiful was not one of them. Otto hadn't married her for her looks. He had married her for her brains, and while her husband liked to think that Fanger's Palace Hotel was thriving as a result of his years of hard work, that was far from the truth. He had no idea how much it cost to keep the hotel running let alone that ridiculous chocolate factory, which was bleeding money like cherry kirsch. If it wasn't for Delphine and her connections, things would have turned out very differently indeed.

Fortunately, when Otto's ancestors had built the hotel many years before, they had the foresight to install a vault. It had steel walls three-feet thick and a patented security system the world's best safecrackers could not penetrate. People paid handsomely to have their most precious possessions securely stored there, and Delphine had recently attracted some serious deposits, although the increasing demands of one client was giving her indigestion. Delphine drained the last drop of her coffee and stood up.

'Where are you going?' Otto asked. He was just beginning to butter his fourth slice of toast.

'There is work to be done,' Delphine said. 'I will see you at the drinks party this evening. Don't forget to collect your suit. I will not have you wear that other one with the buttons bursting off the front.'

'I can fit into my other suit just fine,' Otto sulked.

Gertie growled.

'No, you can't.' Delphine leaned across and kissed her husband's forehead, then picked up her folder and strode off.

Otto sat there for another hour, gobbling down the rest of his toast, which was followed by a large plate of pastries, a second cup of coffee and then two pancakes for good measure. He couldn't think of a more perfect way to spend the day as his guests stopped to say hello and chat about their planned activities. He was the self-proclaimed King of St Moritz and now there was a chance he could be King of Zermatt as well. Life was indeed very good for Herr Fanger.

Chapter 3

The passengers erupted into rapturous applause as the plane slowed to a standstill on the runway at Samedan Airport. Hugh Kennington-Jones's voice came over the intercom from where he was sitting beside the pilot in the cockpit. The man was in the process of gaining his pilot's licence and was co-piloting the jet for the first time. 'Well done, Cyril. That's the hairiest landing we've had in ages.'

Alice-Miranda turned to Millie, whose face was the colour of her mint-green cardigan. 'Are you all right?' she asked.

The girl breathed a huge sigh of relief. 'I didn't think we were going to make it.'

Dolly Oliver looked over at her friend, who gradually released her from a vice-like grip. 'May I have my hand back now, Shilly?'

'I told you we should have stayed home,' the woman said, her face blanched. 'I'd rather clean the entrance-hall chandeliers on stilts than face another flight like that.'

'No offence, anyone, but I'd rather catch a bigger plane next time,' Jacinta squeaked.

The Highton-Smith-Kennington-Joneses' private jet was a luxurious affair but it was true that, in poor conditions, passengers were well aware of every shudder and shake. The jet had bumped and bounced all over the place as it had made its approach through the Alps.

Sloane Sykes looked at them as if they were mad. 'I don't know what you're all whingeing about. It was fantastic. And that view! Those mountains are stunning and the lake shimmered as if it were covered in diamonds.'

Alice-Miranda grinned across the aisle at the girl. 'I'm glad you got to see it, Sloane. I think everyone else had their eyes closed.'

'I know I did,' Hamish McNoughton-McGill agreed. His wife, Pippa, bit her lip and nodded.

Sep and Lucas were busy discussing how they could pass themselves off as eighteen-year-olds so they could do the famous Olympia Bob Run. It was all the boys had thought about since Hugh had informed them that the bobsleigh course was open to the public. They'd both been horribly disappointed when he'd told them there was an age limit.

'Sorry about the rough treatment, everyone – we hit some clear air turbulence up there,' Cyril said over the intercom. 'Samedan is renowned for being a bit tricky. Hopefully it won't be nearly so bad when we fly out.'

'I think I'll walk home,' Millie whispered.

'Me too,' her father said, and everyone laughed.

Millie hadn't realised they'd all heard her, and blushed.

'Now that we're back on solid ground,' Cyril continued, 'welcome to St Moritz, where the current temperature is minus five degrees centigrade with a stiff breeze coming in from the north.'

'If that's what Cyril calls a stiff breeze, I'd hate to see what he makes of a hurricane,' Lucas said to Sep.

'We're here safe and sound and that's the main thing.' Cecelia smiled thinly at the children. For the first time in many flights, she'd been worried too, but she wasn't keen to pass on her concerns lest the children be any more terrified than they already were.

As the plane came to a halt and the engines powered down, Hugh emerged from the cockpit. 'Right then, let's head over to the hotel, shall we?'

'Hats and coats on, kids,' Cecelia instructed.

Everyone stood up and began to gather their belongings.

Sloane turned to her brother, who had suddenly taken on the appearance of a polar bear. 'What *are* you wearing?'

'It's my hat. Cool, isn't it?' Sep said.

Sloane rolled her eyes and pulled on a stylish pink beanie. 'If you're four, maybe.'

Cecelia ushered the children down the steps and onto the freezing tarmac, where they were greeted by an immigration official. The man in a navy puffer jacket and beanie checked the pile of passports Cecelia had gathered together.

'Enjoy your stay,' he said once he was done, nodding at the group politely.

Cyril filled out the necessary paperwork while Hugh and Hamish helped to unload the luggage. It was swiftly collected by three men dressed in red overcoats with gold buttons and navy trim. They all wore peaked caps with the words 'Fanger's Palace Hotel' emblazoned on the brim and quickly deposited the bags into the back of two black mini-vans parked close by.

Cecelia shivered. 'Hop in, everyone. It doesn't matter which van you pick; they're both headed to the same place.'

Soon enough the vehicles were hurtling along the main road towards the famous resort town of St Moritz. It was only a short journey to the hotel, which was positioned right above the frozen lake. Everyone gazed out of the van windows at the picture-postcard views as the sun disappeared over the mountain.

Sloane gasped. 'It's so pretty.'

'People always say that Switzerland has the best scenery,' Millie added, whipping out a guidebook from her jacket pocket. She flipped it open to a dog-eared page. 'Switzerland is famous for its watches, chocolates, alpine pursuits and banks,' she read aloud.

Sloane wrinkled her nose. 'Banks?'

Alice-Miranda nodded. 'Did you know the Swiss didn't fight in either of the world wars? Switzerland is what's called a neutral country. They don't take sides.'

'So they've never had a fight with anyone?' Jacinta asked.

Alice-Miranda shook her head. 'Not for a very long time.'

'Boring,' Sloane quipped. 'What's everyone's favourite colour here? Beige?'

'Does that look beige to you?' Alice-Miranda pointed out the window as they rounded a corner, revealing a backdrop of a glistening lake and soaring mountain peaks.

'Guess not,' Sloane said. 'What's the event your mother's sponsoring again?'

'Alice-Miranda told us at school,' Jacinta interjected.

'Yes, but I wasn't listening properly,' Sloane replied.

Jacinta rolled her eyes. 'How unusual.'

'It's called White Turf,' Alice-Miranda said.

'But how can turf be white?' Sloane asked.

'Well, this time it is,' Millie said mysteriously.

Jacinta shook her head. 'You really didn't listen, did you?'

Sloane thought for a moment. 'Oh, it's the horse-racing in the snow. I remember now.'

'Not the snow – the lake,' Alice-Miranda replied.

'The lake?' Sloane pulled a face. 'But they'll drown!'

'The lake's frozen, you nong,' Jacinta said. 'But I still wonder how they stay upright. I'm bad enough on ice skates with two legs, let alone four.'

Alice-Miranda giggled. 'The horses don't wear skates. They have spikes on their shoes so they can grip onto the ice.'

'That sounds ridiculous,' Sloane said. 'I bet they still fall over.'

'Apparently they've been doing it for a hundred years. There are races with riders and other races where skiers are towed behind the horses,' Alice-Miranda explained. 'It all sounds very exciting.'

'Can you imagine Chops doing that? He'd probably rather build a snowman.' Millie grinned, her eyes on stalks as she drank in the view. 'Look up there!' she exclaimed, pointing to a cable car that was making its way slowly up the mountain.

Sloane's stomach twisted. 'When are we going skiing?' she asked.

Sadly, the girl's alpine ability was a little bit like her horseriding prowess. She'd talked it up a lot but was in actual fact utterly hopeless. Or at least she was on the couple of occasions her parents had taken her and Sep to the snow.

'If I know Hugh, he'll have you children fitted out with your skis this evening and you'll be on the slopes tomorrow morning,' Dolly piped up.

'You know, I'm sure Daddy would be happy to arrange some lessons,' Alice-Miranda said, noticing Sloane's discomfort. 'My parallel turns are abysmal, so I could do with a couple.'

Sloane gave her a nervous smile.

'What about you, Mrs Oliver? Are you going to come up the mountain with us?' Millie asked.

'I don't know, dear. I don't want to risk breaking anything,' the woman replied.

Alice-Miranda peered through the gap in the seats. 'Will you ski, Shilly?'

The old woman nodded and smiled. 'I think I might.'

'Really?' Dolly turned to her friend in surprise. 'I had no idea that was one of your talents.'

Shilly grinned. 'Well, when I was a lot younger I was actually quite good at it and being here has made me wonder, just a little bit.'

Dolly clicked her tongue. 'Oh, well, perhaps I will take a few steady runs then.'

'That's the spirit, ladies,' Millie said as the van pulled into the front of the beautiful Fanger's Palace Hotel.

Chapter 4

The group waited in the large lobby as Cecelia and Pippa organised the keys and room allocations at reception. Alice-Miranda had meanwhile greeted all of the doormen and had now moved on to the staff at the concierge desk.

'We could be here all day if she says hello to *everyone* who works here,' Jacinta whispered to Millie. She glanced around at the huge number of staff that were coming and going.

Millie grinned. 'Just try and stop her.'

A young woman with a neat blonde ponytail gathered the party around her. 'Good afternoon, everyone. My name is Brigitte and I will escort you to your rooms in just a few minutes.' She held out a tray of exquisitely wrapped chocolates. 'Please take one.'

'These look amazing,' Millie said as she peeled off the gold wrapper and popped the treat into her mouth. The girl bit down on the confection and sighed dramatically. 'That's the best chocolate I've ever tasted.'

'They are Fanger's own,' Brigitte said proudly.

Sloane's eyes lit up. 'Is there a chocolate factory *in* the hotel?'

Brigitte chuckled. 'There is a shop downstairs,' she replied, 'but our chocolates are made in a beautiful old monastery in Disentis. The company just won a prestigious award.'

The others eagerly unwrapped their treats and were overcome with the same ecstatic expressions.

Dolly nodded with satisfaction. 'I can well imagine Fanger's being awarded for their chocolate.'

Brigitte shook her head. 'You mistake me. This award was for their innovative climate-controlled reusable packaging,' she said. 'The chocolates can be

33

sent anywhere in the world in any climate and will arrive in perfect condition.'

'Fascinating,' Dolly marvelled, making a mental note to look it up when she was next on the computer. She was always interested in new inventions, particularly when they were anything to do with food.

'Look,' Jacinta whispered to Millie.

A short, round man in a grey suit was walking towards them, his jacket buttons straining against his bulk. He was carrying a small white dog wearing diamond-encrusted hairclips that held back her very long fringe. However, his own hair was a wild affair, with a wave-like section at the front standing straight up in the air.

'Hello, who do we have here?' he asked, approaching the group.

Brigitte smiled at the man. 'Herr Fanger, may I present Mr Kennington-Jones and his party,' she said, before introducing everyone.

'Are those real?' Sloane blurted, ogling the dog's hair accessories.

The man kissed the top of the pooch's head. 'Only diamonds for my little princess.' He shook Hugh's hand firmly. 'Welcome, welcome, it is my great honour to have you here at Fanger's Palace Hotel, the finest establishment in the world.'

Millie thought that was a very bold statement. It looked rather posh from the lobby but whether it was the best hotel in the whole wide world was yet to be seen.

'It's very good to meet you too, Herr Fanger. Who's your friend?' Hugh was about to give the little dog a pat when the creature growled and snapped at him.

'Please forgive my Gertie. She's daddy's girl,' Herr Fanger said, depositing the creature into the arms of a nearby bellboy.

The young lad eyed the terrier warily.

'Take her for potty,' Herr Fanger instructed, 'and make sure that you . . . you know.' The hotelier made a wiping motion with his hand.

The bellboy looked at him blankly.

'Do I have to spell it out for you?' Otto pulled a packet of baby wipes from inside his jacket. 'Wipe her bottom.'

The children giggled. Hamish and Hugh couldn't help but guffaw, though they quickly covered their mouths and pretended to cough.

'My apologies,' Otto Fanger said. He glanced at the empty tray Brigitte was holding. 'I see you have sampled my chocolate.'

'They were the best chocolates ever!' Millie enthused.

'Why, then you must have more,' Otto said, waggling his head up and down.

Brigitte scurried away, returning a minute later with a large gold box. Otto removed the lid and Brigitte offered the chocolates to the group.

'I can personally recommend all of them. I take quality control very seriously,' Otto remarked with utmost sincerity.

Sloane nudged Jacinta and grinned. 'Gee, you could never tell,' she whispered.

The man took a toffee-covered sweet and popped it into his mouth.

'I think we're ready to go up now, darling,' Cecelia called to her husband. 'I've booked dinner for seven-thirty at a pizza place in the village. I thought the children might prefer that tonight.'

Otto Fanger swept towards the women, blocking their path. 'No, no, no, no, no.' He held up both hands, waving them about like windscreen wipers. 'You must not proceed until I have the pleasure of making your acquaintances,' Otto said theatrically.

'Oh, I'm Cecelia Highton-Smith and this is Pippa McLoughlin-McTavish.' The woman looked at the man quizzically, then at her husband, who shrugged. The fellow rather reminded her of Mr Plumpton,

Alice-Miranda's Science teacher, although he was quite a bit wider and a lot more confident.

'I am Otto Fanger and it is my joy to have you here in my hotel.' He smiled at the ladies, then turned back to Hugh and Hamish. 'My dear gentlemen, you are both very lucky men. Your wives are beautiful!' At that moment, Delphine Doerflinger walked into the foyer and shot her husband a dark look. 'So, of course, is my own precious wife and here she is now. Come and meet the Highton-Smith-Kennington-Joneses and their friends, my petal.'

The corners of Delphine's mouth twitched ever so slightly before turning upwards into a smile. She was dressed in a black skirt suit with a crisp white shirt. Her hair, pulled tautly into a French roll, made her angular features seem even more pinched.

'Please allow me to introduce my wife, Delphine Doerflinger,' Otto said as Delphine strode towards them.

'I wonder if she can,' Sep muttered.

Lucas frowned. 'Can what?'

'Fling doors,' Sep said, sniggering.

'Lame.' Sloane shook her head slowly. 'So lame.'

'It is very good to meet you all,' the woman said warmly. 'I do hope you enjoy your stay with us.'

'The children are looking forward to exploring the hotel,' Cecelia said.

'Of course they are,' Delphine replied. 'Now, if you would please excuse me, I have some urgent business to attend to.'

Just as Frau Doerflinger turned to leave, there was a kerfuffle at the entrance to the hotel. Everyone looked over to see the revolving door spinning wildly.

'Come back!' someone shouted.

There was a flash of white as Gertie skidded through several pairs of legs, racing towards the group.

'Stop her!' the young bellboy yelped, clutching a handful of soiled baby wipes.

'Gertie, come to Papa,' Otto called, his arms outstretched.

But the pampered pooch had no intention of coming to Papa. Instead, she barrelled straight into Cecelia's legs. The woman squealed and threw her hands up in the air, knocking into Delphine and sending their key cards sliding all over the floor.

Delphine Doerflinger looked set to explode. 'You naughty mutt,' she hissed.

Otto snatched the dog into his arms. 'Gertie, my precious. What has upset you so?' He glared at the bellboy.

'I d-d-don't know,' the fellow stammered. 'She did not take kindly to my attentions.'

Otto turned to Cecelia. 'My apologies, madame, please let me help you.' He tried to bend down and pick up the cards but negotiating his stomach and the dog was proving too difficult.

Delphine rolled her eyes, then swooped down and gathered the keys herself. 'Here, let me get them sorted for you.'

'No, please don't fuss,' Cecelia insisted. 'It won't take a minute to work it out when we're upstairs. You have somewhere to be.'

'Yes, of course.' Frau Doerflinger smiled tightly and handed over the key cards. 'Otto, please see that our guests have everything they need,' she said sternly before striding away.

'I wouldn't want to be Herr Fanger tonight,' Millie whispered to Alice-Miranda and Sloane.

Sloane nodded. 'She's fierce.'

'I am terribly sorry about that,' Otto said. 'Gertie is a little overly enthusiastic at times. Please, may I personally invite you all to a cocktail reception in the lounge at six o'clock tonight? Might I ask how long you will be staying with us?'

'We'll be here until the weekend,' Hugh replied. 'We usually ski in Zermatt but my wife's company, Highton's, are sponsoring one of the races on Sunday.'

'Ah, Zermatt – another lovely resort,' the man replied. 'But, alas, it does not have the White Turf. It is the most glorious spectacle – all those beautiful people and beautiful horses on that beautiful frozen lake. There is so much beauty your eyes will ache.'

The children giggled.

'Where, may I ask, do you stay when you are in Zermatt?' Otto asked.

'The Grand Hotel Von Zwicky,' Hugh replied.

'It's owned by our dear friend the Baron,' Cecelia added.

'That is a lovely hotel,' Otto agreed. 'I would like to own it myself.'

'Sadly, Herr Fanger, I don't think it will be for sale anytime soon,' Hugh replied. 'The Baron and Baroness love their hotel as much as you love yours.'

Otto chuckled. 'Yes, we will see.'

Hugh frowned, wondering exactly what the man meant by that.

Gertie barked loudly.

'What is it, my princess?' Otto leaned towards the mutt, whose tongue shot out and licked him on the side of his lip.

Sloane screwed up her nose. 'Gross,' she whispered.

'I think my baby is wanting her supper,' Otto said with a grin. 'See you again soon,' he trilled as Brigitte guided the family to the lift at the end of the corridor.

Delphine Doerflinger checked her watch as she rushed down the stairs. Her delivery would be arriving any minute and she still had to check the paperwork. She swiped her key card, then pushed the door open and hurried along to a small lift.

Delphine reached inside her skirt pocket, her fingers searching the folds of the fabric. Her stomach lurched and her heart began to hammer like a drum when she realised the key was gone. Had she left it upstairs? No, she remembered putting it in her pocket as she always did. Delphine breathed deeply.

'Calm down and think,' she muttered to herself. 'Where could you have lost it?'

It must have fallen out when that confounding animal caused all the fuss, Delphine thought. There was no time to search for it now. She'd have to find it later, and thankfully there was the spare in her office safe. Even though she couldn't imagine anyone would know what to do with it, the idea that a key to the Fanger's vault was lost in the hotel was unsettling to say the least.

Chapter 5

Millie pulled back the floor-to-ceiling curtains in the enormous bedroom she and Alice-Miranda were sharing. The windows looked out on the lake with the majestic Alps as a backdrop.

'That view is amazing,' she said, running to get her camera.

'Look at all the marquees over there,' Alice-Miranda said. 'That must be the racetrack.'

'Wow!' Millie snapped away, taking pictures from every angle.

'It looks tiny but I suppose that's just because the lake is enormous,' Jacinta said. She and Sloane had already unpacked and had come to work out where they should go exploring first.

Everyone had been shown to their rooms by Brigitte and was busy settling into their sumptuous accommodation. Shilly and Dolly each had their own rooms at the end of the corridor, with Sloane and Jacinta bunked in together next door to Mrs Oliver. Pippa and Hamish came next and had volunteered to have Sep and Lucas in their spare room, while Millie and Alice-Miranda's bedroom adjoined the sitting room of Hugh and Cecelia's gorgeous suite. The entire wing had its own separate entrance hall from the hotel corridor.

'What do you think, kids?' Cecelia said, poking her head in from the sitting room.

'It's heavenly,' Jacinta gushed, falling back onto the puffy duvet on Millie's bed.

Sep walked into the room, waving a brochure, with Lucas right behind him. 'Hey, have you guys seen this?'

'What is it?' Millie asked, turning away from the window to take his picture.

'Well, you know how they have the bobsleigh

run here?' Sep said excitedly. 'There's this other, even madder thing called the –'

'Cresta,' Hugh said, striding into the room. 'Riders race headfirst down an ice track on little sleds.'

'Headfirst,' Lucas gasped. 'Cool!'

Sloane shuddered.

'Is there an age limit for that too?' Lucas asked.

Sep scanned the page and nodded. 'You have to be eighteen years old and apparently girls aren't allowed to do it at all.'

'What? That's stupid!' Millie protested. 'Girls can do anything boys can. I wonder who made *that* rule.'

'Daddy, can we go and watch the people on the Cresta?' Alice-Miranda asked. 'Even if we can't do it, it would be fun to see.'

Hugh nodded. 'I'd love to. I might even have a go myself.'

'You most certainly will not, Hugh Kennington-Jones,' Cecelia said, shaking her head. 'We need you in one piece.'

Hugh pouted and blinked his big brown eyes.

'Don't even try that puppy-dog look on me,' Cecelia said, wagging her finger. 'It won't work.'

But there was a cheeky glint in Hugh's eye that neither of the boys missed. He gave the lads a wink.

'I'm going to make a suggestion,' Cecelia announced brightly. 'Why don't you kids go and explore the hotel while us oldies rest for half an hour? We're due at Herr Fanger's cocktail party at six o'clock, so you can meet us in the lobby at five to. Just don't leave the hotel. We can go for a walk around the village after dinner.'

'That's a good idea, Mummy,' Alice-Miranda said, hopping off her bed.

'Don't forget to take your key.' Cecelia handed her daughter a swipe card that was sitting on the dressing table.

'I'll get the lift,' Millie called, rushing off ahead of the others.

The hallway was lined with ornate antique armoires, side tables and lamps. Millie pressed the button and waited while the others caught up. As the bell dinged, the doors slid open and Frau Doerflinger strode out, clutching a red folder to her chest.

Millie smiled up at her. 'Hel–'

But the woman turned on her heel and stalked to the end of the hall.

'–lo.' Millie scoffed and pulled a face. 'Lovely to see you again too, Frau Doerflinger.'

'Wow, she's not exactly friendly,' Sloane said as she watched the woman disappear through a door marked 'Private'.

'Perhaps Frau Doerflinger has a lot of things on her mind,' Alice-Miranda said. 'Running a hotel must be a very busy job.'

'Yeah, except that I thought service was the name of the game,' Jacinta pointed out. 'Her husband seemed nice enough, but did you notice that she only paid attention to the adults? I have a feeling she doesn't like kids very much at all.'

Alice-Miranda lingered in the hallway as the children piled into the lift. She had a strange feeling that someone was watching them, and turned to see that the door Frau Doerflinger had gone through was slightly ajar. She peered at it and could have sworn that someone was there.

'Hurry up, Alice-Miranda.' Jacinta beckoned as the lift doors began to close.

Lucas reached out and pressed the button to reopen them.

'Coming,' the girl called, looking back again to find that the door marked 'Private' was now firmly closed.

Chapter 6

The children hurried into the reception area, eager for directions to the hotel swimming pool and to find out if there was a games room too. A concierge looked up and greeted them with a smile. 'Hello there. How may I help you?' he asked.

'Hello,' Alice-Miranda said. 'We were hoping to find the pool.'

While they waited for the man to draw them a map, Millie gazed around admiring the decor in the hotel foyer. Her eyes came to rest upon something shiny poking out from the base of a huge ceramic pot beside the concierge desk. She bent down to pick it up.

'What's that?' Sloane asked.

Millie shrugged. 'It looks like a coin, but I don't know where it's from.' She turned it over in her fingers. There was a mountain goat on one side and a cross on the other.

'You'd better hand it in,' Alice-Miranda suggested.

Millie hesitated for a second. It was so pretty and shiny. 'Excuse me, sir, I just found this on the floor,' she said, holding up her treasure.

The concierge took it from her and examined the little gold disc. 'It must have been attached to a box of chocolates. See, there is the goat of the mountains and the cross for the Swiss flag – the symbol on Fanger's Chocolate.'

'May I keep it?' Millie asked.

'Of course,' he said, dropping it back into the girl's hand with a friendly smile.

Millie grinned and put it into her jacket pocket. 'Maybe it will be my good-luck charm.'

The children thanked the man for his help before weaving through the enormous lounge area with its timber ceilings and comfortable leather couches.

There were several groups of tourists enjoying a late afternoon tea.

They followed the concierge's map to a staircase at the far end of the room and scampered down several flights, where they found the entrance to the hotel spa. Huge glass doors led into a cave-like grotto with a gigantic swimming pool. Along its farthest side were floor-to-ceiling windows that looked out on a magnificent view of the lake and the Alps.

'Look, there's another pool outside,' Sep said as he spied steam rising amid the snow-covered outdoor furniture.

'Wow – we should try it later,' Sloane said.

'It's supposed to be really good for you to run through the snow and then leap into the hot water,' Alice-Miranda said.

Millie shivered at the thought. 'No, thank you.'

Alice-Miranda grinned at her friend. 'Maybe we could ice-skate on the tennis courts instead. Daddy said they freeze over in the winter, so it's impossible to play, and they use it as a skating rink instead.'

The children walked into the pool area to take a closer look.

'It must be boiling.' Millie leaned down and dipped her hand in. 'Yup, it's sort of like the *onsen* in Tokyo except we'll get to keep our clothes on this time.'

Jacinta cringed. 'Don't remind me. That was the most embarrassing day of my life.'

'I wish I could have been there,' Sloane said.

'Trust me,' Millie replied, 'that's one experience you wouldn't mind missing out on.'

Sloane and Sep sat down on two of the reclining lounge chairs beside the pool. The other kids quickly joined them.

'Who wants to go for a swim after dinner?' Jacinta asked.

There was a chorus of yeses as hands shot up in the air.

'Maybe we could go ice-skating tomorrow night,' Alice-Miranda suggested.

'We should visit the Cresta Run tomorrow too, because they don't do it every day,' Sep added.

Alice-Miranda nodded. She glanced at the clock above the door and was surprised to find it was already quarter to six. 'Oops,' she said, jumping up. 'We'd better get going. We have to meet the adults in ten minutes.'

'That looks like a short cut,' Jacinta said. She pointed to a sign on a door labelled 'Lounge', just to the left of the spa reception.

'Are you sure?' Millie said doubtfully. 'What does it say on the map, Alice-Miranda?'

'Well, I can't really tell,' the child replied, trying to decipher the concierge's scribbles.

'We might as well give it a go,' Lucas said, heading for the door.

The rest of them followed him down the passage to a door where a man in black had just walked through. The boy caught the handle before it closed. They scooted inside, none of them noticing the 'Private' sign which had fallen off and was lying face-down on the floor.

They walked along an empty hallway, the decor having deteriorated significantly from the beautifully panelled walls and luxurious light fittings.

Sloane fidgeted nervously. 'Maybe we should just go back the way we came,' she whispered.

'Why? Are you scared?' Jacinta teased.

The girl lifted her chin. 'No. It's just that this doesn't exactly look like the rest of the hotel,' Sloane replied.

The children walked to the end of a hallway and turned left. Halfway along the passage they came upon a lift and piled inside.

Millie frowned at the four buttons on the panel. 'Which level do you think we're on?' she asked.

'Well, our rooms are on the eighth floor,' Alice-Miranda said, 'but I think Daddy mentioned that reception is on the fourth. So . . .'

'Let's try the top one,' Sep said just as his sister hit the button for the second floor.

The doors closed but, instead of going up as they expected, it felt like they were going down. The lift soon shuddered to a halt and the doors peeled back to reveal a large storeroom. There were green sacks piled up in one corner, and crates of wine and champagne, foldaway beds, discarded furniture and various bric-a-brac crammed in all over the place.

'Hold the door and I'll try to figure out where we are,' Lucas said, stepping out of the lift.

'I don't really like it down here,' Sloane said, biting on her thumbnail.

Sep rolled his eyes at her. 'Well, then you shouldn't have pressed the button.'

'We're in the loading dock,' Lucas called back to them. 'I think this is where the chocolate is delivered.'

'How do you know that?' Jacinta asked.

'There's boxes and boxes of it,' the boy replied.

At the mention of chocolate, Millie shot out of the lift and around the corner, with Alice-Miranda and the others following close behind her. Stacks of large white boxes bearing the Fanger's Chocolate logo sat alongside crates of champagne.

Jacinta grinned. 'My mother's two favourite things.'

'These must be the award-winning carriers,' Alice-Miranda said, studying the temperature controls on the side of the sturdy-looking boxes.

'Fancy another taste?' Lucas asked as he undid the clip locks on one of the carriers. Inside were rows of beautifully wrapped chocolate bars. He reached in to take one. 'Whoa, look at the size of them.'

'Lucas!' Alice-Miranda scolded. 'They're not for us.'

The boy looked at his cousin and then at Jacinta, who shook her head at him. He sighed and put the lid back on. 'I guess we couldn't eat that much chocolate, anyway.'

Millie wrinkled her nose. 'I'd have given it a try,' she muttered.

'Come on, we should go,' Sep said. The parents would be wondering where they had got to, and he was beginning to think guests probably weren't supposed to hang out in the loading dock.

As the children turned to leave, the large roller-shutter at the end of the room sprang to life. The beeps of a reversing vehicle filtered in from outside. Panicked, Jacinta grabbed Lucas's hand and ran to the lift. 'Let's get out of here!' she whispered.

'Keep your hair on,' Sloane said, scampering after the pair. 'I thought I was the one who was supposed to be scared.'

Alice-Miranda, Sep and Millie quickly hid behind the mountain of chocolate boxes and watched as the tail-lights of a van came into view. A tall man with a spindly moustache wearing a thick parka and grey beanie jumped out of the driver's seat. He was talking to himself in German and he didn't sound happy.

'*Wo ist die blöde Kuh?*' he grumbled as he opened the back doors of the van.

'Hurry up, you lot,' Jacinta hissed from inside the lift.

The man spun around and peered into the store-room. '*Wer ist da?*' he called out. 'Frau Doerflinger?'

Millie grimaced. 'I really don't want to see that woman again, and I have a feeling she won't be thrilled to see us down here, either.'

The man grunted, then turned back to the van and began to unload the chocolate boxes.

Millie, Sep and Alice-Miranda silently crept towards the lift to join the others. The doors closed, and before anyone could work out which button to press, the lift jolted into action. It came to a halt just one floor up. As it stopped, the children could hear a familiar voice outside.

'I have told you I am about to make an offer he cannot refuse,' the woman said confidently. 'Of course I am aware of what will happen. I do not take kindly to threats.'

The doors sprang open and the children came face to face with Frau Doerflinger. The woman looked as if she had just seen a ghost – or six of them.

'What are *you* doing in here?' she rasped.

Recovering quickly, Alice-Miranda smiled. 'Hello Frau Doerflinger. We thought this might be a short cut to the lounge but I'm afraid we're a little lost.'

The veins in the woman's neck seemed to be pulsating with her every breath. 'This area is private!' she said accusingly. 'The doors are marked as such and they are locked too.'

'I'm so sorry, but we didn't see a sign on the door downstairs,' Alice-Miranda explained. 'And it was open.'

'Liar.' Delphine suddenly remembered the phone in her hand and raised it to her ear. 'I will call you back. I have some *children* to deal with first.'

The way she said 'children' sent a shiver up Jacinta's spine.

'Alice-Miranda's not a liar!' Millie objected. 'There wasn't a sign and the door wasn't locked. Was it, Lucas?'

The boy shook his head, though it occurred to him that perhaps he'd caught it before it had closed properly.

'This is *my* hotel and you will play by *my* rules,' Delphine snapped, her face fast taking on a crimson hue.

'What happened to "the customer is always right"?' Sloane quipped.

Delphine recoiled. 'You are *not* my customers. You are spoiled brats whose parents pay for everything. When you make your own money and stay in my hotel, then I will consider you my customers.'

Sloane gulped and Millie blanched. Frau Doerflinger clearly wasn't to be messed with.

'Where have you been?' the woman demanded.

The children exchanged glances. Lucas stepped forward, keen to diffuse the situation before they ended up on the street for the night. 'We're terribly sorry if we are somewhere we shouldn't be. We just rode the lift down and back up again.'

'And we saw –' Sloane began before Millie swiftly elbowed her in the ribs. 'Ow! What did you do that for?'

Millie made a face at her, willing the girl to keep quiet.

Frau Doerflinger narrowed her eyes at them. 'What did you see?' she demanded.

'Nothing,' Sloane squeaked, shaking her head vigorously.

'Honestly, Frau Doerflinger, there was no sign or we wouldn't have come this way. If you could show us how to get back upstairs, we'd be most appreciative.' Lucas flashed her his winning grin.

Delphine's lips twitched and she sucked in a deep breath through her nostrils. 'For a start, you can get out of that lift,' she snapped.

The children obediently spilled into the hallway. Frau Doerflinger waited for the doors to close before leading them up a staircase at the end of the passage. She flung open a door into a lobby that none of the children recognised.

'Where are we?' Jacinta asked.

Delphine Doerflinger closed the door and pointed at the word 'Private' printed on it in large black letters. 'There was no sign, was there?'

'There wasn't one downstairs,' Jacinta retorted, unrepentant.

The woman huffed and walked off along another timber-panelled corridor.

'Where's the door?' Sloane muttered as they reached the end of it. She was beginning to think Frau Doerflinger was actually leading them to some sort of dungeon.

Delphine waved a white card over an invisible sensor and the panel pivoted.

'Whoa,' Sep marvelled, impressed. He wondered if all hotels had secret passageways like this. It probably helped the staff move around without being noticed.

The children found themselves in the hallway near the concierge desk. Alice-Miranda's parents reached the bottom of the staircase just as the children appeared.

'Goodness, where did you lot come from?' Hugh said, blinking in surprise. 'I could have sworn you weren't there a second ago.'

'We got lost and Frau Doerflinger kindly helped us find our way back upstairs,' Alice-Miranda explained.

Delphine Doerflinger's face melted into a smile as she approached Hugh and Cecelia. 'The poor little mites had got themselves so confused,' she said with a laugh.

Sloane glanced at Jacinta, who shrugged. The woman was clearly unhinged.

'Thank you, Frau Doerflinger. I hope they didn't cause you any trouble,' Hugh said. He did his best to give the children the hairy eyeball but he wasn't very good at it.

'There you are, my darling,' Otto Fanger sang out, waddling into the room. 'I've been looking for you all over the place.'

'I'm afraid the children are to blame,' Cecelia apologised.

'Please, Madame Highton-Smith, Delphine would not have minded one little bit. She loves children. Don't you, my petal?'

'Newsflash,' Millie whispered. 'No, she doesn't.'

Delphine nodded. 'Children are so . . . intriguing.'

'Come, come, everyone, let us get some drinks and canapés. I am starving. It has been a long time since afternoon tea.' Otto patted his stomach and led the way to an area that had been cordoned off for the event.

'Yes, children, follow Herr Fanger,' Frau Doerflinger said. 'I have asked the chef to prepare some delicious treats for you.'

'Probably poisoned apples,' Millie mumbled.

Hugh looked at the girl. 'What was that, Millie?'

'Nothing,' she fibbed.

'I will be back to join you very soon,' Delphine promised. With that, the woman turned on her heel and glided out of the hall.

'I don't think we should have gone that way. Frau Doerflinger had every right to be upset,' Alice-Miranda said, feeling guilty.

Millie shook her head. 'I don't like her. She's mean and she's up to something.'

'We don't know that,' Alice-Miranda said, biting her lip. But she had to admit that there was something about Delphine Doerflinger that didn't quite add up.

Chapter 7

The young woman lazily flicked through the pages of a magazine and slurped on a soda. Her greasy hair was scraped into a messy ponytail and her fingernails bore the remnants of blue polish.

The bell above the door jingled and a man strode in. He glanced around at the peeling paint and mismatched furniture, then gingerly walked up to the reception desk.

Without removing the straw from her mouth, the woman looked up. 'Are you checking in?'

she asked. She sucked the dregs from the bottle, then belched.

He nodded, a grim smile set on his face. 'Yes, thank you.'

'You're not from around here, are you?' the girl said. He didn't look like their usual clientele of backpackers and young skiers. This man was much older, though still handsome. He had a shock of silver hair and wore a black cashmere coat. 'Do you want me to call Fanger's Palace or somewhere a bit more upmarket?' she offered.

The man shook his head. 'No, no, this is fine,' he insisted. 'The booking should be under the name Florian.'

'Florian . . .?'

'Oh, von . . . no, um, Epple,' he said. 'Florian Epple.'

'Are you sure?' the receptionist asked.

'Yes, my name is Florian Epple,' he said firmly.

The woman flicked through the guest register. 'Here it is,' she said, scribbling something down next to the booking. She placed a key on the desk. 'I think this is for your room, but if you get up there and find that it doesn't work just come back and I will look again.'

'Thank you.' Florian glanced at the number on the key. *Thirteen.* Of course it was, he thought to himself.

'That will be two hundred and fifty francs,' the woman said.

Florian swallowed. 'Are you sure it's as much as that?' he asked.

The receptionist nodded. 'High season. You should see what they charge over at Fanger's. I heard from a friend of a friend who works there that some rooms are thousands of francs a night. It would want to be good for that much money.'

Florian took out his wallet and peered inside. He'd have to pay cash as his credit card had already been declined at the train station.

'By the way, your toilet is blocked, so you'll have to use the communal bathroom down the hall,' the woman added. 'Sorry about that, but the plumber only visits once a week and it clogged up a couple of nights ago.'

Florian was tempted to head back to the station and take the first train home. And what then, pray? he chastised himself. There had been some difficult times before, from which they had emerged relatively unscathed, but this he could not understand.

Florian's stomach grumbled. 'I don't suppose you have room service?' he asked, then wondered why he had even bothered. This was the last place he'd choose to eat something from.

'No, but there's a convenience store just across the road where you can get some takeaway,' the girl replied.

Florian nodded and picked up his small leather suitcase. 'Could you tell me how to get to my room?' he asked.

'It's on the third floor,' she said, looking up. 'The lift is just through there, but you'll have to take the stairs because –'

'The lift man only comes once a week,' Florian finished.

The receptionist grinned. '*Ja*, sorry about that.'

'Daddy, isn't that the Baron?' Alice-Miranda asked as her family and friends strolled along the snowy street. She pointed at a man climbing the steps to a building across the road. He was holding a small takeaway pizza box.

'The Baron from Zermatt?' Millie asked.

Hugh immediately looked over. 'Florian!' he called, waving to the man.

Just as he did a bus rounded the corner. The driver blasted the horn and screeched to a halt as another car swerved into the roundabout. For a few seconds the bus completely blocked their view. By the time it moved, the man was gone.

'Yes,' Alice-Miranda said to Millie, 'but I must have been imagining things.'

'No, I thought it looked like him too,' her father said. 'And it's quite possible he and Giselle have come over for the racing.'

Alice-Miranda skipped along beside her father with Millie. They crossed the street and reached the building they had seen the man enter.

'It's a guesthouse,' Millie said, spotting the two stars on its signage.

'Do you think Uncle Florian could be staying here?' Alice-Miranda asked, taking in the flaking paintwork on the door and cracked window beside it.

'Anything's possible, I suppose,' Hugh replied, though he had his doubts. It wasn't the sort of accommodation the Baron and his wife would normally frequent.

'You could ask,' Millie suggested.

'Good idea,' Hugh said. He turned to Cecelia, who was walking behind them and chatting to Pippa. 'Darling, why don't you all go on to the restaurant?' he said. 'I'll be there in a minute.'

'What are you up to?' the woman asked.

'Alice-Miranda and I thought we spotted the Baron, so I just want to check,' Hugh explained.

Cecelia smiled. 'Oh, that would be a lovely coincidence. We'll see you in a minute, then.'

'We'll come too, Daddy.' Alice-Miranda grabbed Millie's hand and the pair followed Hugh inside.

The reception area was sparsely furnished, almost bare apart from a bicycle and a rack of ski boots off to the left.

Millie pinched her nose. 'Pooh!'

Hugh looked at the boots. 'I quite agree, Millie. It isn't ideal to have a drying rack in the lobby.'

A young woman emerged from the back room, carrying a steaming mug. 'Hello, are you checking in?' she asked.

'No, I just wanted to inquire about a friend of ours that might be staying here,' Hugh said.

The woman took a sip from the mug and opened up the guest register. 'Sure, what's the name?'

'Baron von Zwicky,' Hugh said.

The girl almost spat out her drink. 'As in a real baron?'

'Yes,' Hugh replied, smiling patiently.

'I don't think so but I'll check for you.' She ran her finger down the list of names and then shrugged. 'No barons. There are no dukes or kings, either, for that matter.'

'Sorry to have troubled you,' Hugh said, clearly disappointed. 'Come on, girls, we should get going.'

They turned to leave and were hit with another wave of the pungent odour of sweaty feet. Millie turned back to the woman, unable to hold her tongue any longer. 'You should really find a better place for those boots,' she said. 'They stink.'

The receptionist nodded. 'I know, but someone locked the door to the drying room downstairs and I can't find the spare key.' She held up a handful of keychains with keys of all shapes and sizes.

'Wouldn't it be a good idea to sort them out?' Millie asked.

'*Ja*, I just don't have time.' The woman flipped open the pages of a magazine and sat down on the stool.

Millie frowned. 'I'd have thought sorting out the smelly boots would be more important than reading that rubbish.'

The woman shook her head. 'It's not rubbish, and you never know who might be in St Moritz. Lawrence Ridley was here a few years ago but I didn't get to meet him because he was constantly surrounded by pesky photographers.'

'That always happens,' Alice-Miranda said, taking her friend by the arm. 'Come on, Millie.'

Hugh waited by the door, hoping neither of the girls elaborated on Lawrence.

'Goodbye.' Alice-Miranda waved, but the woman's eyes were glued to the magazine.

'Well, I still think you should get rid of those boots,' Millie huffed, walking to the door. 'First impressions count, you know, and I wouldn't want to stay here.'

The receptionist looked up. 'Me either.'

Millie stepped out onto the street, shaking her head. 'There's *no* way I'd want her working for me.'

'I couldn't agree more, Millie,' Hugh said with a chuckle.

'You have to ask yourself: what's wrong with the kids of today?' Millie tsked.

Alice-Miranda and Hugh laughed.

'What?' Millie said, looking at them.

'*You* are a kid of today, Millie.' Alice-Miranda grinned.

'Oh, yeah.' Millie smiled back. 'But hopefully not like her.'

'You can come and work for me anytime, Millie.' Hugh wrapped an arm around each girl and led the way down the street.

'I might just take you up on that one day,' Millie replied, 'after I open my rescue stables and write a bestselling book.'

Hugh smiled, holding open the door of the restaurant a few shops down. 'Just say the word. Anyway, I don't know about you two but I can feel a pepperoni pizza coming on.'

'Me too,' Millie said.

'Me three,' Alice-Miranda agreed as they walked inside.

Chapter 8

'Whoa, look at that course!' Lucas exclaimed as the children trudged up the hill to the top of the Cresta Run. The idea of hurtling headfirst down an icy track on little more than a plastic tea tray and some metal runners sent shivers of excitement down the boy's spine.

Dolly looked at the frozen runway and shuddered.

'I wish we could do it,' Lucas said, gazing at the track longingly.

Jacinta gripped the boy's arm. 'I'm very glad that you can't. It looks deadly.'

'It says here,' Millie said, reading the brochure, 'that women *were* allowed to ride the Cresta until nineteen twenty-nine, when a vote was taken to exclude them, and the general membership hasn't sought to change the rules since. That's so unfair.'

'Why?' Sloane asked, raising an eyebrow. 'Do you want to have a go?'

Millie looked down at the track just as a rider flew up over the edge, his arms and legs flailing out of control. He grabbed at the piles of loose straw that were strewn all over the ground to slow down crashing riders, before somersaulting headfirst into a row of foam barriers. 'Mm, I think I'd prefer to have a nosebleed in a shark tank,' she conceded with a grimace. 'It might be safer.'

Pippa McLoughlin-McTavish chuckled. 'I don't know about that.'

The man stood up and dusted himself off, then grabbed his sled and began to trek back up the mountain.

Jacinta shook her head in disbelief. 'He's crazy.'

'So, what do you think, kids? Should Hamish and I give it a whirl?' Hugh said, giving Alice-Miranda a wink.

She winked back. 'Go on, Daddy. You'll be brilliant.'

Millie considered her father. Hamish was a big man, not overweight but tall and solid. 'Don't be ridiculous, Daddy,' she scoffed. 'It would be like driving a Mini Minor to the top of the track, releasing the brakes and hoping for the best.'

'I'm not that big, Mill!' Hamish said, slightly wounded.

Cecelia Highton-Smith gulped. 'You're not serious, are you? The last thing we need is for the two of you to be laid up with broken bones for the next three months.'

'Exactly,' Pippa echoed.

Alice-Miranda looked towards the starting area, where a giant banner hung over the track. Several officials wearing headsets were standing nearby and there was a man about to start. 'Is that Cyril?' she said, squinting into the sun.

'Oh my word!' Shilly exclaimed.

Cecelia gasped. 'What on earth is he doing?' she said, clutching her husband's arm.

Hugh shrugged helplessly. 'He's on leave, so he can do whatever he wants.' He hadn't realised Cyril would indulge in anything more than a spot of skiing when he'd given the fellow the week off.

The children and adults raced towards him. As they arrived at the start of the course Cyril was receiving his final instructions.

'Don't forget to use your boots to slow down. If you do go off the edge, you'll want to try to land as far away from the skeleton as possible. Remember, those things can kill you,' one of the officials warned him.

'Why would you want to land away from your skeleton?' Jacinta said, perplexed.

Millie giggled. 'That's what they call the sled.'

'Oh.' Jacinta grimaced all the same.

'Cyril!' Cecelia called out, waving both her arms.

The man looked up and grinned. 'Hello there. I thought you'd be hitting the slopes this morning.'

'We will after lunch but we were all curious about this thing,' Hugh replied.

'What are you doing, man?' Dolly demanded, her voice tight. Cyril seemed awfully relaxed about the whole thing, which put her even more on edge.

'Don't worry, Dolly. I've done it before,' Cyril assured her.

Cecelia turned to her husband. 'Did you know about this?'

Hugh shook his head. 'Afraid not, but we might as well cheer him on.'

'You should watch from the clubhouse,' Cyril suggested. 'You'll have a great view of the whole course from the balcony. I'll wait until you get there.'

'You be careful, Cyril,' Shilly warned. 'Last time I checked, none of us was licensed to fly that jet except for you.'

The family and friends made their way down to the white building, where they were ushered upstairs to a wide veranda which afforded a stunning view. They positioned themselves along the balustrade, looking down at the glistening snake-like track that curved its way for just over a kilometre down the mountainside.

Cyril gave them a thumbs up, then swayed back and forth several times before hurling himself onto the small sled. He fidgeted about for a few seconds and then straightened out his body. The sled clattered down the track. The group lost sight of him as he hit the first corner, only to reappear at the top of the ice, whizzing around the bend.

Hugh glanced at the giant stopwatch on the commentary box above them. 'My goodness, he's quick.'

'Go, Cyril!' Alice-Miranda shouted, and Millie joined in, cheering him on. Soon the entire group was calling the pilot's name.

'He's going too fast,' said an older chap standing beside Alice-Miranda. 'He'll never make it around Shuttlecock.'

'What's that?' Alice-Miranda asked, suddenly concerned.

'It's where most amateur riders crash out,' the man replied. 'At least he'll get to join the club.'

Millie looked at him. 'What club?'

'Everyone who crashes at that corner joins the Shuttlecock Club,' the man said impatiently, craning his neck to see if he could spot the human missile.

All of a sudden the whooshing of the sled stopped.

'Look! There he is!' Lucas pointed at the figure in the air.

The crowd gasped.

Shilly covered her eyes. 'I can't watch.'

'Stupid man,' Dolly muttered, wringing her hands.

Time seemed to expand in the seconds that followed as the spectators watched the events unfold in slow motion. Cyril hurtled through the air and disappeared into a cloud of snow.

'Is he all right?' Shilly asked, still hiding behind her hands.

The group looked towards the commentator's box above them.

'Medics,' the loudspeaker blared. 'Could we get the medics to Shuttlecock immediately?'

Shilly placed her hands across her chest. 'Good heavens.'

'He's going to be fine,' Cecelia told the group, hoping it were true.

'Can we get to him?' Mrs Oliver asked the man who had foretold Cyril's fate.

'Leave it to the professionals,' the fellow replied calmly. 'They've got all the equipment down there, and if he has to be taken to hospital they'll have a snowmobile ready. Believe me, he's not the first to come off there and he won't be the last.'

'Hospital!' Shilly gasped. 'He shouldn't have been on that course in the first place. Why are men so . . . so . . . stubborn?'

No one spoke a word as all eyes were focused on the middle section of the track.

'He's moving,' the announcer said, looking through his binoculars. 'Although, that shoulder seems to be at a very strange angle. They're loading him onto the snowmobile and . . .'

'Come on!' Shilly shouted up at the commentator. 'Don't give us half the story, man!'

'He's raised his good arm and he's giving the thumbs up,' the man blurted.

There was a huge cheer from the small crowd.

Dolly and Shilly hugged one another, and Cecelia allowed herself to breathe again. 'Thank heavens for that,' she said to her husband. 'So are you still keen to have a go?'

Hugh looked at her sheepishly. 'Maybe not today.'

'He was never going to do it, Mummy,' Alice-Miranda said. 'He was only teasing.'

Cecelia smiled and squeezed her daughter's shoulder. 'When it comes to your father, I can never be too sure.'

The mosquito motor of the snowmobile buzzed as the vehicle carried Cyril to the top of the track. The family rushed down from the balcony and up the course to meet them. The wailing of an ambulance siren sounded in the distance.

'Good Lord, Cyril, you were flying,' Hugh said with a grin. 'Pity you stacked it.'

'Looks like that's the end of my Cresta ambitions,' the man said wryly.

'You were awesome,' Lucas said. 'Did you know you were on track to beat the record?'

'Seriously?' Cyril looked at the lad.

Sep nodded. 'We couldn't believe how fast you were going.'

'Neither could I. I lost my footing not long after the start and then I just couldn't get it again. Thank heavens for that corner or I think you might have been scraping me off the barrier at the end,' Cyril joked, then winced as two medics began to examine his injuries.

'We're going to have to pop that shoulder back in,' one of them said.

'And you'll need to go to hospital so they can check if you have a concussion,' the other added. She directed Cyril to watch her pointer finger as she moved it from side to side.

'I'll go with him,' Hugh said, watching the medics ready the snowmobile.

'No, sir, leave it to me. I'll look after him,' Dolly said, bustling forward. 'You go and enjoy your afternoon on the slopes.'

'I'll come with you,' Shilly offered.

Dolly shook her head. 'He doesn't need both of us. I'll make sure he's okay, then head straight back to the hotel.'

'Excuse me, how far away is the hospital?' Cecelia asked the track marshal.

'Only a few minutes,' the man replied. 'Faster if they put the siren on.'

'And is it far from Fanger's Palace Hotel?'

'Not even a minute,' the man said.

'Thank you.' Cecelia smiled at him. 'Well, at least Cyril doesn't have to be taken down the mountain.'

Dolly headed over to the waiting ambulance and climbed into the back with Cyril. He had been given some strong medication to relieve the pain and was now telling Dolly a long story about how he used to race billycarts with his brother as a boy.

Chapter 9

Nina took the key from the small timber cupboard in the kitchen where every key for every lock in their rambling old house was neatly lined up, labelled and hanging on a hook. Labelling had been one of her mother's obsessions, which was just as well as her father wouldn't have had the first clue where anything was without it. She raced downstairs and through the red velvet curtain that partitioned the museum from the rest of the house. Nina unlocked the wide timber door, making sure to leave it open. Her father would not be home for a while yet.

The girl walked among the cabinets with their strange and wonderful workings. Most of the instruments in the museum were so rare that they didn't exist anywhere else in the world. She stopped in front of her favourite piece.

Nina thought back to the time when she was just five years old, visiting the market fair in Basel with her grandfather. She had been so excited to take the long journey by train, to wander past the colourful stalls and exotic foods. She remembered rounding the corner and seeing it for the very first time. A timber-and-glass case with miniature musicians – men and women dressed in once-fine clothes, monkeys with tarnished cymbals and ballerinas in moth-eaten tutus, their faces dull and grimy from the spectre of time. The sounds it made were terrible too. She had blocked her ears at the ghastly clash of percussion and organ pipes. She hadn't known why they had travelled so far until that very case was delivered to their door several weeks later.

For months Nina watched her grandfather work on it, first pulling the whole thing apart, then painstakingly putting it back together until, finally, it was perfect. Her mother had sewn new clothes for the figurines so they were once again suitably attired. The spinning ballerinas with bright eyes and rosy cheeks stood alongside monkeys with plush fur and gleaming cymbals. Nina's father had looked in on the pair's progress from time to time but he knew nothing of the inner workings of such contraptions. Sebastien Ebersold spent his days outdoors on the mountainside unlike Nina's grandfather, who had been a watchmaker – a man who understood the precision required to restore such splendid creations.

The unveiling had been spectacular. Her grandfather, wearing his lucky black hat, had called the family down one evening after dinner. Nina had leapt about all over the place as excited as the day she'd first spotted the cabinet in the market.

'Is it ready, Opa?' she'd said. 'Is it really ready?'

'I think so.' He'd smiled at her, then walked around to the side of the cabinet and pulled the handle.

It had begun slowly as though the figurines were awakening from a deep, enchanted sleep. The tempo gradually quickened and the men, women, ballerinas and monkeys were soon twirling and prancing and strumming and plucking as the tune took hold.

Nina remembered how her grandfather had tears in his eyes as he watched the tableau come to life. Nina and her mother danced a jig arm in arm and her father stood shaking his head, wondering at his father-in-law's skill and his wife's eye for such fine detail.

That was long ago, when all had been right in Nina's world. Tourists would come to see Lars Dettwiller's Mechanical Musical Cabinet Museum filled with violinas, orchestrions, symphonions, organs for grinding, musical chairs and all other manner of automats. The museum was a renowned Alpine attraction, no doubt helped by its location across the cobblestoned street from the most beautiful hotel in all of Zermatt, the Grand Hotel Von Zwicky. The Baron and Baroness visited often and recommended the museum far and wide. There was always something new arriving from a far-flung corner of the globe, often in pieces, tarnished, broken and neglected, until her grandfather set to work restoring it.

But then almost a year ago, just after her tenth birthday, Nina had arrived home from school to find her grandfather sitting opposite her father at the kitchen table; the old man's eyes wet and his face ashen, her father looking like a ghost. Nina would never forget the moment she discovered her mother had died. They called it an aneurysm, but she called it the end of the world.

Her grandfather closed the museum the very next day and had not stepped foot in it since. They had lost him to despair. But surely, Nina thought, the music box had been a sign that Opa wanted to live again – she just had to help him find the way.

Her father was wrong. Opa shouldn't go to a home where old people ate their suppers at four in the afternoon and sat around all day, suspended in a no-man's-land between life and death. She knew about those places. Her father's mother had been in one. Nina didn't remember much about the woman but she could recall the building and its antiseptic smell, as if she had gone there a thousand times, instead of just the two visits her parents had taken her on. She wasn't going to let her grandfather suffer the same fate.

Nina looked at the dusty orchestrion. 'Are you ready?' she asked the figurines.

The girl walked to the side of the machine and pulled the lever. Slowly, as always, the performers took up their instruments and the tune began. She stared through the glass at the motley band of players and crossed her fingers. If he heard them, she thought, maybe it would be enough to bring him back to them.

Chapter 10

Millie and Alice-Miranda were riding the chair-lift to the top of the run. After lunch Hugh and Hamish had decided to take the children up onto the mountain while Cecelia and Pippa did a bit of shopping. Mrs Shillingsworth had opted to go for a leisurely walk in the village to see if she could spot the famous Heidi hut and leaning tower, both well-known landmarks.

'I think my turns were getting better on the last run,' Millie said.

'You were fast,' Alice-Miranda said as she clacked her skis together, sending a little shower of snow onto the slope below.

Millie wrinkled her nose as a stiff breeze blew an overpowering fragrance towards them. She pointed at the stylishly dressed woman with a mane of bouncy brunette curls in the chair in front. 'Do you think her perfume's strong enough?'

Alice-Miranda sniffed the air. 'It is a bit much, isn't it?'

'It smells like cloves mixed with something else I can't stand,' Millie said, trying to think what it was.

'Ginger,' Alice-Miranda suggested.

'Urgh, that's it,' Millie agreed. 'It's gross.'

The woman had spent the entire ride whining loudly as she tousled her hair and fiddled with her headband while the man beside her talked nonstop on his phone. He was gesticulating wildly and at one point almost dropped his stocks.

The woman's strongly accented baby voice floated on the wind as she turned to face the man. 'Vincenzo, when are you taking me shopping? You promised me diamonds.'

'Not now, Sancia,' he hissed. 'I am working.'

She pouted her bee-stung lips at him. 'But you are always working. I want to go shopping.'

Millie and Alice-Miranda looked at one another and giggled.

'Vincenzo,' Millie said, perfectly mimicking the woman's Italian accent, 'when are you going to buy me the world?'

The girl hadn't thought her voice would carry forward at all and was shocked when the woman swivelled her heavily made-up face to glare at her.

'Oops,' she gulped and looked away, pretending to wave at some skiers down below.

Alice-Miranda saw her father and Hamish reach the top of the lift and ski off to the left. 'Daddy, wait for us,' she called.

The men were two chairs ahead of the girls, while Lucas and Jacinta were in the chair behind. Sep and Sloane had decided to start their ski lessons straight away. As the girls neared the top of the mountain, they pushed the bar up over their heads and wriggled forward on the seat, holding their poles together in front of them.

'Push,' Millie said as their skis made contact with the snowy platform.

The pair whizzed down the slope, and realised too late that Vincenzo and his whiny girlfriend had stopped to adjust their gear, right in the middle of the runway.

'Look out!' Alice-Miranda shouted. She managed to avoid them but Millie wasn't so lucky. With nowhere to go, the girl ran straight over the back of the man's skis.

'What are you doing? These are brand-new,' Vincenzo barked. 'Children who cannot ski should not be allowed up here.'

'Sorry,' Millie squeaked. If the stupid man hadn't stopped where he did, it wouldn't have happened. She sped over to her father, turning dramatically to send a powdery spray all over his legs.

'Look at you, Mill. When did you become such a good skier?' Hamish said with a grin.

Millie grimaced. 'That's not what the man over there said.' As the others turned to see if they could spot Lucas and Jacinta, Millie leaned down and made a snowball. She patted it into shape, then promptly threw it at her father, whacking him on the nose.

'Right, you little monster, that's it!' Hamish declared, clicking his boots out of his skis and staking his poles into the snow. 'Snowball fight!'

Millie squealed as her father pelted a handful of snow in her direction. She ducked out of the way, leaving it to smack Lucas on the mouth.

'You call *that* a snowball, Hamish?' Lucas said, wiping it off his face. I'll show you a snowball.' The boy grabbed a handful of snow and moulded it into a missile the size of a bowling ball.

'Look out, Alice-Miranda!' Jacinta yelled as Hugh dumped a clump of snow on his daughter's head.

'Daddy, I'm going to get you for that!' The tiny child turned around and zoomed towards him on her skis, knocking him off his feet and into a deep snow-drift. Jacinta and Millie went in for the kill, hurtling snowballs as quickly as they could make them.

'Stop, stop!' Hugh held his hands in the air. 'I surrender!'

Lucas had managed to cover Hamish in snow too. The man collapsed on his knees, his sides heaving with laughter. 'Gosh, I haven't had this much fun in years.'

'Me either,' Hugh gasped as the girls and Lucas all fell about in the snow.

Jacinta fanned out her arms and legs. 'Look, I'm an angel,' she said.

'You? An angel?' Millie laughed.

'She's my angel,' Lucas whispered, and Jacinta felt her heart skip a beat.

Millie's jaw dropped in disbelief. 'Did you really just say that?'

'What?' Lucas said sheepishly. 'I didn't say anything.'

'Yes, you did.' Millie nudged the boy.

Lucas blushed and pressed his finger to his lips.

Millie nodded. 'Don't worry, your secret's safe with me, sappy pants.'

Alice-Miranda was still wiping the snow out of her goggles when a ski instructor in his instantly recognisable red parka whizzed past. 'Snowplough, snowplough,' he called to the two children following him.

'Hey, that's Sep!' Lucas said, sitting up.

'And Sloane. Look how well they're doing.' Alice-Miranda picked up her poles. 'Come on, let's join them.'

The threesome traversed the slope back and forth until Sloane and Sep stopped beside their instructor. Alice-Miranda sped towards them.

'Hi there,' she said with a wave.

'Oh, hi,' Sloane said. Her grin couldn't have been any wider.

'Did you see us?' Sep said, beaming. 'We rode the chairlift up and neither of us has crashed at all.'

Hugh had a quick word with their instructor, whose name was Gunter. An older man, his tanned face was lined from years of winter sun.

'These two are very impressive,' he said, nodding at the Sykes children. 'If they continue with their lessons, I think they might even be able to conquer one of the black trails before they leave.'

Sep's eyes widened. 'Did you guys hear that?' he gasped. 'A black run at St Moritz – awesome!'

'Alice-Miranda, weren't you keen to have some lessons too?' Hugh asked.

The girl nodded. 'Could we all go together? I don't think we're that much better than Sloane and Sep and then we can help each other.'

Gunter nodded. 'I don't mind and these two won't hold you back. I think Sloane is a lot better and braver than she gives herself credit for, and Sep is already a star.'

Sloane and Sep were positively glowing.

'Why don't you all have a run now so Gunter can let us know if that would work?' Hugh suggested.

'Come on, kids. Show me what you're made of,' Gunter called, whizzing off down the mountain. He stopped to watch the children as they followed in his tracks. He then led them to a series of little jumps.

'You can do it, Sloane,' Millie called to the girl, who was the last to come down the course.

'Here goes nothing,' Sloane yelled as she let rip. She hit the jump and leaned forward the way Gunter had taught them. For a few seconds Sloane felt as if she were flying.

'Wow, she's awesome,' Lucas said.

The kids held their breath as Sloane sailed through the air. She nailed the landing but soon began to wobble. She was balancing on her left ski, then on her right, unable to get them both on the ground at the same time.

'Look out!' she cried, before collecting the back of Millie's skis and sending the line of children toppling like dominoes. Gunter managed to leap out of the way just in time. The children were all in fits of giggles and completely covered in snow.

'Is everyone all right?' Gunter called, skating over to them.

'Good one, Sloane,' Sep said, giving his sister a push.

'I didn't mean it. I'm sorry,' she said, dusting herself off and getting back up onto her feet.

'That was nothing,' Gunter reassured her. 'Are you hurt?'

Sloane shook her head.

'Are you scared?' he asked.

Sloane shook her head again.

'Do you want to show that jump what you're made of?'

Sloane nodded.

'Okay, kids, let's ski down and do it all over again.' Gunter pointed his stock towards the chairlift.

The children took off after him, shrieking as they raced each other to the bottom of the slope.

Chapter 11

Delphine Doerflinger sat in the lounge sipping her tea. From her vantage point in a high wingback chair, she could see everyone coming and going while she herself could not be easily seen.

'There you are, my petal,' Otto said, looking over the top of her chair.

Delphine glanced up and found herself nose to nose with Gertie. 'Get that creature out of my face,' she hissed.

Gertie growled and Otto clutched her closer to him. 'Be nice to your mama,' he cooed.

'I am not that beast's mama,' Delphine huffed.

Otto walked around the settee to join his wife. 'You should have told me you were having afternoon tea,' he said. 'I will join you.'

'I'd rather you didn't,' Delphine said.

Otto looked wounded. 'Why? Do I embarrass you so much that you won't be seen with me these days?'

Delphine sighed, her face softening. 'Don't be stupid,' she said. 'I am working.'

'Oh, is it . . . what we spoke of yesterday?' he asked, grinning.

Gertie growled again.

'Otto, take her upstairs. She should not be down here upsetting the guests,' Delphine sniffed.

'She doesn't upset anyone. Do you, my little princess?' The man pursed his lips and made a kissing noise as the dog's tongue shot out towards him.

Delphine cringed. 'Honestly, you will catch something from that mutt one of these days. Now, why don't you go for a walk? Then tonight we will celebrate.'

Otto's face lit up. 'Will it be ours so soon?'

'I am hoping so, but I cannot afford any distractions. Hurry up, Otto,' she instructed under her breath.

'You are such a good wife. I will do as you wish. Come along, Gertie, we must get changed.' He held the dog and scurried away just as Delphine spotted her target.

She stood up and walked towards him, pretending to make notes in an open folder. He had his coat collar drawn up around his neck and wore a stylish fedora, which cast a shadow across his face.

Delphine spun around, almost bumping into him. 'Baron, is that you?' she said, feigning surprise. 'I nearly didn't recognise you with that hat on.'

He flinched and tightened his grip on the briefcase. 'Frau Doerflinger, how lovely to see you.'

'I hadn't realised that you were staying with us,' the woman said, smiling sweetly.

'Oh no, I am just here for a meeting,' he replied as beads of perspiration formed on his brow.

'Do you have time for tea?' she asked, gesturing to the lounge.

The man gulped and shook his head. 'No, sadly not. I must be going.'

'What a pity,' Delphine said. Out of the corner of her eye, she saw two men enter the room. One of them was nudging five feet and dressed in a flamboyant navy pinstriped suit. His slick grey hair looked as oily as he did. The other, who was bald, wore a plain black suit and towered over his associate. 'Well, I mustn't keep you,' she said with a note of finality.

'*Auf Wiedersehen*, Frau Doerflinger.' The Baron took a deep breath and walked away.

With the slightest signal from Delphine, the two men nodded and followed him.

Sloane grinned as she clicked out of her bindings and picked up her skis. 'That was awesome.'

'You were amazing,' Alice-Miranda said.

'I think I amazed myself,' Sloane said with a laugh.

'Especially when you stacked into us,' Millie teased.

'At least it only happened once,' the girl said as the rest of the group reached the bottom of the Chantarella funicular.

'Well done, kids,' Hugh called as he and Hamish brought up the rear. 'Who's ready for a swim?'

The children's hands shot up in the air as they jumped up and down yelling 'me'.

Hamish chuckled. 'Let's get moving then.'

Everyone carried their skis down to the roadway, where the shuttle bus was waiting for them. It was a short drive through the village, past the town square and to the hotel. Several doormen helped to unpack the gear and, despite the men's offer, Hugh, Hamish and the children insisted on carrying everything to the lockers themselves.

The group quickly changed out of their ski boots and charged back upstairs. Aside from the well-stocked ski shop two floors below street level, the hotel also boasted its very own subterranean shopping mall.

'Look at those clothes,' Millie gushed, admiring the sparkling dresses in the window of the first boutique. 'That cloth looks as if it's made from spun silver.'

Hugh spotted the figure on the price tag and let out a low whistle. 'Whoa, for that many francs, you would want it to be.'

Millie's eyes bulged when she saw it too. 'No! That can't say what I think it does,' she gasped.

Hugh nodded. 'I'm afraid it does.'

'Who wears a dress that costs more than a car?' Sloane said incredulously.

'Even if I had that much money, I'd never spend it on a dress,' Millie said. 'What if you sat on chewing gum or something?'

'Because that happens all the time,' Sloane said with a grin.

Millie rolled her eyes. 'You know what I mean.'

The group continued down the mall, past shops selling fine art and jewels.

'Now, that's more like it,' Sloane said. She stopped to ogle the diamonds and other precious stones in the window.

'When would you ever wear those?' Millie said. She eyed a pair of diamond-and-ruby earrings the size of small chandeliers.

'Well, if I became a famous actor like Lawrence Ridley, I'd wear them to all those red-carpet events. Imagine how jealous my mother would be! She'd beg me to come along and I'd just say, "No, I'm taking Sep."'

'Really?' Her brother looked at her in surprise.

'No, not really, but you were the first person that came into my head,' Sloane replied.

Everyone laughed as the group made their way up another flight of stairs and emerged into the hotel foyer, where they bumped into Otto Fanger and Gertie.

'Hello there.' The hotelier smiled at them. 'Did you have a good time on the slopes?'

The children nodded.

'Yes, thank you, Herr Fanger,' Alice-Miranda said. 'It was lovely. The snow was delicious.'

Herr Fanger's eyes widened in alarm. 'You didn't eat it, did you?'

Alice-Miranda shook her head and grinned. 'No, of course not.'

'Thank goodness for that,' the man said. 'There are far too many dogs in St Moritz. Sometimes the snow is yellow, if you catch my drift.'

The children nodded and giggled.

'Where are you off to now?' Otto asked.

'We're going for a swim,' Millie said.

'A swim,' Otto sighed. 'I was just about to take Princess Gertie for a walk, but perhaps we will swim instead.'

Jacinta cupped her hand and whispered in Sloane's ear. 'I don't think I want to see Herr Fanger in his swimming trunks.'

Sloane nodded in agreement, green at the thought of it too.

'Well, come along, Gertie,' the rotund man cooed into the creature's ear. 'Papa will get your swimming trunks.'

None of the children attempted to pat the dog this time, having seen her reaction the day before. They waved goodbye and piled into the lift.

Chapter 12

Alice-Miranda and her friends gathered outside their rooms, dressed as if they were on a summer holiday. Although it was below freezing outside, the temperature was almost balmy inside the hotel.

'Daddy had a few calls to make and told us to go ahead without him,' Alice-Miranda said.

Millie nodded her head. 'Same with my dad, though, knowing him he'll probably have a nap. He was yawning *a lot*.'

The children made their way down to the hotel spa. Lucas pushed open the heavy glass door into the humid room. The boy dumped his towel on a lounge chair and quickly stripped off his T-shirt and shoes and raced to the water's edge.

'Last one in's a rotten egg,' he called out as he leapt high into the air and tucked his legs beneath him, showering water all over the place.

The others followed, diving into the steaming pool like missiles.

'Oh, that chlorine's strong,' Alice-Miranda said as she came up for air, her eyes stinging.

'Do you want to play Marco Polo?' Jacinta asked.

'Yes!' Millie replied. 'You're in.'

Jacinta pouted. 'Why do I have to be in? It was my idea.'

'That's why you're in,' Millie said with a nod before swimming away.

'Whatever,' Jacinta huffed. The girl stood at the shallow end of the pool with her eyes closed, then spun around five times. She could hear the water sploshing and splashing and sensed that one of her friends was near. 'Marco,' she called, pushing away from the edge.

'Polo,' the children chorused.

Jacinta dove all over the place trying to find them. She came close to catching Sep but the boy was like a seal and zoomed to the bottom just in time.

'Where is everyone?' she moaned after a while. 'You're all being way too tricky.'

'Stop cheating,' Sloane called.

Jacinta grinned. Her plan had worked – she now knew that her friends had all swum to the other end of the massive pool. She plunged under the water and swam as far as she could in one breath.

Just as she did, Otto Fanger arrived dressed in a long white robe and matching slippers. He already had on his white swimming cap and red goggles and was carrying Gertie, who was dressed identically, down to the cap and goggles, although hers were pink and looked to be dotted with diamonds.

Millie had to duck under the water to stop herself from laughing out loud.

Otto took off his robe to reveal a much-too-tiny pair of red-and-white striped swimming trunks and a thicket of wiry chest hair that would have put an old English sheepdog to shame. He set Gertie down on a sun lounger with her towel laid out, then took off her robe to reveal a one-piece swimsuit in the exact same fabric.

'He can't be serious,' Sep whispered to Lucas.

'Stay there, my princess, and watch Papa perform his aquarobics,' he instructed before padding over to the deep end.

Otto dipped his toe into the water and pulled it out again, mumbling to himself about the perfect temperature. Then he took several steps backwards, before he began a run-up towards the pool. The hairs on the man's chest parted down the middle as he propelled himself into the air, like an oversized squirrel in mid-flight. All the children, except for Jacinta, winced in anticipation. Their fears were answered when the man's enormous belly slapped hard against the surface, creating a tsunami.

'Ooooh!' The children cringed in unison, diving under to avoid the rolling wave.

At that moment, Jacinta came up for air and copped a mouthful of chlorine. The girl sputtered and coughed, trying to catch her breath. 'Where are you?' she whined. 'I've been in for ages. It's not fair.'

She lunged towards Millie and missed, then sank under the water again.

Herr Fanger paddled to the shallow end of the pool, where he stood up and fiddled with his swimming cap. From somewhere underneath it he pulled out two earphones. Music blared into his ears and he began to wave his arms in the air and stretch from side to side.

Jacinta burst through the surface. 'Marco!'

'Polo,' the children shouted.

Jacinta pushed off the bottom of the pool and pounced, grabbing hold of something huge and hairy.

Otto squealed.

'Eew! What's that?' Jacinta screamed, opening her eyes to see she was clutching the hotelier's hairy arm. She immediately let go, her face flushing the same colour as the man's goggles. 'S-sorry, Herr Fanger, I didn't realise you were here.'

'It is all right, Miss Jacinta,' the man replied. 'I am just doing my exercises.'

Millie and Sloane were treading water in the middle of the pool, biting their fists to stop themselves from howling with laughter.

'Does Gertie go in the water?' Alice-Miranda asked, swimming over to the man. She gestured to the dog, who was now stretched out full-length on the sun lounger, fast asleep.

'Oh, goodness no,' Otto replied. 'She does not like to get wet at all but she loves to dress up.'

Millie rolled her eyes, imagining what the dog's groomers must go through.

'Does Frau Doerflinger enjoy swimming?' Alice-Miranda asked.

'My poor Delphine never has time to relax. She is so busy with the hotel and the chocolate factory and soon we will have another . . . Oops!' The man tittered and covered his mouth. 'Anyway, soon we will celebrate.'

Alice-Miranda frowned, wondering what Herr Fanger was talking about.

'Your eyes are really red,' Millie said, looking at her friend. 'Do they hurt?'

Alice-Miranda nodded. 'They are stinging a bit. I'll go upstairs and find my goggles and see where Daddy has got to,' she replied, swimming over to the pool's edge and climbing out of the water. 'Bye, Herr Fanger.'

The man waved goodbye and put his earphones back in. He thrust his arms into the air and began to sing along with the music, perfectly executing every move to 'YMCA'.

Chapter 13

Alice-Miranda hurried up the stairs. As she reached the top, a tall man in a dark suit and hat, with an overcoat slung across his left arm and a briefcase in his right hand, walked out of a doorway ahead of her and along the hall.

'Uncle Florian!' the girl gasped and rushed towards him.

The man's jaw dropped.

'It's so lovely to see you,' Alice-Miranda said, throwing her arms around his waist.

Florian von Zwicky leaned down and hugged the girl back. She kissed him on one cheek then the other and then the first again. For a moment Florian's face seemed frozen. 'W-whatever are you doing here?' he whispered.

'We came for the White Turf racing,' the child explained. 'Highton's is one of the sponsors. Daddy's been trying to get in touch with you for ages but he says that your phone doesn't let him leave a message. He and Mummy had hoped we could come to Zermatt for some of the time too but your hotel was fully booked.'

The Baron's brow creased at this. 'There must be something wrong with that confounding phone. The hotel is certainly not full.'

'That's strange.' Alice-Miranda frowned for a split second before breaking into a smile. 'It doesn't matter. Mummy and Daddy will be so excited to see you. Is Aunt Giselle here too?'

Florian took a deep breath and shook his head. 'No, Aunt Giselle is at home. I'm just doing some business and . . . I'd rather you didn't tell your parents.'

Alice-Miranda was surprised to hear this. She looked at the Baron with new eyes. The man seemed drawn and tired and not at all like the jolly, old fellow she knew. 'Is everything all right?' she asked him.

'Of course, of course. I just have a lot of things on my mind and I'd rather not burden your parents with any of it,' Florian replied with a smile. 'Is it too much to ask that you keep our meeting between us?'

Alice-Miranda considered this. 'I can keep a secret, if that's what you want.'

The Baron exhaled, visibly relieved. 'Yes, it is. Thank you, sweet girl.'

'Are you going home now?' Alice-Miranda asked.

'Tomorrow,' he said.

'You might not be able to avoid us if we're staying in the same hotel,' Alice-Miranda said. 'It's not that big, really.'

'Oh, I'm not staying here,' Florian replied. He heard a noise and turned to see a door opening back along the hall. 'I have to go. Goodbye, my dear.' He planted a kiss on Alice-Miranda's head and dashed away.

As Alice-Miranda stood there wondering about the Baron's reason for keeping his visit a secret, two men emerged from the same room she'd seen Uncle Florian leaving. They walked right past her as if she were invisible. Deep in thought, Alice-Miranda set off for the lift in the foyer. The men, it seemed, were headed there too. The three of them stood together waiting for the carriage.

'He is desperate,' the taller of the two men said.

The other man nodded. 'It is sad to see a great man brought to his knees like that, but one man's loss is another's gain.'

The tall, bald man grinned. 'Yes, I think the boss will be very happy.'

The lift doors opened and the taller of the two men held out his arm for Alice-Miranda. She stepped inside and waited to see which floor they were going to.

The shorter man in the flashy pinstriped suit pressed the number eight and looked around at Alice-Miranda. 'Which level do you need, little girl?' he asked.

'Same, thank you,' she replied, hoping they would continue their conversation.

The short man examined his reflection in the mirror and smoothed his grey hair. 'I just wish he had signed the papers. Do you think he will understand the fine print?'

The tall man shook his head. 'I am a lawyer and I could hardly understand it.'

'Are you sure it's binding? What if he finds out and takes legal action?' the other man said, his tone growing serious.

The bald man raised his eyebrows. 'With what? He has no money left and he will be paid for the sale – just at our rate, not his. Any longwinded legal battle will likely go badly for him. He should take the money and run.'

The short man chuckled. 'He looked like he wanted to run out of our meeting.'

Alice-Miranda glanced at him in the mirror. She knew she shouldn't be listening but she couldn't help it and it wasn't as if they were being particularly discreet.

'Tomorrow morning he will deliver the papers to the office,' the taller man said, 'and in a week we should be getting some nice, fat bonuses.'

The shorter man pressed his finger to his lips as he caught sight of Alice-Miranda looking at his reflection.

'She's just a kid,' the taller man whispered.

Alice-Miranda immediately looked away, She didn't like the sound of this. Uncle Florian would never sell the Grand Hotel Von Zwicky, not unless something was terribly wrong. She had promised not to tell her parents he was in St Moritz but now she wasn't so sure that was the best idea.

The lift shuddered to a halt and the doors slid open. The shorter man stepped aside and motioned for Alice-Miranda to go ahead of them. She smiled and scurried into the hallway, taking the first right and almost colliding with Frau Doerflinger.

'Watch where you're going, child,' the woman snapped.

Alice-Miranda apologised and continued down the corridor. She had far more important things on her mind than the cranky hotelier. She had to find her father and track down Uncle Florian right away.

Alice-Miranda burst into the suite. She rushed to her parent's bedroom and knocked gently on the door before pushing it open.

'Daddy,' she said, scurrying over to the bed and tapping her snoozing father on the shoulder.

Hugh's whole body tensed and he sat bolt upright. 'Hello darling. I was just coming down to the pool,' he said as he swivelled his legs to the floor.

Alice-Miranda looked at him. 'You were sound asleep.'

'I'm sorry,' he said, grinning at her. 'I just put my head down for a minute. I guess I'm not as young as I used to be.'

'Daddy, I just saw Uncle Florian downstairs –'

'Oh, how wonderful!' Hugh exclaimed. 'Your mother will be so pleased.'

Alice-Miranda shook her head. 'It's not wonderful, Daddy. He asked me not to tell you that I saw him.'

Hugh frowned. 'Why would he do that?'

'I wasn't sure at first, but I think I have an idea,' the child said urgently. 'When he left, I overheard a conversation between two men I think he had just had a meeting with, and it didn't sound good. We've got to find the Baron before it's too late.'

'Too late for what?' Hugh said. He wondered if he was still dreaming.

'I'll tell you as soon as I'm dressed,' Alice-Miranda said, racing off to her bedroom.

Hugh pulled a grey sweater over his shirt. 'Where are the others?'

'At the pool,' she shouted back.

'I'll call down and let them know something's come up or else they'll be worried about you,' Hugh said, trying to locate his boots.

'Thank you,' Alice-Miranda yelled, changing as quickly as she could. Uncle Florian was somewhere in St Moritz and she had a pretty good idea where they should look first.

Chapter 14

Mrs Oliver had just come through the revolving door and was brushing snowflakes from her shoulders when she spotted Alice-Miranda and Hugh charging across the foyer.

'Hello there. Where are you two going in such a hurry?' the woman asked.

'We'll have to tell you later as we're in a bit of a rush,' Hugh replied. 'How's Cyril?'

'I'm afraid he has a dislocated shoulder and a severe concussion. The doctor said that if it wasn't for his helmet he'd be in a very bad state.' Dolly sighed, shaking her head. 'He will have to stay in the hospital for at least a couple of days and he's not to fly for another week.'

'Poor Cyril,' Alice-Miranda said.

'He's worried about how we're going to get home but I told him not to fret about that at all,' Dolly said. 'You know how he hates letting anyone else take charge when it comes to flying the family.'

Hugh nodded. 'We'll work something out.'

Alice-Miranda looked at her father. 'I've got an idea, Daddy.'

'You can tell me on the way,' Hugh said, pulling on his gloves. 'And everything else too. See you later, Dolly.'

With that, the pair bundled out into the cold, leaving Mrs Oliver wondering what on earth was going on.

'I hope Uncle Florian won't be too cross with me, Daddy,' Alice-Miranda said.

'Don't worry, darling, it was right of you to tell me,' Hugh assured her. 'He's a proud man, but I won't let him lose the hotel. It's been in his family for over a century.' He pushed open the door to the guesthouse they had visited the day before. 'After you.'

The pungent smell of sweaty ski boots made an immediate assault on the pair's nostrils.

Hugh grimaced. 'Good grief. I think that's worse than yesterday.'

The receptionist seemed to be in the exact same position and possibly reading the same magazine. She didn't even look up when Hugh cleared his throat and Alice-Miranda called out hello. Hugh promptly picked up the little bell on the countertop and gave it a very loud tinkle.

The young woman finally glanced up. 'Oh, hello. Sorry, still no barons or princes or kings.'

'I think our friend might have checked in under a different name,' Hugh said.

'Ooh, he must be super-important then,' the woman replied, perking up. 'I love it when celebrities use pseudonyms. Is he a celebrity? I've heard Lawrence Ridley calls himself George Grant.'

Alice-Miranda frowned. 'Is that true, Daddy? I've never heard Uncle Lawrence do that.'

'I wouldn't count on the reliability of the information you get in *Gloss and Goss*,' Hugh said, eyeing the open tabloid on the counter.

The woman's eyes almost popped out of her head. 'Uncle Lawrence?'

'He's married to my Aunt Charlotte,' Alice-Miranda explained.

The woman's face began to contort and she looked as if she might cry.

'Are you all right?' Alice-Miranda asked her.

'I just can't believe you're related to Lawrence Ridley,' the woman said, fanning herself. 'He's so dreamy.'

Alice-Miranda grinned. 'My friend Jacinta thinks so too. He and Aunt Charlotte were hoping to come to St Moritz but he's busy shooting a movie and Aunt Charlotte thought the babies were still too little for a ski trip. I can't wait until they're old enough to learn,' she gushed.

'But we're not here to talk about Uncle Lawrence, are we, darling?' her father said, giving Alice-Miranda a nudge. He was worried the woman might pass out before they had time to ask her about the Baron. 'Do you have anyone registered under the name of Florian?' he asked.

The receptionist pushed away the magazine and pulled the guest register towards her. She scanned the page. 'Mmm, so your friend might be using an assumed name.'

Hugh nodded. 'Yes, I imagine so.'

'Then I probably shouldn't tell you,' the girl replied. 'It sounds as if he doesn't want anyone to know that he's here.'

Hugh smiled at the woman. 'Yes, you're probably right.'

'But, Daddy, we have to find Uncle Florian or else he's going to do something he'll regret,' Alice-Miranda implored her father.

'I can't make . . . I'm sorry, I don't know your name,' he said, turning back to the receptionist.

'It's Christiane,' she replied. 'Christiane Birchler.'

'Darling, I can't make Christiane tell us if she doesn't want to,' Hugh said, giving his daughter a meaningful look.

Alice-Miranda's eyes grew wide as she cottoned on. 'What about . . .' She glanced at her father. 'What if I asked Uncle Lawrence to send Miss Birchler an autographed picture?'

Hugh shook his head forlornly. 'Oh, I'm sure she wouldn't tell us, not even for that.'

'A signed photograph of Lawrence Ridley with my name on it?' Christiane stared at the pair of them as if they were mad. 'I'd tell you the name of every guest in this hotel for that.'

Hugh grinned. 'There's no need to go overboard.'

'I'll send Uncle Lawrence a message as soon as we get back to the hotel,' Alice-Miranda said.

'Really?' Christiane's eyes were brimming with tears.

'Please don't cry, Miss Birchler,' Alice-Miranda said. 'Uncle Lawrence wouldn't like that at all.'

The bell above the front door jingled as someone came in from the street. Alice-Miranda looked around and gasped. 'Hello Uncle Florian,' she said quietly.

'Oh no,' Christiane sighed dramatically. 'Now I won't get my autograph.'

Hugh quickly went to greet his friend. 'Before you say a word, Alice-Miranda only told me you were here because of something she overheard.'

The child nodded. 'I promise, Uncle Florian. I wasn't going to tell, but I had to.'

The Baron shook his head. 'It is fine. It is just a short-term loan.'

'It's not,' Alice-Miranda insisted, taking him by the hand. 'They're going to seize the hotel.'

'What are you talking about?' Florian said, his forehead creasing.

'Is there somewhere we can go to talk in private?' Hugh asked Christiane, who seemed to be much more interested in what was going on now that she realised her guest was using an assumed name.

'The breakfast room is empty,' she replied reluctantly. She considered snapping a couple of photographs to see if she could interest *Gloss and Goss* in the niece and brother-in-law of Lawrence Ridley.

'Through there.' Florian pointed at a doorway off to the left.

'It's good to see you, Florian,' Hugh said.

The Baron smiled. 'It is good to see you too, my friend.'

The two men embraced and followed Alice-Miranda into the room.

Chapter 15

Giselle von Zwicky made her way through the hotel lobby, turning off the lights as she went. The bar had closed an hour ago and she had sent the chef home just after nine. There was no point having staff in the kitchen to cook for an empty dining room. She could hear the happy shouts of holiday-makers, and looked out the window. Snow had been falling steadily since midday and tomorrow was forecast to be fine. It would be a beautiful day on the mountain. She wondered if she should abandon her post – at least if she was skiing she could forget about their troubles, even if it was just for a little while.

Giselle walked to the huge double front doors with their ornate iron lacework set against carved mahogany panels and turned the lock. The handful of guests who were staying had keys to the side door.

She wondered if Florian had called. He had left the day before with a spring in his step – something she hadn't seen for a long time. He had kissed her softly and told her that everything would be all right, to trust him. Of course she did. They had been married for more than forty years and never once had he let her down. But this – this was inexplicable. In all the years they had run the hotel, never had there been so few guests. None of it made sense. They hadn't let things slide, the place was as beautiful as it ever was – better, really, with their ongoing program of refurbishments. Even good friends seemed to have abandoned them. She had thought they might see Hugh and Cecelia this season but there had been no booking and no word. Though she could have telephoned Cecelia, the truth was she couldn't bear another rejection.

As she crossed the foyer, Giselle noticed a beam of light shining along the bottom of the office door.

She pushed it open and gasped. 'Valerie, my dear, you scared me half to death.'

A young woman looked up from one of the desks. 'My apologies, Baroness. I was just catching up on some work,' she said.

The cuckoo clock above the fireplace sprang to life, the little bird popping in and out of its house eleven times.

Giselle patted her chest and took a deep breath to steady her racing heart. 'You should go home. It is far too late and I am afraid I cannot pay you any overtime at the moment.'

'You mustn't worry about that, Baroness,' Valerie said. 'I'm happy to do what I can to help. I've been looking into some cheap advertising options.'

'You are very kind. Do you think it might be those silly reviews? Florian has told me there are several which are unflattering to say the least.'

Valerie shrugged. 'I don't know. Perhaps. But we will get to the bottom of the problem. I know how much this place means to both of you.'

'Yes. It means everything. We are fortunate to have good people around us.' The Baroness smiled. 'Now, go home before I feel even more guilty for making you work around the clock.'

'Just ten more minutes,' Valerie promised.

Giselle nodded. 'If you must, but we will do something to make it up to you.' Her eyes felt heavy and she knew that if she didn't head up to bed soon it would be that much harder to get up in the morning. 'Goodnight, dear.'

'Goodnight.' Valerie smiled at the old woman until the door was firmly closed. Then she turned back to the computer and wiggled the mouse, bringing the screen to life. She had been in the middle of composing an email when the Baroness walked in and she wanted to finish it quickly. She began to type.

> . . . *unfortunately the hotel is fully booked. However, should things change, we will let you know immediately. I highly recommend our sister hotel in St Moritz, Fanger's Palace Hotel, which appears to have some availability at that time.*
> *Sincerely,*
> *Giselle von Zwicky*

Valerie wondered if that was getting a bit too cheeky. Fanger's wasn't their sister hotel yet, though it would be soon. She had always dreamed of running her own place, and now, at thirty-two years of age, her dream was about to come true. She reread the email and deleted the last line before clicking 'Send'. The cursor raced around the screen as she covered her tracks, just as she had done every night for the past year.

Chapter 16

Delphine Doerflinger pushed herself up straight in the chair and stretched her back. She was about to call for some tea when the phone on her desk rang. She picked up the receiver before the second ring sounded.

'Is it done?' she asked. There was a short pause before the woman's face lit up like a bonfire. 'What do you mean he hasn't delivered the papers? What's keeping him?' There was another short silence. 'You told me he would sign them overnight and now *this*?' she hissed. 'Find him!'

She slammed down the phone and leaned her elbows on the desk, massaging her temples. Her mind was swimming and she had a horrible feeling this was not going to end well.

There was a knock on the door.

'Enter!' she boomed.

The door opened and a man poked his head in.

Delphine eyed him warily. 'I hope you have good news for me.'

'Not exactly, Frau Doerflinger,' the man replied, dropping his gaze. He scooted into the room, closing the door behind him.

'Your partner tells me that the papers have not yet been returned. What are you doing here?'

The man's bald head glistened with perspiration. 'It seems the Baron . . . left for Zermatt this morning.'

'What?' Delphine screeched. 'He cannot leave!'

'Frau Doerflinger, please, try to calm yourself.' The man couldn't help noticing the throbbing vein that had popped out of her neck.

'You have no idea what this deal means to me.' Her breathing became laboured and she seemed to be swallowing air.

'We do not know for sure that the deal is dead,' the man said. He hurriedly poured a glass of water and passed it to her.

Frau Doerflinger gulped it down. 'Dead,' she muttered over and over. 'It's not just the deal that is dead.'

There was another knock at the door. The man's partner entered the room holding an envelope.

'Ah, good, you have it,' the taller man said, breathing a sigh of relief.

His partner grimaced and shook his head.

Delphine stood up and raced towards him. She snatched the envelope from his hand and tore it open. Instead of a signed contract, she pulled out a handwritten note. As her eyes scanned the page, she collapsed into a nearby armchair.

'What does it say, Frau?' the taller man asked tentatively.

'He says he would rather go bankrupt than borrow money from two shysters such as yourselves,' she said, her eyes wild.

'But he wasn't borrowing the money from us,' the short man said. 'He was borrowing it from you.'

'He didn't know that, did he?' Frau Doerflinger scrunched the page into a ball and threw it at him.

Both men shook their heads. 'N-no, of course not,' the taller man stammered. 'He thought we were a reputable loan company.'

'Something must have tipped him off,' the woman said. 'Get out, the pair of you. Consider yourselves terminated, just as I will be.'

'But, Frau, he is desperate,' the shorter man pleaded. 'He will have to sell sooner or later.'

'You will stay away from the Baron. I should have known that if I wanted this job done properly I would have to do it myself. Get out! NOW!' she howled.

The men scurried from the room. The shorter of the two bumped into the coffee table on the way and let out a yowl of pain.

Delphine slumped into the chair and looked at the crumpled note. 'Idiots,' she whispered.

Chapter 17

'I don't ever want to leave this place,' Millie said as her family and friends sat on a long table outside a restaurant perched high above the village and the lake. The children had spent the morning with Gunter while their parents, Mrs Shillingsworth and Mrs Oliver had enjoyed some time together on the slopes – all except Hugh. Cecelia had made apologies for her husband's absence, citing some urgent business.

When Alice-Miranda and her father had returned to the hotel the previous night, Cecelia had been shocked to learn of the Baron's predicament. Hugh had immediately scanned the contract and sent it to his lawyers to review. There was no mistake: the financiers were poised to seize the Grand Hotel Von Zwicky as soon as Florian signed the papers and there would have been nothing he could do to stop them. The Baron had been stunned at the news. In his desperation to raise the funds to keep his hotel running, he'd allowed himself to be enticed by crooks. After some research, they'd found the loan company didn't even exist and it was impossible to trace who was behind it.

Despite the Baron's protests, Hugh and Cecelia arranged to lend him the funds to carry the hotel through the next few months. Hugh had also insisted on going with Florian to Zermatt to try to get to the bottom of things. There was just so much that didn't add up. Why they had no guests was the biggest mystery of all.

Hamish stared out across the glistening ski field. 'I agree, Millie. This place is breathtaking.'

'How are the legs, Shilly?' Cecelia asked. The woman had surprised them all by taking the lead on several runs.

Mrs Shillingsworth rubbed the tops of her thighs. 'Well, I'm bound to be sore, but it's nothing that a 'soak in that gorgeous pool won't fix,' she replied with a smile.

'What about you, Mrs Oliver?' Alice-Miranda asked. 'Did you have fun out there?'

'Goodness, dear, I can hardly believe I remembered how to ski. I'll leave you all to it this afternoon and go and spend some time with Cyril,' Dolly Oliver replied. 'I don't want him to think we've abandoned him.'

'We made him a card,' Alice-Miranda said. 'It's on the coffee table in our suite. Lucas drew the Cresta Run and Jacinta added Cyril flying up into the air. It's a really good drawing.'

'We wrote a funny poem too,' Millie added.

Dolly chuckled. 'I'm sure he'll appreciate being reminded of the reason he's spending the next week in bed.'

'Have you decided what we'll do about getting home, ma'am?' Shilly asked.

'No, and we might have a slight change of plans if everyone's agreeable,' Cecelia replied. She shot Alice-Miranda a knowing look.

Hamish took a sip of his drink. 'What do you have in mind, Cee?'

'Well, Hugh saw our dear friend Baron von Zwicky last night and it seems the hotel in Zermatt has some rooms available after all. So, we were thinking of catching the Glacier Express and heading over there for another week until Cyril is ready to fly again,' Cecelia explained. 'Sloane, Sep, I've called your parents and they're happy for you to stay on with us.'

'Really?' Sloane said in surprise.

'Your mother is fine with it too, Jacinta,' Cecelia added. 'She was hoping to be home from New York to meet us when we got back but a wonderful opportunity has come up for her to spend a week behind the scenes with Christian Fontaine in Paris, so she's flying directly there. She was worried you'd be upset.'

Jacinta shook her head. 'That's a great scoop. Mummy's not that keen on the cold, anyway, and she's so much happier now that she's working.'

Millie grinned at the girl.

'What are you looking at me like that for?' Jacinta asked.

'Sometimes I wonder what happened to you. It's like you suddenly grew up and now you're the most understanding daughter in the world,' Millie said.

Jacinta shrugged. 'I'm really proud of Mummy. She's changed completely and I know she'd rather be with me, but sometimes you have to make sacrifices if you're going to succeed in life.'

The adults laughed.

'It's going to be so much fun in Zermatt,' Alice-Miranda said dreamily. 'I can't wait for you all to see it. I think it's even prettier than St Moritz.'

'Isn't that near where Caprice skis with her family?' Sloane asked.

Alice-Miranda nodded. 'I think she said her family has a lodge in Cervinia, which is just over the border in Italy.'

'Thankfully, she's staying home these holidays,' Millie said. 'She wouldn't stop bragging about taping some episodes for the next season of *Sweet Things*.'

Sloane rolled her eyes. 'What doesn't that girl brag about?'

'So, what does everyone think about a few more days away?' Cecelia asked. 'I hope getting back a bit later than we planned isn't a problem for anyone.'

'It's fine by us,' Pippa said cheerfully. 'We were thinking of having a weekend in the caravan but I'm just starting to feel my ski legs and I'd love to stay longer.'

Hamish nodded. 'Absolutely. I haven't had this much fun in years.'

'Well,' Dolly began, 'Shilly and I were just saying yesterday that we'd have loved to have time to visit Zurich and perhaps even get to Geneva too.'

'The Large Hadron Collider isn't far from Geneva,' Alice-Miranda piped up. 'I remember in the laboratory one day you told me how much you'd like to see that, Mrs Oliver.'

Dolly nodded eagerly. 'I wouldn't want to bore Shilly to death with it, but perhaps I could take a side trip there on my own.'

Cecelia clapped her hands together. 'Oh, yes, you must. What a wonderful idea.'

'We'll miss you, of course,' Alice-Miranda chimed in.

'Dear girl, you'll be so busy you won't give us two oldies a second thought,' Shilly teased.

'That's not true and you know it.' Alice-Miranda slipped off her chair and wrapped her arms around the woman.

'I'm glad you're not too big for hugs yet,' Shilly said and pecked Alice-Miranda's cheek.

'Never,' Alice-Miranda replied, giving Shilly another squeeze.

'Will Hugh be joining us this afternoon?' Hamish asked. He had enjoyed their skiing yesterday and was keen to tackle a few of the more challenging runs with him.

'Actually, Hugh's already gone over to Zermatt this morning,' Cecelia replied. 'We'll meet him again on Monday.'

'Oh,' Hamish said, 'I'm sorry he had to go.'

'Yes, it's a pity Daddy won't get to see the racing,' Alice-Miranda said.

'I'll take loads of photographs.' Millie whipped her camera out of her jacket pocket as proof.

'All right then, who wants to hit a couple of red runs with me?' Hamish asked.

'Me! Me! Me!' the children shouted over the top of one another.

'Can we find some black trails too?' Lucas asked.

Sloane grimaced. 'I don't know if I'm ready for that yet.'

'How about we manage a couple of reds and then see how everyone feels?' Hamish suggested.

'It's all right,' Alice-Miranda said to Sloane. 'If you don't want to go on the black runs, I'll come back down here with you. But after Gunter took us on that mogul course this morning, I'm pretty sure you wouldn't have any trouble handling it at all.'

'Yeah, you were amazing,' Jacinta agreed. 'And you beat your brother, remember.'

The boy wrinkled his nose. 'Don't remind me.'

'Okay, I'll give it a try,' Sloane said, perking up considerably. 'But if I die, I'm never speaking to any of you ever again.'

Everyone laughed.

'Well, der!' Millie said.

'You know what I mean!' Sloane jammed her helmet on her head and snapped her goggles on over the top as she and her friends charged off to get their skis.

Chapter 18

Hugh Kennington-Jones took the mug of steaming-hot tea from the old woman. In her youth, the Baroness had been a renowned beauty and, even now, the years had been kind.

'Have you learned anything, Hugh?' she asked.

'Not really,' he replied wearily. He'd been working his way through the booking sheets and was waiting for Florian to bring him the past guest registers. 'I can't wrap my head around the gradual decline in occupancy. I want to try to pinpoint when it started.'

Giselle shook her head, her brow creasing into a thousand tiny worries. 'We cannot understand it, either. Surely a couple of ghastly online reviews are not responsible for turning our clientele against us.'

'What I don't understand is that those reviews are completely untrue and anonymous. I mean, there's no credibility in that.' Hugh gave the woman a reassuring smile. 'Don't worry, we'll get to the bottom of it.'

'What if we can't?' Giselle asked, her eyes glistening. 'What then?'

Hugh patted her hand. 'One way or another, we'll work things out,' he said. 'I'm just glad that Alice-Miranda saw Florian when she did, though I do wish he'd told me earlier.'

'I am glad she saw him too.' The Baroness sighed. 'I had asked Florian many times to call you, but you know my husband better than most. He is a proud man and used to being in control. This whole thing just seemed like a bad dream. I really think he believed that one day we would wake up and everything would be back to normal,' she said. 'But now I have Monday to look forward to. Alice-Miranda will be getting a very big hug from her Aunt Giselle, and it will be lovely to see Cecelia.'

'I hope you don't mind but there are twelve in our party, so you're about to be overrun,' Hugh said.

Giselle smiled. 'May there be many more.'

Hugh glanced at the clock on the wall. 'You should get to bed. It's after midnight.'

Florian walked back into reception carrying a pile of guest registers. They were bound in red leather, each with a frayed silk ribbon stitched into the spine. 'I found these downstairs,' he said, lowering them onto the counter with a thump.

'I shall leave you to your task,' Giselle said. She turned and looked into her husband's eyes.

'I will be up as soon as I can,' the Baron said, kissing her forehead.

Giselle waved a hand at Hugh. 'Goodnight, dear.'

'Sleep well,' the man replied as the Baroness walked off.

Florian flipped open the first register. 'Alice-Miranda mentioned that you thought the hotel was fully booked when you checked online,' he said.

Hugh nodded. 'When I couldn't get through to you I thought I'd just book but I couldn't get any of the dates I was after.'

'And yet we have plenty of availability,' Florian said.

'It has to be a bug in the system,' Hugh said. 'Do you have an IT person?'

'Valerie handles all that,' the Baron replied. 'I am afraid Giselle and I are both dinosaurs when it comes to any form of technology – as shown by the fact that I cannot even get my phone to work. You can talk to Valerie tomorrow.'

Hugh moved the lamp closer to illuminate the register. 'I'd like to talk to all the staff, if I may?'

Florian nodded. 'Yes, of course.'

The men turned back to the register. It was going to be a long night.

'Mummy, are you awake?' Alice-Miranda tapped at the door before pushing it open. Her mother was lying in the giant bed, reading.

Cecelia Highton-Smith set aside her book and pushed herself higher against the mountain of pillows. 'What is it, darling?' she asked. The woman held up the covers and Alice-Miranda climbed in beside her.

'I'm sorry Daddy's not here,' Alice-Miranda said, looking up at her mother. 'He would have loved skating on the tennis courts tonight. It was so much fun, although I think poor Millie is going to have a very big bruise on her bottom.'

'Yes, poor Millie indeed,' Cecelia said, chuckling at the memory. The child had been racing Sep when she tripped and, despite almost saving herself, fell heavily onto her bottom and skidded the full length of the arena. Her pants were soaked through and her pride was a little damaged. 'I wish your father was here too, but he's done the right thing going to help Florian.' Cecelia ran her fingers through Alice-Miranda's curls.

'Did *I* do the right thing?' the child asked.

Her mother frowned. 'What do you mean?'

'Should I have kept Uncle Florian's secret?' Alice-Miranda said.

'I know you didn't want to break Uncle Florian's trust, but, because of you, your father can help him now and hopefully he and Giselle won't have to sell the hotel. If they do have to, at least it will be on their own terms and no one else's,' Cecelia explained.

'But I made a promise and I broke it and now I feel all mixed up inside,' Alice-Miranda said. 'When I was younger I felt like I always knew the right thing to do, but now I worry that I meddle when perhaps

I shouldn't. The older I get, the less sure I am about lots of things.'

'Oh, darling, how wonderful to know that at your age,' Cecelia said with a smile. 'It happens to all of us, usually not until we're much older with a lot more mistakes under our belts.'

'Is that true?' Alice-Miranda asked.

Cecelia nodded. 'The thing about you, my precious girl,' Cecelia said, looking into her daughter's big brown eyes, 'is that you have the best instincts of anyone I've ever known. If your first reaction was to tell Daddy so that he could help Uncle Florian, then I have no doubts whatsoever that you did the right thing.'

Alice-Miranda snuggled in next to her mother. 'I love you, Mummy.'

Cecelia felt a lump rising in her throat. Tears pricked at the back of her eyes. 'I love you too, my darling girl, and I couldn't be more proud.'

Cecelia reached across and snatched a tissue from beside the bed. She was fully expecting a scolding from her daughter, who often told her she was far too sentimental for her own good, but when she turned back the child's eyes were closed. Cecelia gently took out the extra pillows and Alice-Miranda nestled under the feather-down duvet, fast asleep.

Chapter 19

'Good afternoon, ladies and gentlemen, and welcome to the final day of White Turf for the year,' a voice boomed over the loudspeakers. 'And what a beautiful day it is.'

'I didn't realise it would be like a carnival,' Jacinta said, her eyes dancing across the ocean-blue sky and craggy mountain peaks. Although the children had seen the marquees and the racetrack from the hotel, it was all so much bigger up close.

'Looks like fun, doesn't it?' Cecelia said with a grin.

White tents were clustered together like a snowy Bedouin village, interspersed among food stalls selling all manner of Swiss treats. The crowd had been steadily building since the gates opened a couple of hours before; a rainbow of coats and hats providing splashes of colour against the frosty backdrop.

Lucas marvelled at a man who walked past with what looked like a raccoon on top of his head. 'I want that hat,' he announced.

Jacinta grimaced. 'No, you don't.'

'How come there are so many dogs here?' Sloane said. She pointed to an enormous Bernese mountain dog being led by a girl who was not much bigger than her pet. 'Isn't he gorgeous?'

The girl stopped for the children to admire him.

'What's his name?' Alice-Miranda asked.

'He's Groβ,' the child replied.

'He's lovely,' Millie said. 'Much better mannered than that horrible Princess Gertie.'

'Do you mean Herr Fanger's dog?' the little girl asked.

Millie winced, wishing she'd kept quiet. St Moritz wasn't a very big place. It stood to reason that all the locals knew each other.

'My mama owns the grooming salon that Princess Gertie comes to.' The girl smiled and lowered her voice conspiratorially. 'I do not like her, either. She has got a very bad temper.'

'She sure does,' Millie said, nodding. 'Herr Fanger told us she doesn't like getting wet. I feel sorry for your poor mother.'

With that, the little girl bid them goodbye and walked on, stopping again after a few steps as more patrons admired her dog.

Coloured flags and sponsors' signboards adorned the railings of the racetrack and a jazz band could be heard in the distance.

Sep's stomach grumbled. 'Can you smell that apple strudel?' he asked, sniffing the air.

'I want to find some potato rösti,' Lucas said. The boy had fallen in love with the Swiss dish after devouring a huge plate of the grated-potato cake topped with a fried egg and bacon for lunch the day before.

A man wearing a thick parka and a navy beanie walked towards them. 'Good morning, Madame

Highton-Smith, I am Klaus Gerber. I will be looking after you and your party for the day.'

'Hello Herr Gerber,' Cecelia said, giving the man a warm handshake. 'Let me introduce everyone.'

'Welcome, welcome,' the man said, greeting them all. 'Would you like to follow me to the sponsors' tent? From there I can direct you to any of the things you might like to see.'

'Thank you,' Cecelia said. 'This is our first time at White Turf and I know we're all keen to see pretty much everything.'

The entourage followed Herr Gerber to a large white marquee, where they entered past a security man with a furry hat and a headset over the top. Once they were all inside Herr Gerber located their passes.

'Wear these at all times and you will have complete access to the tents and the VIP areas as well as the track for the presentation,' he instructed. He then passed out programs and alerted them to the signature event, the Highton's Cup, which was to be the last race of the day.

The marquee was beautifully decorated with sumptuous white lounges, plush rugs and a draped ceiling. There was a bar set up at one end and a long marble countertop where chefs were busily preparing food. Expensive-looking watches were displayed in glass cabinets. Already there was quite a crowd inside.

'Wow,' Sloane whispered to Jacinta, giving the girl a nudge. 'She looks like she escaped from the henhouse.'

The woman's jacket was made of copper-coloured feathers, which, coupled with her deeply tanned face, gave her the appearance of an unplucked rotisserie chicken. 'Who would wear that?' Jacinta giggled.

Sloane winced. 'Not me.'

'This is lovely,' Dolly Oliver gushed as a young man offered her and Shilly drinks from a tray. The woman grinned and reached for a glass of champagne. 'Why not?'

Shilly took one too. 'Thank you.'

The two older women clinked their crystal champagne flutes.

'Mummy, can we have a look outside?' Alice-Miranda asked.

'Of course, darling. Just check in here again in a couple of hours if you like – or whenever you get hungry,' Cecelia said.

'We'll probably see you out there,' Pippa said. 'According to the program, the first race is due to start in about twenty minutes.'

'What sort is it?' Millie asked.

'It's a flat race, so a regular horserace,' Pippa said. 'They have one skijoring race later in the afternoon and one trotting race too.'

'That skijoring sounds nuts,' Lucas said. 'Can you imagine being towed on skis by a galloping horse around a frozen racetrack?'

'It's no crazier than racing horses with spiked shoes on ice, if you ask me,' Jacinta said.

The children bid their farewells and charged off out into the sunshine, eager to find out what else was on offer.

'Where should we go first?' Millie said.

'Do you want to have a look at the horses?' Lucas asked, remembering the parade ring they'd seen on the way to the hospitality tent.

'Sounds good,' Millie said. 'I want to see the shoes. I've been trying to imagine horseshoes like mountain-climbing cleats and I just don't understand how they'd work at all.'

The children made their way through the crowd and emerged at the entrance to an oval-shaped enclosure. Several of the entrants of the first race were being led around inside and one of the beasts stopped right in front of them. The groom gently ran his hand over the creature's foreleg before picking it up to check something in its hoof.

'That's not what I imagined at all,' Millie said. The spikes on the shoes were rounded and only a centimetre long.

'Are you looking at the shoes?' a man beside her asked. He was tall and wore a thick blue-and-green checked coat and a Tyrolean hat.

Millie nodded. 'I was curious as to how the horses could get a grip on the ice,' she replied.

'There is actually a very thick layer of snow on top of the ice,' the man explained. 'The groomers compact it to just the right consistency, so the horses are running on snow, not ice. There is very little danger to them all.'

'That's good to know,' Millie said, relieved. 'I'd been imagining their shoes with great big metal spikes and wondering how the poor creatures didn't cut themselves.'

'Do you ride?' the man asked.

Millie nodded. 'I do and so does Alice-Miranda.' She gestured towards her friend, who was standing beside her.

He eyed the girls closely. 'Can you gallop?'

'Of course,' Millie said.

'Millie's amazing,' Alice-Miranda enthused. 'Her pony, Chops, is really fast. He always beats me and Bony. I'm Alice-Miranda Highton-Smith-Kennington-Jones.' She held out her gloved hand, which the man shook.

'Johan Heffelfinger at your service,' the man said with a smile.

'I'm Millie,' the child said, 'and this is Sloane and Jacinta and Sep and Lucas.'

'They're both brilliant riders,' Sloane piped up. 'They win ribbons and compete and race each other like maniacs. And, just so you know, I'm not a rider and neither are they,' she said, pointing at the others.

'How would you two like to compete today?' the man said with a glint in his eye.

'As if that could happen,' Millie scoffed. 'You're joking, right?'

Herr Heffelfinger shook his head.

'It would be amazing but I imagine the jockeys have to train for ages to race on the snow and no one in their right mind would put a child on a million-dollar racehorse,' Alice-Miranda said.

Millie stepped forward. 'I'd give it a go.'

'All right then, as long as your parents agree, would you like to race for me?' Johan grinned at the girls and adjusted his hat.

Millie blanched. 'I didn't think you were serious!'

'Two of my riders have come down with colds and, well, it is hard to find kids who can ride at short notice,' the man replied.

'Why do you need kids?' Millie asked. 'Can't you afford grown-ups?'

The man laughed heartily. 'I could hardly ask a fully grown adult to race a Shetland pony for me, could I?'

Alice-Miranda's eyes widened. 'Is it a children's race?' she asked.

Johan nodded. '*Ja*, it is only down the straight and it is lots of fun.'

'Shetlands!' Millie exclaimed. 'I'm in.'

Alice-Miranda nodded. 'Me too.'

Just as the girls turned to run back to the sponsors' tent, Cecelia, Hamish and Pippa walked towards them.

Pippa looked at the pair, who were jumping up and down as if they were on springs. 'What are you two so excited about?'

'See that man there?' Millie pointed and he gave a wave. 'His name is Johan and he needs two riders for the program and he asked if we'd like to do it.'

Pippa shook her head. 'You've got be kidding, Millie. There is no way you're going out onto that track on a racehorse.'

'But, Pippa, it's not on a racehorse. There's a kids' race on Shetland ponies, so it won't be too fast at all.' Alice-Miranda's eyes were pleading.

'Pleeeeeease,' Millie begged.

Cecelia looked at Pippa, then at Hamish. 'What do you think?'

Pippa shrugged. 'I'm fine with it if you two are.'

'I'd do it!' Hamish said, grinning widely.

Millie rolled her eyes. 'You'd squash the pony, Daddy.'

Cecelia laughed. 'Okay. Just promise you'll be careful.'

Millie and Alice-Miranda squealed with delight and hugged each other tightly. Then they rushed forward and hugged their mothers.

'You guys are the best!' Millie exclaimed, high-fiving her father.

Johan Heffelfinger walked towards the group and Alice-Miranda introduced him to the parents. 'Thank you for letting me borrow your girls,' he said. 'It sounds as if they are both very accomplished riders. Would you like to come with me and we can get them ready?'

'Yes, of course,' Pippa said.

'If you see Dolly and Shilly, it's probably best not to mention anything just yet,' Cecelia said to the other children. 'I wouldn't want them worrying unnecessarily.'

Lucas grinned. 'We won't say a word, but we'll make sure that they're trackside for the big event.'

'According to the program it's on right after this first race, which is about to start,' Cecelia said, consulting the timetable of events. 'Why don't you all go and watch and we'll see you as soon as the girls are ready?'

'Wish us luck,' Alice-Miranda said.

'Good luck,' the four friends chorused and disappeared into the sea of people.

'Isn't that Grouchy Doerflinger?' Sloane said, looking at a woman dressed in a long brown fur coat with a matching hat and large sunglasses.

'How did you recognise her?' Jacinta said.

Sloane pointed at the man several steps behind Delphine. Otto Fanger was holding Gertie. This time the pooch was wearing a white fur coat with pompoms tied under her neck and matching white sunglasses.

'She's got booties too!' Sep exclaimed.

'That's ridiculous,' Lucas said, as he and the others convulsed with laughter.

Chapter 20

Sloane, Sep, Jacinta and Lucas forged their way to the edge of the track, and then up into one of the temporary grandstands that had been erected for the event.

'Hurry up,' Sloane said. 'The race has already started.'

'There's some space over there,' Lucas said, pointing to the back row.

The children shuffled past the seated patrons, who grumbled about them blocking their view.

'They're so fast,' Sloane gasped, her tummy fluttering at the thought of her friends riding next.

As the field rounded the bend and charged down the straight towards the finish line, it was neck and neck between a jockey in red and another in blue. A huge bay horse with a jockey in green silks surged to the front, leaving the rest of the field in its powdery cloud.

Jacinta shouted and waved at Mrs Oliver and Mrs Shillingsworth, who made their way up into the stand to join them.

'Well, that was exciting, wasn't it?' Mrs Shillingsworth panted. 'Oh dear, I have to catch my breath.'

'Not as exciting as the next race is going to be,' Sloane said with a sly grin.

'Why is that, dear?' Shilly asked.

'Our very special race is soon to begin,' the announcer said as a huge cheer went up around the track, 'but first we will have the presentation for the last race.'

It only seemed to take minutes for the jockeys and their owners to gather onto the podium, where they were presented with exquisite crystal trophies and a giant novelty cheque to the winner.

'What's everyone so excited about now?' Dolly said, craning her neck to see.

As the ground crew cleared away the podium, several stumpy ponies trotted out from behind one of the tents and onto the track.

Shilly smiled. 'Oh, aren't they precious?'

A roar of laughter echoed through the crowd as a pony carrying a rather large rider appeared and darted all over the racecourse.

Dolly giggled. 'Good grief, I hope the lad gets a headstart to give him a fighting chance.'

'Can you see them yet?' Jacinta asked, leaning out around the other spectators.

'See who?' Dolly asked.

The little ponies ran all over the track towards the finish line, warming up.

'There's Alice-Miranda!' Sloane yelled, jumping to her feet and calling out to the girl.

'No!' Shilly's jaw dropped. 'What on earth is she doing down there?'

The tiny child waved up at the crowd. She was wearing lilac silks with a white star in the middle of her back and her Shetland pony was a small bay steed with a very jaunty gait.

'There's Millie,' Sep called out as the child cantered past on a grey pony. Millie's silks were red with white stripes.

Dolly's eyes were the size of dinner plates as she struggled to understand. 'Does Cecelia know about this?'

Lucas nodded. 'She and Pippa told them they could do it.'

'Mad! Stark-raving mad, the pair of them,' Shilly blustered. 'What if they fall?'

'Then they can keep Cyril company,' Sloane said cheekily.

The other children stared at the girl.

'What? I didn't mean it,' she protested.

'I can't believe Cecelia would have encouraged them,' Dolly Oliver tutted. 'I wish Hugh was still here. He'd have talked sense into the woman.'

'Have you ever seen Bony and Chops at full gallop? Shetlands will be a walk in the park for those two,' Jacinta said, trying to reassure the distressed woman.

Mrs Oliver shook her head. 'Not on an icy track.'

'There's Cecelia now,' Shilly said. She waved to the woman, who was walking along with Pippa and Hamish.

Hamish shielded his eyes from the sun. 'You've got the perfect position up there.'

The three of them bounded up to join the others at the top of the grandstand.

'What were you thinking, Cecelia?' Dolly Oliver said, shaking her head. 'This can't be safe.'

'It's all right, Dolly.' Cecelia patted the woman's arm. 'Pippa and I watched them warm up. I have to say their ponies are two of the sweetest tempered little things I've ever encountered. Shetlands aren't always known for their agreeable manners but those two are darlings.'

At that moment the PA system blared again, calling the riders back to the start.

'We are just about ready to start a new race on our program. It's one for the young riders, the Shetland Stakes, sponsored by our very own Fanger's Palace Hotel,' said the announcer.

A cheer went up around the course as Otto Fanger blew kisses to the crowd from the edge of the track. Every inch of him exuded Alpine royalty. He was cradling Princess Gertie in the crook of his arm and soaking up the adoration. His wife, as pinched as ever, stood by his side and gave a half-hearted wave.

'She doesn't look very happy to be here,' Jacinta observed.

'She doesn't look very happy full stop,' Lucas said with a grin.

'We have a fabulous field of eight runners and their very brave riders, two of whom I am told have never ridden on the snow before,' the announcer continued. 'We wish them the best of luck on their dash down the straight.'

The ponies, too small for the barrier, were assembled behind a red line that had been sprayed onto the snow.

'I can see the starter having his last words with the group,' the announcer said, talking the crowd through the activity at the starting line. 'And they're off! Itty Bitty got away quickly, followed closely by Tiny Dancer. Then we have Strudel and Ladybird, next I can see Twinkletoes and coming up on the outside is Hula Hoop. As they reach the halfway mark, Bumblebee is making up ground and after her is Lollylegs. Our newcomers are doing well . . .'

'I can't look,' Shilly moaned, covering her eyes. A moment later she spread her fingers ever so slightly, unable to resist a tiny peek. 'It's just like Cyril all over again.'

The crowd went wild as the ponies drew closer to the finish line.

'Go, Alice-Miranda! Go, Millie!' Cecelia yelled, echoed by their friends.

'I think Millie's going to win,' Sep said, holding his breath as her little grey mare, Bumblebee, flashed ahead of the rest.

'Oh dear, Itty Bitty looks to be tiring and Tiny Dancer has fallen to the back of the field. What's Strudel up to?' the announcer pondered aloud.

The little cream-coloured beast was throwing his head in the air. There was a groan from the crowd as the pony stopped in its tracks, made a sharp left turn and then tore off back towards the starting line. The spectators roared with laughter when the pony pulled up at the rail and stole a plate of apple strudel from a little boy who had, up until that second, been enjoying his afternoon snack.

'Now we know why she is called Strudel, eh?' The announcer chuckled. 'But, look, we have a new leader. Bumblebee has some sting in her tail today! She's followed by Lollylegs, and here comes Tiny Dancer,' the man's voice reached a crescendo, as the crowd clapped and cheered. 'They've hit the line and it's Bumblebee in first place! I think we will have to check the photo for second and third.'

'Millie won!' Hamish cried. He hugged Pippa and jumped up and down. 'Our little girl won!'

Mrs Oliver and Shilly embraced with relief. Sloane and Sep did too until they realised what they were doing and quickly withdrew from one another.

'Ew, don't touch me,' Sloane grouched.

Sep was mortified. 'I didn't mean to.'

'It looks like Alice-Miranda came third,' Hamish said, pointing to the track.

Jacinta disentangled herself from Lucas's arms. 'I told you those two are amazing,' she said to Mrs Oliver and Mrs Shillingsworth, who were both fanning themselves and gasping for breath.

'Please put your hands together for Herr Fanger and his lovely wife, Frau Doerflinger, here to present the prizes to our winners,' the announcer boomed.

Millie and Alice-Miranda both jumped off their mounts and hugged each other.

'You were unbelievable!' Alice-Miranda said, beaming at her friend.

'You were too,' Millie said, her smile stretching across her face.

Johan Heffelfinger jogged onto the track and shook hands with both children as two grooms took the ponies from them. 'Well done, girls!' he exclaimed.

'That was the best!' Millie said. 'We'll ride for you anytime.'

'Please come back again next year,' Herr Heffel-finger said with a wink.

A man holding a microphone invited the children onto the stage. Otto Fanger and Delphine Doerflinger were standing on either side of him, behind an array of trophies. Otto had put Princess Gertie on the ground and, judging by the disdain on the little dog's face, she didn't seem particularly impressed about it.

'I think we should congratulate all our runners for their courage,' the man said. The crowd responded with enthusiastic applause. 'And now to our placegetters. Congratulations to Alice-Miranda Highton-Smith-Kennington-Jones, for coming third riding the lovely Lollylegs.' Alice-Miranda, who was standing to the right of Frau Doerflinger, stepped forward as Herr Fanger handed her a small silver trophy in the shape of a cup.

'Thank you, Herr Fanger.' She shook the man's hand and smiled at his wife. 'Thank you, Frau Doerflinger.' Alice-Miranda looked at the woman, who seemed much more interested in the crowd.

Delphine grunted in reply.

A small boy with a mop of white-blond curls named Piers was given a slightly larger trophy for second place. He raised his riding crop into the air in victory.

'I am sure that we all hope the Shetland Stakes becomes a regular feature on the White Turf calendar,' the presenter said, looking to Herr Fanger.

The hotelier nodded vigorously while his wife plastered a grin on her face.

'Well, there can only be one winner, so I would like to ask Millie . . .' The man leaned around and whispered to the girl. 'I'm sorry I don't know your full name,' he apologised.

'Just Millie is fine,' the girl said.

'Millie, please come and accept your trophy,' the presenter said into the microphone.

As the girl walked to the middle of the stage, the crowd cheered. None more enthusiastically than the group at the top of the central grandstand, who were whistling and whooping.

'It seems you have a lot of fans, Miss Millie,' the man said.

The child's freckles exploded into a burst of crimson confetti.

'Well done, Miss Millie. I did not know you had such talents,' Otto said with a grin. He passed her a trophy that was almost as tall as she was.

'Thank you, Herr Fanger.' Millie shook his hand and the pair posed for the photographers.

Alice-Miranda smiled at her friend but was soon distracted by Frau Doerflinger. The woman appeared to be scouring the crowd for someone. Her complexion was pallid and even though the temperature was a crisp minus eight degrees, a trickle of perspiration ran down her temple.

Alice-Miranda tried to work out what Frau Doerflinger was looking at. She followed the woman's line of sight until her eyes came to rest on a very glamorous couple. The man wore a long black coat and a sneer, while the woman's waterfall of glossy brunette curls framed an almost perfectly proportioned face. She wore a black fur coat with a row of pearls the size of quail eggs around her neck. Alice-Miranda recognised her as the whiny woman from the chairlift the other day. The man raised a glass of champagne in Frau Doerflinger's direction and Alice-Miranda could have sworn the woman began to tremble.

'Let's give all of these brave children another round of applause,' the presenter boomed into the microphone.

Millie grinned at Alice-Miranda, who smiled back at her. When she looked out into the crowd again, the couple were gone.

Chapter 21

Delphine Doerflinger pinched the tips of her gloves, easing them off before she swiped her key card against the panel. She pushed open the door and began to take off her coat when she noticed an unmistakable scent – one that had no business being inside her home. She quickly turned to leave, pulling her coat back on.

'Going somewhere, Frau Doerflinger?' the intruder said.

Delphine stopped in her tracks and swallowed hard. 'How did you get in here?' she asked.

'That is none of your concern,' the man said coolly. 'You are home early.'

Delphine spotted a suitcase in the hall. She looked at it and back at the intruder. 'I have a headache,' she replied.

'You certainly do.' The man raised his eyebrow at her. 'Now, what's this I hear about the Baron deciding not to borrow *our* money?'

'He is a smart man. He must have read the fine print,' Delphine said, her temperature rising.

'Then you must find another way to honour your agreements,' the man said.

The sound of heels striking the timber floor bounced around the walls, followed soon after by the voice of a young woman.

'For such an ugly hag she has many beautiful things,' she trilled. The young woman reached the hallway, twirling the silk Hermès scarf around her neck, and saw the man was no longer alone. 'Oh, I didn't know you were here,' she said, fingering the diamond teardrops dangling from her lobes.

'Take them off at once,' Delphine demanded. Otto had given her those earrings for their tenth wedding anniversary and the sight of them on that gold-digger made her stomach churn.

'Or what?' The young woman smiled. 'I'm sure you would agree that they look much better on me.'

'Otto will be back any minute now. You cannot be here,' Delphine said, hating the pleading note in her voice.

'You clearly don't know your husband as well as I do,' the man scoffed. 'Herr Fanger loves nothing more than to be the centre of attention. He will not leave the racetrack when everyone in St Moritz is falling all over themselves to congratulate him. But perhaps there is one thing he loves even more than an adoring crowd . . . Is it his wife?' The man looked at the young woman, who shook her head.

'No, no, no,' she giggled, fluttering her fingers.

'Is it his hotel?' the man asked, sweeping his arm around the room.

Sancia pouted. 'I don't think so,' she said in a singsong voice.

'Oh, I know!' The man grinned. 'It's that stupid little dog.'

The brunette reached into her pocket and pulled out Gertie's diamond hairclips, which she displayed on her palm for Delphine to see. 'Can I keep these, Vincenzo?'

'Of course you can,' he sneered. 'Princess Gertie may not be needing them if someone refuses to cooperate.'

Delphine's heart thumped in her chest. 'What did you do?' she rasped.

'Poor little Gertie. I think she has run away,' the man said.

'Please don't hurt her,' Delphine begged.

'What do you care?' the man replied. 'You despise that mutt.'

'But . . . Otto loves her,' Delphine said. She despised *herself* for getting into this mess.

The man glared at her. 'I thought you hated him too.'

Delphine's mouth grew dry. Otto was an annoyance, a buffoon, but he was a good man with the kindest heart and he didn't deserve to lose everything because of her stupidity.

The young woman walked into the lounge and plonked down on the largest of the sofas. 'Vincenzo, can we go now? I am so bored,' she whined loudly. 'And you promised me chocolate.'

'We will leave soon enough,' Vincenzo replied. He gestured to the suitcase. 'We don't want to keep Frau Doerflinger from her train.'

Delphine baulked. 'What are you talking about? I have a hotel to run!'

'You have a hotel to *buy*,' Vincenzo said. 'I suggest you get to the other side of the mountains right away and close that deal, or you know what will happen.'

'I can't just leave. What will I tell Otto?' Delphine protested.

Vincenzo shrugged. 'You take regular trips to the chocolate factory. Isn't that what you always tell him?'

Delphine inhaled sharply. It was, but she had never told Vincenzo that. 'I have to write Otto a note.'

Sancia tripped out to the kitchen and opened the refrigerator. 'I can't believe you don't have any chocolate in this house,' she called.

'It is peculiar given the amount of chocolate downstairs,' Vincenzo agreed. He turned to follow Delphine to her study.

'You don't need to accompany me,' she snapped.

Vincenzo tilted his head to one side and smiled. 'On the contrary, Frau. It would not do me well to leave you to your own devices.'

Chapter 22

Alice-Miranda and Millie walked across the snowy roadway to the rear entrance of Fanger's Palace Hotel.

'Can you hold this?' Millie asked, passing the girl her trophy. Alice-Miranda balanced the huge cup on her hip. Millie rummaged around in her pocket and pulled out the little disc she'd found in the foyer the other morning. 'Oh drat, I forgot our room key,' she said. 'I don't suppose this will be of any use, although maybe it really was my lucky charm in the race.'

Alice-Miranda smiled. 'I think sheer talent, guts and determination probably had a lot to do with it too.'

'We'll have to go back and get the key from your mother.' Millie sighed and took her trophy.

The girls were on their way to the hotel to deposit their winnings and change out of their silks. They had just turned around when they saw Lucas racing towards them.

'Hey, wait for me,' he yelled as he sped up to the hotel gate.

'What are you doing here?' Alice-Miranda asked. 'I thought you and the others were getting something to eat.'

'I need my gloves,' the boy said. He pulled his hands out of his jacket pockets, revealing two pale sets of digits, which looked distinctly blue on the tips.

'Have you got your key?' Millie asked. 'I forgot mine.'

Lucas pulled out his card and swiped the keypad next to the gate. The children walked through a small garden and into a foyer, where they found a lift. The hotel seemed deserted compared to the early-morning bustle. Lucas pushed the button.

'That trophy is enormous,' Lucas said to Millie as they waited.

Millie held up the silver cup and studied it closely. 'I still can't believe I won.'

Lucas nodded. 'You were incredible. You too, Alice-Miranda.'

'It was so much fun,' Alice-Miranda said, grinning at the memory.

After several minutes had gone by, Lucas pushed the button again.

'Do you think it's out of order?' Millie said. Her arms were beginning to ache from holding her prize.

Lucas walked to the other end of the vestibule. 'That's weird,' he said, glancing around. 'You'd think there'd be a staircase down here somewhere. Otherwise, how would you get up and down if the lift's not working?'

'What about through that door?' Alice-Miranda said, pointing at a panel in the wall.

'Where?' Lucas asked, trying to see what his cousin was looking at.

'There.' The girl ran her finger around the outline of a door that was almost completely camouflaged in the timber wall.

'Good spotting,' Millie said. She pushed on the panel and it pivoted, opening out onto a staircase.

'The sign must have fallen off,' Lucas remarked. 'Again.'

He and Alice-Miranda bounded up the stairs two at a time like a pair of thumping elephants. Millie was slower, taking care not to drop her trophy. Fortunately, each floor was clearly marked on the back of the exit doors. They passed the spa and swimming pool, which they knew was only a couple flights below reception.

'Finally,' Alice-Miranda puffed as they reached the fourth floor. She was about to turn the door-handle when she was startled by loud voices. They were coming from the other side of the wall, and whoever was speaking didn't sound happy.

Millie pressed her finger to her lips.

'Where are they?' Lucas whispered.

Alice-Miranda pointed to a vent high up on the wall. 'It's coming from in there.'

'Otto will be worried, you know,' they heard a woman say. 'I always tell him my travel plans in advance.'

'You wrote him a note,' a man replied.

'It's Frau Doerflinger,' Alice-Miranda said. 'But I'm not sure about the other person.'

Millie and Lucas nodded.

'He knows about your acquisition, doesn't he?' the man said.

'Yes,' Delphine replied. 'He wants to know why we didn't celebrate last night.'

'Then, surely, he will not even bat an eyelid. You are a businesswoman going away to do business,' the man said. 'I expect to hear from you in the next few days. Good news only, please, or else – *poof* – she will be gone forever.'

'You have no business speaking to me like that,' Frau Doerflinger said.

'On the contrary, your business depends on our business, does it not?' the man said archly.

There was the sound of shuffling feet and the voices ceased.

The children looked at one another.

'What was all that about?' Millie said.

'If I didn't think she was the biggest dragon in the world, I'd have said that Frau Doerflinger almost sounded scared,' Lucas said.

Alice-Miranda nodded. 'I wonder where she's going and who will be gone forever.'

'Who cares?' Millie huffed. 'Hopefully it's her and she's going far, far away and we'll never have to see her again.'

Alice-Miranda looked at her friends. 'Come on, we should hurry up and get changed.'

The tiny girl pushed open the door and was surprised to see Delphine Doerflinger come out of the invisible doorway she'd taken the children through the other day. The woman was wearing the same heavy fur coat they'd seen her in at the races but was now trundling a small leather suitcase.

'Hello Frau Doerflinger,' Alice-Miranda said, greeting the woman. 'Are you going somewhere?'

Delphine spun around as if she'd been poked in the bottom with a pin. 'Hasn't anyone ever told you it is rude to sneak up on people?' she snapped, signalling to a porter.

A young man strode forward.

'Take this to the car,' Delphine barked. 'I am going to the station.'

The porter looked as if he had just swallowed a slug. 'I-I'm afraid that the car is at the track. Herr Fanger requested it be on standby for his use.'

'Then get me another,' she demanded.

'There are none available at the moment,' the porter said, his voice quivering. 'Many of our guests booked them as their transport to the races. We weren't aware you would be needing a vehicle today.'

'*Faulpelz*,' Delphine muttered under her breath. 'I have an unexpected business trip. Call me a taxi!'

'I will do my best, Frau,' the young man replied, relieved for the excuse to get away.

Frau Doerflinger turned to see Millie and Lucas staring at her. 'What are you lot gawking at?' she snapped.

The children shook their heads. 'Nothing,' Millie squeaked.

Alice-Miranda rejoined them after having asked for another key at reception. 'Got it,' she said, triumphantly holding up the white card. She paused, noticing the woman's vexed state. 'Are you all right, Frau Doerflinger?' she asked.

'Of course I am all right,' the woman said. 'Stop minding other people's business. Nobody likes a *Schnüffler*.'

'I didn't mean to upset you,' Alice-Miranda apologised. 'Have a good trip.'

She walked off with Millie and Lucas, still troubled by the woman's demeanour. They stopped at a door on the first landing, which provided a barrier between the hotel's public areas and guestrooms.

'I don't know why you bother being nice to her,' Lucas said, stopping to swipe the keypad by the big glass door.

'She's so mean,' Millie said indignantly. 'Seriously, she doesn't know the first thing about being hospitable – at least not to kids.'

The children continued upstairs until they reached the entrance to their wing.

'I'll get my gloves and meet you back here in a minute,' Lucas said, racing off to his room while Alice-Miranda and Millie headed into their suite.

The girls arranged their trophies on the coffee table and Millie took a few photos before they got changed and folded Herr Heffelfinger's silks. They emerged from their room a few minutes later to find Lucas waiting for them in the corridor.

'Is Zermatt really as lovely as St Moritz?' Millie asked as the three children walked downstairs.

Alice-Miranda nodded. 'It's even lovelier, although there isn't a beautiful lake like here. The skiing is amazing and there's the most wonderful museum. It's across the road from Uncle Florian's hotel and it's full of bizarre mechanical instruments. I've been there lots of times. My friend Nina lives there – you'll get to meet her. She's a bit older than I am and she's really sweet.'

When they reached the reception area, Frau Doerflinger was still waiting for her car. She seemed to be staring off into the distance, deep in thought. Alice-Miranda hesitated as Millie and Lucas charged past, eager to avoid being on the receiving end of the woman's sharp tongue again.

'Excuse me, Frau Doerflinger, we're just on our way back to the racing. Would you like me to ask Herr Fanger to have the car sent back for you?' the child asked.

Something resembling fear flashed in the woman's eyes. 'You will not say a word to Herr Fanger,' she ordered.

'Of course.' The child smiled. 'I just thought –'

The same porter from before scampered towards them and picked up the woman's suitcase. 'Frau Doerflinger, your car has arrived,' he announced breathlessly.

'About time,' Delphine muttered.

'Thank you for having us,' Alice-Miranda said. 'Fanger's Palace is such a lovely hotel. We'll be leaving tomorrow to catch the Glacier Express over to see Uncle Florian and Aunt Giselle. Daddy's there already.'

The woman leaned down and peered into the girl's eyes. 'What did you say?'

'We're going to Zermatt in the morning,' the child repeated. She wondered if the hotelier had met the Von Zwickys.

'Not that. The other part,' Delphine said impatiently.

'E-excuse me, Frau, but your train will be leaving soon,' said the fidgety porter.

The woman turned and glared at him. 'I'm coming!' she barked, then turned back to the little girl. 'Continue.'

'Oh, Daddy had to go and help Uncle Florian with some urgent business yesterday,' Alice-Miranda said, slightly disconcerted. She eyed the flecks of spittle that had begun to gather around the woman's mouth. 'He was sorry to miss the White Turf. He would have loved it too, although I think he might have been less enthusiastic about Millie and me racing in the Shetland Stakes,' she added.

Delphine drew herself up to her full height. 'How very interesting,' she murmured. Without a backward glance, she turned on her heel and glided out the revolving door.

'Have a lovely trip,' Alice-Miranda called as she ran to catch up to her friends.

Chapter 23

The children wove their way through the food stalls, past gleaming luxury cars on plinths and along a line of marquees hosting various events. There looked to be a fashion parade going on in one of them, while in another a large crowd was being serenaded by a string quartet. As they neared their destination, the children heard a loud sob.

'You must find her, you simply must!' It was Herr Fanger and he was surrounded by a circle of grim-faced onlookers.

'When did you see her last?' asked a well-meaning woman in a black fluffy coat and red turban.

'She was here just a minute ago and now she is gone,' the man moaned, cradling his face in his hands.

Alice-Miranda walked up to the man. 'Excuse me, Herr Fanger, who are you looking for?'

He turned to the child, tears welling in his eyes. 'My little Gertie has disappeared.'

'Oh dear, we can help look for her,' she offered. 'Millie, do you want to see if Sloane and the others are in the tent? They can help with the search too.'

Millie wrinkled her nose, thinking of all the treats she would miss out on. 'All right, but I want something really yummy to eat as soon as we find her,' she said, before scurrying away.

Alice-Miranda turned back to the distraught man. 'She can't have gone too far.'

'It is not like her to wander off,' Herr Fanger said, dabbing at his cheeks with a handkerchief.

Millie reappeared with their friends in tow.

'We'd better find that spoilt pooch fast. I was just about to eat the biggest, most delicious-looking slice of strudel you have ever seen. It had cream *and* ice-cream,' Jacinta blustered.

Millie cleared her throat and gestured towards Herr Fanger, who was sniffing quietly to himself.

'I mean, that sweet little dog,' Jacinta mumbled, hoping the man hadn't heard her the first time.

'Why don't we split up and each take a couple of rows of tents?' Alice-Miranda suggested. 'Gertie might have wandered into one of them and found something yummy to eat, like Jacinta's strudel.'

'My princess does not like strudel at all,' Herr Fanger whimpered. 'She is a very fussy eater.'

The children split up into pairs and Lucas allocated their search zones. 'Remember,' he instructed in a low voice, 'if you do find the snappy mutt, she's a princess in looks only. Take care of your hands – you're likely to lose a finger if you go in too quickly.'

Sep grinned and the girls giggled.

Alice-Miranda and Millie headed around to the back of the sponsors' tent while Lucas and Sep charged off to the other end of the food stalls. Lucas considered that, if they didn't end up finding the dog, he could at least grab himself that rösti he'd been hankering after.

Sloane and Jacinta darted to the back of the grandstands. As the children scattered, the afternoon train could be heard pulling out of the station.

Millie and Alice-Miranda didn't find anything, so they decided to try the outdoor cafe that fronted the jazz band. A U-shape of smaller tents and marquees created a square, which was packed with elegant people sitting at tables or standing in the sunshine sipping champagne.

'Excuse me,' Millie said as she poked her head under one of the tables.

'What in heaven's name are you doing, child?' a woman reproached. Her wrinkled hands didn't appear to belong to her flat, ironed face.

'We're looking for Herr Fanger's dog,' Millie replied. She stood up and walked over to the next table, where she crouched down again.

Alice-Miranda glanced around the edge of the crowd. Out of the corner of her eye she spotted a woman in a long white fur coat. She was holding a phone to her ear and, as she put it away, she dropped something onto the ground. At first Alice-Miranda thought it was a furry hat but she soon realised it wasn't a hat at all.

'Gertie!' the child shouted, racing towards the woman. 'That's Princess Gertie, Herr Fanger's dog!'

Millie's head jerked up, thumping the underside of the table. 'Ow,' she said, rubbing her crown. She scrambled out and ran towards her friend.

'Thank goodness you found her,' Alice-Miranda said. 'Herr Fanger will be so happy.'

'I don't know what you're talking about,' the woman said, stepping away from the dog. 'I didn't find her.'

'Then why do you have her?' Alice-Miranda asked.

The woman shrugged. 'A man paid me five hundred francs to look after her until he called, which he just did. Then he told me to let her go.'

Gertie was dancing about, the pompoms on her coat jiggling.

Alice-Miranda frowned. 'Why would anyone do that?' she wondered aloud. She grabbed an abandoned half-eaten sausage from a nearby table and knelt down in the snow. The little white fur ball wagged her tail as the girl inched closer. 'Gertie, look what I've got,' she cooed, dangling the bratwurst in the air.

Gertie dashed towards Alice-Miranda and snatched the sausage from her hand. As she did, the child scooped the dog into her arms.

'So much for Gertie being a fussy eater,' Millie said, joining them. 'Where was she?'

'This lady was . . .' Alice-Miranda turned around to find that the woman had gone.

'What lady?' Millie asked.

'She was here just a second ago. She said that someone had paid her to hold onto Gertie,' Alice-Miranda said.

Millie eyes grew wide. 'Like dognapping? We have to find her and call the police.'

'I think we should take Gertie back to Herr Fanger first. He'll be so relieved.' Alice-Miranda held on to the little dog, who had now finished the sausage and was squirming like a worm.

The girls hurried through the crowd and discovered the poor man sitting at a table sobbing into his handkerchief and blowing his nose loudly. 'My baby. Someone find my baby,' he wailed through hiccuping gulps.

'Herr Fanger, we found her,' Alice-Miranda called as the girls rushed towards him.

Otto immediately stopped crying and leapt to his feet, almost knocking Alice-Miranda over as he seized Gertie. 'My darling, where did you go?' he said, hugging her close to him. 'Are you hurt, my princess?'

The creature sniffed her master's face.

Otto's jaw dropped. 'Where are her hairclips? She was wearing her diamonds and now they are gone.'

'That woman must have stolen them,' Millie said.

'What woman? Where?' Otto demanded.

Alice-Miranda relayed what had happened and everything the woman had told her.

'We must find her at once,' Otto said. 'I will alert security. What did she look like?'

'She was tall with long blonde hair and she was wearing sunglasses and a white fur coat,' Alice-Miranda reported.

Millie glanced around. 'Sort of like every other woman here at the moment.'

Several of the ladies who had been comforting Herr Fanger shot Millie snooty glances and quickly moved away.

'If she was after Gertie's jewels, Herr Fanger, she's probably long gone by now, especially as she knows I've seen her up close,' Alice-Miranda said.

Otto nodded and turned to one of his minders. 'Get Gertie a fillet steak and caviar. You know she won't eat anything less.'

'Actually she just ate someone's leftover sausage,' Millie piped up. 'She didn't seem to mind that at all.'

Otto's jaw dropped. 'My princess doesn't eat leftovers!' He looked at the dog, who licked her lips.

'Did you find her?' Lucas called as he and Sep ran over to them, with Jacinta and Sloane in tow.

'Sure did,' Millie said with a satisfied smile. She turned to Otto. 'Good thing too, as you would have been lonely tonight without Gertie and Frau Doerflinger.'

Otto looked at her blankly. 'What do you mean?' he asked.

Millie bit her lip. 'Oh, just that Frau Doerflinger has gone away on business,' she said, wishing she'd kept quiet.

Otto Fanger's brows knotted. It wasn't like his wife to disappear without any notice. What on earth was going on today?

Chapter 24

Millie gazed through the glass roof at the snow-covered peaks above. 'Whoa,' she gasped.

'Just look at the beautiful mountains and the beautiful snow and all those beautiful little villages with their beautiful churches,' Sloane trilled, mimicking Herr Fanger's accent and mannerisms perfectly. 'There is so much beauty it is hurting my eyes.'

The others giggled.

Alice-Miranda grinned. 'Poor Herr Fanger. He's so sweet.'

'Pity about his wife,' Millie added.

The six children were seated together at one end of the train carriage while the adults sat behind them.

'How good was that skijoring yesterday?' Lucas said.

Sloane nodded. 'My heart was beating so fast I thought I had a bomb in my chest.'

'It was fantastic,' Millie agreed. 'I'd love to have a go at it one day – but I think I might need to improve my skiing first.'

Once they had recovered Gertie, the rest of the afternoon had gone by in a flash. Lucas had finally got his rösti for dinner and Millie was able to indulge her new-found love of Fanger's Chocolate, although she was disappointed that there weren't any of the giant blocks Lucas had discovered in the loading dock. Herr Fanger had sent boxes of the mouth-watering confections to each of the children to thank them for helping him find his beloved Gertie.

The party on the lake had continued long after the horses had been trucked back to their stables and, to top it all off, there was a huge fireworks display which lit up the whole village and half the mountain. By the time their party had wandered back to the hotel, it was well past nine o'clock.

Suffice to say there were a few tired travellers the following morning.

After the group had farewelled Mrs Oliver and Mrs Shillingsworth, who were catching a train to Zurich an hour later, they boarded the Glacier Express, bound for Zermatt and another week of skiing.

All of the passengers were given headsets so they could listen to the commentary about the history of the train and some of the locations and landmarks they passed along the way. A gong conveniently sounded each time an audio recording began.

'Do we have to listen to every bit?' Sloane griped. 'These things hurt my ears.'

'Do what you like,' Sep said, 'but I'm not going to miss any of it.' He put the earbuds in and turned up the volume.

The train had just travelled through a section of track that seemed to go around in circles and was now approaching the famous Landwasser Viaduct, a long curved stone bridge over a deep ravine. Its pillars rose from the valley below, creating another picturesque scene. Millie snapped away with her camera, trying to get as many shots as she could, although the reflection on the window was making it a tad tricky.

'It's a pity your father's not here,' Millie said to Alice-Miranda as the train forged on through a pretty village with a tall church spire and A-framed houses.

'Oh, he had to go this way to Zermatt. Even though the train's slow, this is still the most direct route from St Moritz,' Alice-Miranda replied.

'Will we be coming back this way as well?' Sloane asked.

Alice-Miranda nodded. 'I think so, unless Daddy would prefer to drive.'

Cecelia had been worried that the children might get bored as the journey would take almost eight hours but there was no sign of it as they played cards, took photographs and listened to the commentary. At one stage, she thought it was far too quiet and was surprised to see that Millie and Sloane had fallen asleep. Sep was reading the guidebook and Alice-Miranda, Lucas and Jacinta were all staring out the windows, mesmerised by the landscape.

'Look at that stunning building!' Alice-Miranda exclaimed as the train drew into a station.

Lucas read the name on the platform. 'Disentis. Isn't this where the Fanger's Chocolate factory is?'

Millie roused at the sound of her favourite sweet. 'Did someone say chocolate factory?' she said sleepily. 'Can you see it?'

Lucas shook his head. 'I think it was that building Alice-Miranda spotted just before the station.'

'Keep an eye out for Grouchy Doerflinger. She's probably lurking around here somewhere,' Millie said, before falling back to sleep.

It was mid-afternoon by the time the train started to climb high into the mountains, towards Andermatt, where the snow was thick and the extra-toothed track in the centre of the rail lines clawed at the circular cogs beneath the carriages, propelling the train forward on the icy rails. Sep was fascinated by the engineering of the railway and had borrowed Millie's guidebook to read about it.

Millie's stomach grumbled. 'Do they have snacks in the dining car?' she asked Alice-Miranda.

'I'm sure they will,' the child replied. 'Do you want to go and have a look?'

Millie nodded. The girls stood up and asked if anyone wanted anything. The others were keen for a walk, so they all headed off together. The dining car was only one carriage along from where they were sitting.

'Who wants a hot chocolate?' Millie asked, scanning the menu. She ordered six of them and some cakes too. The children sat together at the tables, which were mostly empty apart from one couple, who were staring into one another's eyes while holding hands.

'Do you want to walk to the end of the train before we go back to our seats?' Sep asked. 'I think my backside's numb from all that sitting.'

There was a murmur of agreement and the children finished their drinks and set off towards the front of the train. They weren't sure how far they'd get but calculated there were at least four passenger carriages ahead.

A young man in a uniform stepped in front of them as they reached the door to the engine. 'May I help you?' he asked.

'Hello,' Alice-Miranda said. 'We were just stretching our legs. I'm Alice-Miranda Highton-Smith-Kennington-Jones and these are my friends.' Alice-Miranda proceeded to introduce everyone.

'I'm Anton,' the man said with a smile. He was a short fellow with a kind face and an air of calm about him.

'We know,' Millie said, pointing at his name badge.

'Yes, of course,' the man replied with a chuckle. 'I'm afraid you can't go any further unless you'd like to drive the train.'

'That would be awesome,' Sep gasped.

The train guard grinned. 'Sorry, you can't *actually* do that.'

Sep nodded, a little disappointed. 'How many carriages are there?' he inquired.

'It can vary, depending on how many passengers we have and if there are any goods being transported over the mountains,' the man replied. 'Sometimes we need to hitch on extra carriages. We have two engines as well.'

'Two? Why?' Millie asked.

'Well, sometimes we need pulling power at the back as well as the front, so there's an engine up front and another at the back. That way, we can reverse the train at any time,' Anton explained, impressed by the children's curiosity.

At that moment a huge plume of snow flew up past the windows and over the roof. The passengers in the carriage sat to attention, peering outside.

'See that?' Anton said. 'That was the train ploughing the snow. They had a big dump up here last night, so there's a scoop on the front of the engine that throws the snow up off the track.'

'Cool,' Sep breathed as another huge spray of powder slapped at the roof.

'Does the train really cross a glacier?' Alice-Miranda asked.

Anton chuckled again. 'No, they're much higher up in the mountains. The train used to travel overland the whole way but it was too dangerous in winter. There's now a network of tunnels so that it can run all year round.'

'Hey, it's snowing,' Lucas said, pointing to the fat flakes pouring from the sky. It looked as if someone was standing on the roof with a bucket of white confetti and shaking it onto the ground.

'Can we walk to the other end of the train too?' Sep asked.

'Sure,' the man replied cheerfully. 'Just watch out for Andreas.'

Sloane frowned. 'Who's that?'

'You'll see,' Anton said with a wink.

The children waved goodbye to him and headed back the other way. They passed Hamish and Pippa having a coffee in the dining car, then Cecelia, who had her head firmly buried in a book. They continued on through another few carriages until they reached a door with the word 'Private' emblazoned across it.

'End of the line,' Sep announced. 'So to speak.'

Just as they were about to head back, the door opened and a tall man with thick caterpillar-like eyebrows and crow-black hair walked out. He had a thin moustache and wore a sneer on his lips.

'What are you doing?' he barked, eyeing Sep suspiciously. He glanced over the boy's shoulder at the others. 'Go back to your seats. Children are not allowed to wander around unsupervised.'

'Do you think Grouchy Doerflinger has a brother?' Millie whispered to Sloane, who smothered a giggle.

'Are you an engine driver?' Alice-Miranda asked.

'Yes,' the man said gruffly. 'Now, move along.'

Alice-Miranda thought the fellow seemed vaguely familiar, but before she had time to ask him anything else, he disappeared through the door, closing it behind him.

'He's not the friendliest member of staff, is he?' Millie grumbled as the children returned to their carriage.

'No,' Sep agreed, shaking his head.

'Must be why Anton warned us to watch out for him,' Sloane said.

'Come on, who wants to play cards?' Lucas asked.

There were nods all around.

While the group walked to their carriage, swaying with the motion of the train, something about the engine driver niggled at Alice-Miranda. It was as if a memory were scratching at the back of her mind, refusing to come into focus. She wondered if she had seen him somewhere before. If only she could remember.

Chapter 25

The sun had long disappeared by the time the train pulled into the station at Zermatt.

'Hello everyone,' Hugh greeted them once they were all on the platform. 'How was the trip?'

Alice-Miranda ran up and hugged her father.

'Stunning,' Pippa said with a sigh. 'I don't think I've ever seen so much gorgeousness in one day.'

Alice-Miranda tugged on her father's sleeve. 'Have you and Uncle Florian sorted out the problem yet?' she asked quietly.

'I'm afraid not, sweetheart,' Hugh replied. 'It's a real mystery, but don't you worry, we'll figure it out.'

'I can't believe it took eight hours to get here,' Hamish said. 'It was all over in a blink, really.'

Millie rolled her eyes. 'That's because you were asleep for half the time, Daddy.'

'I spoke to Cyril last night,' Cecelia said. 'He was being released from the hospital this morning and he's promised me he's going to get plenty of rest so he's fit to fly by the weekend.'

Hugh grinned and gave his wife a kiss on the cheek. 'That's good news.'

'Dolly sent a message to say that she and Shilly arrived in Zurich and have already done the red bus tour and visited several galleries. I think they're going to need a holiday from their holiday once we get home,' Cecelia laughed.

A man with a thin moustache and eyes as black as coals approached the group. He was dressed in a long navy coat with capelet shoulders and a peaked cap. 'Excuse me, sir, would you like me to load the bags?' he asked Hugh.

'Yes, thank you, Marius,' Hugh replied. 'Come on, everyone, that's our ride over there.' Hugh pointed to a shiny navy-blue carriage pulled by two handsome grey horses.

'Wow!' Millie exclaimed. 'That's gorgeous.'

'You're right about it being different to St Moritz,' Jacinta said.

She looked around at the railway station, where several horse-drawn carriages were being loaded. A line of electric minibuses resembling oversized golf carts sat nose to tail on the roadway. The lights in the village twinkled, revealing the wash of houses and chalets halfway up the mountainside. It all seemed more intimate and modest than the sprawl of St Moritz.

'Where's the hotel?' Sloane asked.

'It's that way.' Alice-Miranda pointed to their right. 'We could walk – it's not very far.'

'Can we go in the carriage just this once?' Sloane pleaded.

Alice-Miranda grinned at her friend. 'Of course.'

The man in the long coat began to load the bags onto the top of the carriage. Alice-Miranda wondered why he didn't just use the little trailer which was attached to the back. It seemed like it would be more troublesome to haul the cases onto the roof.

'Hello,' Alice-Miranda said as she passed her small red suitcase to him. 'My name is Alice-Miranda Highton-Smith-Kennington-Jones. I don't think we met last time we were here, Herr . . .?'

'Roten,' the man said.

Millie guffawed but was quickly silenced by the glare he threw her way.

'How do you spell that?' Alice-Miranda asked.

'As it sounds,' the man said through gritted teeth. 'Why don't you get into the carriage? I have many bags to secure.'

'Perhaps you could use the trailer instead,' the child suggested. 'It would be much easier to load.'

Millie shook her head. 'It's full of those big white Fanger's Chocolate carriers,' she said.

'What are you doing looking back there?' The man jumped down and stormed around to secure the lock on the trailer.

'It's only chocolate,' Millie muttered. 'You'd think he was carting around gold or something.'

Marius returned to the pile of bags.

'Well, it's lovely to meet you, Herr Roten. Thank you for driving us,' Alice-Miranda said. She was just about to walk away when she stopped. 'You know, you look a lot like a man we met on the train. His name was Andreas.'

Marius grunted. 'I don't know anyone on the Glacier Express.'

'That's uncanny,' the child said. 'Don't you think so, Millie?'

But Millie wasn't listening. She was watching the funicular head slowly up the mountain. 'Sorry, what did you say?' she asked.

'Don't you think Herr Roten looks a lot like Andreas?' Alice-Miranda repeated.

Millie raised her eyebrows. 'Yes,' she said, studying Marius closely. 'You could almost be his twin.'

'I don't have a twin,' Marius said sharply. 'Now, if you wouldn't mind moving along, I know that your party would like to get to the hotel before dinner.'

'His name suits him that's for sure,' Millie mumbled.

The two girls walked around to give the horses a pat. 'If I remember correctly, I think this old boy is Harry and that's Hazel,' Alice-Miranda said.

'Do they belong to your Uncle Florian?' Millie asked.

Alice-Miranda nodded. 'They live in the stables at the back of the hotel.'

Millie reached up to give one of the horses a rub. The beast whinnied and threw its head back and forth, jerking the carriage and almost causing Marius to fall off the back.

'Hey!' Marius shouted. 'Don't touch the horses!'

Millie stepped away and cooed at the creature. 'It's all right. You don't have to be scared.' But it was clear the beast was terrified. 'Look at him – he's shaking,' Millie said. She spied a long whip sitting vertically in an ornate bracket beside the driver's seat and pointed to it. 'Maybe Herr Roten uses that on them.'

'I don't think so,' Alice-Miranda said, horrified at the thought of it. 'All the carriages have whips but I'm almost certain they're just for show. I've never seen any of the drivers here use one. Besides, they can't do more than a slow trot in the village or they'd run people over.' She stood in front of the other horse. It was pawing the ground, its eyes wild. 'Come on, Hazel, you're all right,' the girl whispered.

'You'd think these two would be used to having lots of people patting them,' Millie said.

Alice-Miranda thought so too. She didn't remember them being skittish the last time she and her parents visited.

'All aboard,' Hugh called.

Millie and Alice-Miranda scurried around to the open door and hauled themselves up. The carriage was large enough to take the whole party together, although Hugh and Hamish elected to walk.

'We'll see you up there in a minute,' Hugh said as Marius climbed into the driver's seat and grabbed the reins.

Alice-Miranda looked out of the window at the station.

'I'll be back soon,' she heard Marius shout. She couldn't see who he was talking to but, when they pulled away, she caught a glimpse of Andreas standing by the tourist office and she could have sworn he'd nodded his head.

The children stared out at the shops and cafes that lined the main street of Zermatt. The carriage moved slowly along the roadway as hordes of skiers walked back to their hotels and chalets. Some were even skiing along the snowy footpaths.

'I can't wait to get up on the mountain tomorrow,'

Lucas said, peering out the window. 'I think I might give snowboarding a try.'

'I'll snowboard with you, if it's all right with Mummy and Daddy,' Millie said, looking to her mother.

'I don't see why not,' Pippa replied. 'You've done fabulously well on your skis this past week, so I'm sure you'll be great on a board too.'

'What about you, Alice-Miranda?' Millie asked, turning to her friend.

The girl shook her head. 'It's skis all the way for me – at least for this year.'

'I'm with Alice-Miranda,' Sep chimed in. 'I need to get better on two planks before I try one.'

The carriage continued up the hill before turning left into the driveway of the Grand Hotel Von Zwicky. Right next door was the Matterhorn Museum, which was mostly underground and accessed by a glass entrance at road level, and further along was a beautiful church with a tall spire. They were surprised to see Hugh and Hamish standing beside the Baron and Baroness.

Giselle von Zwicky held her arms wide as Cecelia stepped down from the carriage.

'Are you all right, my dear?' Cecelia whispered when the two women embraced.

'All the better for seeing you,' Giselle replied softly. She stepped back, her eyes shining.

Cecelia then embraced Florian and proceeded to introduce everyone as they spilled out onto the hotel steps.

The Baroness hugged Alice-Miranda tightly. 'My darling girl.'

'Hello Aunt Giselle.' Alice-Miranda kissed the old woman several times on both cheeks.

'Five kisses!' the Baroness gasped. 'To what do I owe such grand affection?'

'Just because,' the child replied as the Baron scooped her into a big bear hug. 'Uncle Florian, I'm sorry I didn't keep your secret,' she said.

The Baron shook his head. 'It is I who am sorry. I should not have asked that of you,' he said, returning her to the ground. 'Come, everyone,' he called, 'supper will be ready soon. Marius will take your bags.' With a sweep of his arms, he gestured for them to follow.

'Where is Schlappi?' Marius asked hotly.

'I have given him the night off,' the Baron replied.

Marius scowled. 'But I have to return some boxes to the train.'

Millie's eyes lit up. 'Oh, the chocolate boxes?' she said. 'We went past the Fanger's Chocolate factory in Disentis.'

Alice-Miranda nodded. 'Brigitte at Fanger's told us all about the big award they won for their innovative packaging and recycling.'

'Fanger's boxes?' The Baron frowned. 'I cannot imagine we would have many of them – we are certainly not going through chocolate the way we used to. Besides, the train will not leave until the morning.'

Marius gulped and looked daggers at the girls before trudging away to deal with the luggage.

'Is he always so accommodating?' Hugh chuckled, slapping the Baron on the back.

'My friend, you of all people know that not all employees are happy all of the time,' the Baron replied with a grin.

'How long has Marius been working for you?' Hugh asked as the pair walked inside.

'Only about a year,' Florian replied.

Hugh nodded. He couldn't help but wonder about the timing.

The party followed the Baroness through the hotel foyer and into a vast lounge that was every bit as grand as Fanger's Palace.

'Where is everyone?' Millie whispered to Alice-Miranda, surveying the empty room.

Alice-Miranda glanced around, her face grim. 'It wasn't like this last time we were here.'

'You must all be exhausted,' Giselle said, clasping her hands together. 'I'll arrange some refreshments, then we can have an early dinner so that everyone is well rested for a full day of skiing tomorrow.'

As the group settled onto the plush couches in the lounge, Alice-Miranda and Millie excused themselves and headed to the powder room.

'I wasn't joking before,' Millie said, turning to her friend. 'Where are all the people?'

Alice-Miranda shrugged. 'No one knows. That's why Daddy came over with Uncle Florian a couple of days ago – to see if they could work out why there are hardly any guests.'

Millie gazed around at the elegant decor. 'It's so weird. This hotel is gorgeous.'

'I know,' Alice-Miranda replied. 'Hopefully Daddy and Mummy can help sort it out before it's too late.'

'Too late for what?' Millie asked as she pushed open the powder-room door.

The room was huge, with a double row of toilets and an expanse of marble countertop with inlaid porcelain sinks and brass taps. Millie marvelled at the luxurious lounges and coffee table at the end of the room, although she couldn't imagine why anyone would want to stay in the loo any longer than necessary, no matter how lovely it was.

'Well, they can't run a hotel without guests,' Alice-Miranda replied, walking into one of the cubicles and closing the door.

'Good point,' Millie said, ducking into the next stall.

The girls heard the clacking of heels across the marble floor and the sound of a tap running.

Alice-Miranda flushed the toilet and walked out to find a slim woman in a smart uniform applying lipstick in front of the mirror. With her hair pulled into an elegant French roll, she was pretty in a sharp sort of way. The child smiled at her. 'Hello, I'm Alice-Miranda.'

'Good evening,' the woman said cordially. 'I'm Valerie. I work in reception.'

Millie walked out of the cubicle and smiled at the woman before washing her hands. Just as Alice-Miranda was about to say something, Valerie's pocket began to ring. The receptionist packed away her lipstick and pulled out her phone.

'Don't mind us,' Alice-Miranda said, wiping her hands with a fresh handtowel.

Valerie shrugged, then rejected the call with a swipe of her manicured hand. 'Aunt Delph—' she said, swallowing the rest of the word, 'can wait.'

'Delph?' Alice-Miranda said, her ears perking up at the name. 'We just met a lady called Delphine Doerflinger in St Moritz. She's not your aunt, is she?'

Valerie laughed delicately, blotting her lips with a tissue. 'No, everyone in Switzerland has an Aunt Delphine.'

'Really?' Millie said, surprised that the guide-book had left out such an interesting bit of trivia.

Alice-Miranda shook her head, grinning. 'Valerie just means that it's a very common name here, that's all. Like everyone has an Aunt Mary at home.'

Millie raised an eyebrow. 'I don't.'

Valerie checked her lipstick one last time before walking out of the room. 'Enjoy your holiday, girls,' she trilled.

'She seems nice,' Millie said, drying her hands. 'It can't be the staff that's the problem then, unless you count Rotten Marius.'

Alice-Miranda grinned. 'He's not *that* bad.'

Millie rolled her eyes.

The pair walked back to the lounge, where Sloane and Jacinta were sipping tall glasses of lemonade and laughing with the boys.

Chapter 26

The next morning Alice-Miranda skipped into the hotel foyer to find the Baroness standing beside the grand oval table. She looked to be deep in thought as she removed several wilted roses from a huge floral arrangement. 'Good morning, Aunt Giselle,' the child sang.

The old woman looked up and smiled. 'Hello my darling. Did you sleep well?'

Alice-Miranda nodded. 'The bed was heavenly and the duvet made me feel like I was sleeping under a cloud.'

'I am glad,' Giselle said. 'Are you off to the slopes this morning?'

'Yes, but I thought I'd visit Nina first,' Alice-Miranda said. She spotted a drooping bloom and plucked it from the vase. 'I've missed her, and I can't wait to introduce her to my friends.'

'Ah, lovely Nina.' The old woman sighed, releasing a handful of roses into the basket at her feet. 'I am afraid I have some bad news.'

Alice-Miranda looked up at the Baroness, wondering what was the matter.

'I am sorry I did not tell you sooner,' Giselle said, taking Alice-Miranda's hands in hers. 'Nina's mother passed away almost a year ago. It was a terrible tragedy.'

Alice-Miranda caught her breath, her eyes pricking with tears. 'What happened?'

The Baroness shook her head. 'She suffered an aneurysm one morning, after Sebastien had left for work. Lars was downstairs in the museum and Nina was at school. Tragically, no one found Sandrine until it was too late.'

Alice-Miranda pulled a tissue from her pocket and wiped her eyes.

'Oh, my darling.' Giselle wrapped her arms around the girl.

'How are Nina and her family?' Alice-Miranda asked.

'Her grandfather is not coping well at all. There is talk that he may have to be moved into a nursing home,' the old woman said.

Alice-Miranda couldn't believe what she was hearing. 'But what about the museum?' she asked.

'It is closed,' the Baroness said gently.

A tear ran down Alice-Miranda's cheek. 'It's horrible and so unfair.'

'Life is not fair,' Giselle said, touching the girl's cheek and brushing a tear away. 'There are things we will never understand and sometimes I think it is even too hard to try.'

'I should go and see her. Will you let Mummy and the others know where I am?' Alice-Miranda said, looking up at the Baroness.

Giselle nodded. 'Of course.'

Alice-Miranda hurried out the front door and across the snowy street. The fresh powder crunched under her feet while the sun shone brightly overhead. To her left, the Matterhorn towered above the village, a vast crag of white under a winter blanket.

She knocked on one of the mint-green doors. A handwritten sign taped to the other door declared the museum closed. Alice-Miranda waited for a minute before knocking again. This time she could hear movement on the stairs and the sound of running feet. The door opened to reveal a girl with two long plaits tumbling over her shoulders. She was dressed in jeans and a long-sleeved navy shirt with tiny white spots on it.

Alice-Miranda smiled at her friend. 'Hello Nina.'

'Alice-Miranda! What are you doing here?' Nina exclaimed. She rushed out onto the front step, and the two children hugged each other fiercely. 'It is so good to see you.'

The girls stepped back and looked at one another. 'Aunt Giselle just told me,' Alice-Miranda said. 'I am so sorry.'

Nina nodded, her eyes filling with tears which she hastily brushed away. 'Me too.'

'I don't know what to say.' Alice-Miranda reached into her pocket for a tissue and dabbed at her eyes. 'Your mother was always so kind to me.'

'She was kind to everyone.' Nina smiled. 'How long are you staying for?'

'We'll be here until next weekend, then we go back to St Moritz,' Alice-Miranda said. She thought for a moment. 'Do you have school today?'

Nina shook her head. 'We are on a break this week.'

'Who is it, Nina?' The sound of Sebastian Ebersold's footsteps echoed on the stairs.

'Papa, it's Alice-Miranda.' The girl turned to her father. He didn't miss the look of delight on her face – something he hadn't seen for a long time.

'Hello Herr Ebersold,' Alice-Miranda said. She stepped forward, unable to help herself from giving Nina's father a hug. 'I am so sorry about Frau Ebersold.'

The man's kind eyes glistened. 'Thank you, my dear,' he said, his voice thick with emotion. 'It is lovely to see you.'

'Likewise,' Alice-Miranda said with a grin. 'Would you mind if Nina joins me and my friends today?'

'That sounds wonderful,' Sebastien said. He knew his daughter hadn't been on the mountain since her mother had passed away. It was almost as if she were afraid to leave the house unnecessarily lest she lose another loved one.

'We'll be leaving as soon as everyone has finished their breakfast. We were a bit late getting up today,' Alice-Miranda said.

Nina bit her lip. 'I'm sorry, I can't go. Unless you are not working today, Papa?'

She knew it was unlikely as her father oversaw a large team in charge of resort maintenance. They were responsible for ensuring the chairlifts were in good order, the runs were clearly marked and just about everything else to do with creating a safe environment for the skiers.

Nina's father shook his head. 'You should ski,' he insisted. 'I want you to have some fun. I will ask Frau Gisler if she can sit with Opa.' He ran down the front steps and over to a cluster of houses down the street.

Nina turned to Alice-Miranda. 'Opa has started to wander,' she said by way of explanation. 'Frau Gisler used to babysit me when I was small. It seems strange that it is now Opa who needs a babysitter.'

The ringing of bells sounded as the town clock struck nine. 'I'd better go and find everyone,' Alice-Miranda said, giving her friend another hug before turning to leave. 'I'll be back in half an hour. I hope you can come with us.'

'Me too,' Nina smiled, waving from the doorway.

★

Delphine Doerflinger held the phone away from her ear and waited for her husband to stop talking.

'I am sorry I had to leave so suddenly, but there has been a small hiccup with our acquisition,' she said. 'No, no, there is absolutely no need for you to come here. I will be home again very soon.' After saying goodbye, Delphine ended the call.

She stood up and paced around the room. The last thing she needed was for Otto to interfere. Delphine sighed and returned to the matter at hand. There could only be one explanation for Von Zwicky backing out of the deal: someone else was helping him, and that someone was Hugh Kennington-Jones. She remembered bumping into his infernally happy child while on the way to meet her colleagues. Knowing those *Dummkopfs*, they'd probably been boasting and the girl overheard them. Why else would her father have hurried to Zermatt to help the Baron with his business?

The woman flipped open her purse and rummaged around for some headache tablets. She rubbed her temples, aware that if she didn't catch it now, the dull throb would turn into something much worse and she couldn't afford to be laid up for the rest of the day.

So far Delphine had managed to avoid the brat and her family, but it was such a cumbersome affair. It would have been easier if only there were more guests, but that was a problem of her own making. More than ever, she needed to find that access route. Otherwise, everything she had been working so hard to gain would be lost.

Chapter 27

The children stood shoulder to shoulder with over one hundred other passengers as they rode the cable car to the top of the mountain. They were accompanied by their ski instructor, a young woman called Michaela. She worked for the oldest ski school in Zermatt, which was affectionately known as 'the Reds' due to their bright red jackets. Michaela had taught Alice-Miranda a couple of times before and the child was thrilled that they were going to have her all to themselves for the whole week.

'You were right about this place, Alice-Miranda,' Millie gushed. 'It's incredible.'

Michaela looked over and grinned. 'Glad you are enjoying it, Millie.'

Earlier in the day Millie and Lucas had revelled in their first snowboarding lessons but had decided to switch back to skis after lunch so the whole group could be together.

'I'm so happy you could come out with us,' Alice-Miranda said, peering around Millie at Nina.

The girl was wearing a white ski suit with pink trim. Underneath her pink hat, her long brown plaits fell down almost to her waist. 'Me too,' she said, nodding. 'I haven't been up on the mountain much lately.'

When Alice-Miranda had returned to the hotel that morning, she had relayed Nina's sad news to her friends. They had all felt terribly sorry for the girl, prompting Sloane to try to keep her usual litany of whinges about her own mother to a minimum.

'This will be our last run of the day,' Michaela announced as the cable car pulled into the station.

Jacinta pouted. 'Already?'

'Don't worry, we will do it all again tomorrow,' the woman assured her. 'Besides, it will take us a while to get back to the village.'

This was the group's first ride to the very top of the Klein Matterhorn, having spent most of the day on some of the lower slopes closer to where Millie and Lucas were learning to snowboard.

'Whoa!' Sloane gasped as she caught sight of the view. She had been sandwiched between several adults on the way up and only just realised that the village had been reduced to a speck down below. 'Is it safe up here?' she asked, her stomach lurching.

'You'll be fine.' Michaela gave the girl a smile and a wink. 'Just follow me.'

The children walked out onto the snow, slapping their skis on the ground and clicking into their bindings. Goggles were adjusted and straps tightened in anticipation of the marathon run to the bottom.

When everyone was ready, Michaela waved her pole in the air and pushed off. She traversed a steep dip and swung up onto a flatter section of snow on the other side. 'Come on, kids!' she called.

Alice-Miranda took off after her, with Nina close behind. But just as Millie pushed herself forward, a skier dressed in head-to-toe black flew over the top of the rise and missed hitting her by mere millimetres.

'Watch out, you lunatic!' the child yelled, waving her pole at the man. She was about to go again when a stream of identically dressed skiers hurtled towards her.

Lucas lunged forward and grabbed Millie's arm, hauling her out of harm's way. Sloane's knees were trembling and Sep shook his fist at the interlopers. Down below, Michaela was signalling for the children to join them.

Millie craned her neck to see if anyone else was about to zoom over the top. When she was convinced the coast was clear, she pushed off. Lucas, Sep, Jacinta and Sloane followed her, their skis pointing straight ahead to gather as much speed as possible and avoid any other maniacs.

'Are you guys okay?' Michaela asked as Millie turned sharply to stop.

Millie nodded. 'Who were they?' she asked.

'They call themselves the Black Diamonds,' Michaela said disapprovingly. 'They're a new ski school, but I only ever see them racing each other over the mountain with their little backpacks on. I don't know how they expect to stay in business without any students.'

'I wouldn't want them teaching me,' Sloane said. 'Did you see how out of control some of them were?'

'Oh, I know them,' Nina piped up. 'They're always hanging around with the driver from the hotel.'

'Rotten Marius?' Millie said.

Alice-Miranda giggled. 'Millie means Marius Roten.'

Nina nodded. 'That's him. I've seen them at the stables. They make lots of noise.'

'No wonder Hazel and Harry seemed a bit uptight,' Millie said.

But Alice-Miranda wasn't listening. Something – or someone – had caught her eye. 'Caprice! Is that you?' she called out.

Jacinta's jaw just about hit the ground. 'What?'

Alice-Miranda pointed to a skier below them. A girl was sitting in the snow, her arms and legs flailing.

Millie groaned. 'She's not supposed to be here.'

'Do you know that person?' Michaela asked.

'I think it's a girl from our school,' Alice-Miranda replied, tilting her head to the side. It almost looked as if she was punching the snow.

'You mean a monster,' Sloane said.

'Let's see if she needs some help,' Michaela suggested.

'I'll help her,' Millie grumbled, 'right over the edge.'

Sloane snorted.

Michaela took off down the mountain with her students snaking along behind her. They pulled up, with Millie sending a spray of snow all over the girl.

'Hey! What did you do that for?' Caprice grouched, then looked up and realised who she was yelling at. 'You!' she exclaimed, glaring at Millie. Caprice stood up and dusted the snow from her pale pink pants. 'Go away!'

'What's the matter?' Alice-Miranda asked, clearly concerned. 'Where's your group?'

Caprice staked her poles hard into the ground. 'I don't care,' she huffed. 'Somewhere in Italy.'

'Where are you staying?' Michaela asked gently. 'You can ski down with us and I'll make sure that you get home.'

'Our chalet isn't in stupid Switzerland,' the girl said tersely. 'It's in Cervinia.'

'Oh.' Michaela looked up at the cable cars, then glanced at her watch. 'That's going to be a bit of a problem.'

'Why?' Millie asked, her voice wavering.

'The cable car has closed for the day,' said Michaela, 'and that is unfortunately the only way high enough to go over to Italy.'

Caprice kicked at the snow. 'Great. I'll just stay up here for the night then.'

'What are you having a tantrum about, anyway?' Jacinta said. She was fast losing patience with the girl. She had been, in fact, ever since Caprice had arrived at school.

'It's none of your business,' Caprice spat.

'Well, if you're happy to stay here, then *we* should go. We don't want to get stuck on the mountain too,' Jacinta replied, keeping her cool.

Lucas and Sep grimaced at one another, and Nina watched on quietly, wondering what catastrophe had befallen the girl to make her so upset.

'I'm afraid I can't do that,' Michaela said. 'Come with us and I'll telephone your parents once we're in the village to let them know where you are. They must be very worried.'

'Serves Mummy right for being so mean,' Caprice fumed.

'Sorry, Caprice, but you won't be seeing your parents tonight. It's a full day's drive from Cervinia,' Michaela explained.

'What?' Millie looked as if she'd been slapped with a wet fish.

'It's all right,' Alice-Miranda said to Caprice. 'You can bunk with me and Millie tonight. I'm sure your parents will be happy to meet you at the top of the mountain tomorrow.'

'I'm not going back tomorrow,' the girl replied, crossing her arms defiantly.

'I don't think you'll have a choice,' Millie said through gritted teeth.

Caprice sniffed, her nose pointed in the air. 'Just watch me.'

Worried about the fading light, Michaela turned on the speed for their homeward journey. But she had an ulterior motive too. A good, long run would take the wind out of Caprice's sails so that by the time they reached the bottom the child might be able to conduct a civil conversation.

Michaela stopped at the top of the final descent into the village and waited for the children to catch up. 'Is everyone okay?' she called.

'That was awesome!' Sep enthused. The boy could hardly believe how much he'd improved in just a few days on the slopes.

'What about you, Caprice? Are you feeling better?' Michaela asked, but the girl just shrugged in response. Her plan seemed to be working and, at the very least, she was glad the child was no longer hurling herself about like a three-year-old. 'Well, we've only got this last part to go and then we're going to have to skate back to the middle of the village,' she said.

'I'm bored,' Caprice whined. 'Why don't we have a race?'

Lucas grinned. 'I'm up for it.'

'Me too,' Nina said with a shrug.

'How does everyone else feel?' Michaela glanced at the children, who nodded and smiled. Only Sloane looked unsure. 'It's settled then. I'll ski ahead so you can follow my path – no going off-piste,' the young woman said.

'What's the prize?' Caprice asked.

Millie and Lucas groaned.

'You don't always have to win something, you know,' Sloane said.

'Yeah,' Lucas chimed in, 'why don't we just have some fun for once?'

'It's not a proper race if you don't win a prize,' Caprice griped.

'Okay, I'll buy the winner a chocolate,' Michaela relented, eager to call it a day.

'Only if it's Fanger's,' Millie agreed. 'I love that stuff.'

Michaela smiled. 'Deal.'

Lucas drew a starting line in the snow with his stock. 'Someone has to say "go" or else it won't be fair,' he pointed out.

'I will,' Sloane volunteerd. 'I'm not going to win, so I don't mind being the starter.'

'Right, I will see you all at the bottom.' Michaela gave them a wave before speeding off down the mountain.

The children arranged themselves on the make-shift line, with Sloane at one end and Caprice at the other. Sloane took off her scarf and waved it in the air. 'Ready . . . set . . . go!'

Caprice leaned across and shoved Alice-Miranda so hard that the girl fell into Nina, who fell into Millie. The whole row tumbled, with only Sep and Sloane managing to avoid the chaos and stay upright.

'Oh no, did all the little Humpties fall down?' Caprice laughed as she zoomed away.

Sep and Sloane took off after her, both determined to not let her win.

'You're asking for it, Caprice,' Millie grumbled, pushing herself to her feet. She helped Nina up and seconds later the girls were charging down the slope with Alice-Miranda in hot pursuit.

'Go, Nina!' Lucas yelled as the girl flew off a jump that propelled her almost level with Caprice.

Caprice glanced over her shoulder and shrieked. 'Where did you come from?'

'You're not so clever now, Miss Smartypants.' Nina's hips swung from side to side as she powered down the snowy terrain.

'Don't let her win!' Sloane shouted as Nina overtook Caprice.

Millie and Alice-Miranda were gaining fast. They could see Michaela at the bottom, waving her stock in the air. Suddenly, Caprice let out a scream. Everyone turned to see her hit a jump and fly into the air. She flipped backwards and miraculously landed on her feet.

Nina crossed the line first with Millie close behind.

'It's all your fault!' Caprice wailed as the rest of the children zoomed past her. 'You forced me over that jump.'

'Nobody made you do anything,' Millie yelled at the girl. 'It's called karma.'

'Whatever,' Caprice said, shoving Millie on the shoulder. 'It was a stupid race, anyway.'

'Stop it!' Michaela ordered. 'You were lucky that Alice-Miranda saw you, Caprice. You would have frozen up there overnight, and your parents must be worried sick – although, if I were them, I'd be glad for a night off.'

Caprice's mouth opened, then closed again.

'Now, stop your nastiness, or I'll hand you over to the ski patrol and they can look after you until the morning,' Michaela said.

'She's fantastic,' Millie whispered to the others. 'Do you think she'd be open to teaching at our school?'

Nina grinned. 'I'm sure Caprice is not the first spoilt brat Michaela has had to deal with up there.'

Chapter 28

Cecelia Highton-Smith and her husband had spent the day with the Von Zwickys, going through their financial statements and trying to pinpoint exactly when the hotel's occupancy had begun to decline. There had been a steady drop-off in clientele for the past year but the crisis had really become apparent at the beginning of what should have been their busiest time.

'Have you telephoned any of your regulars who haven't turned up this year?' Cecelia asked.

'I've tried a couple,' Florian said, 'but I've had no luck getting through.'

Cecelia pointed to a name on the list. 'What about this chap? He seems to have been coming here for the past few seasons.'

'Ah, yes, Herr Schwieserhof,' Florian said. 'He and his family have been guests for a long time. I do remember that Valerie telephoned him and found out he was having a knee reconstruction.'

'Fair enough,' Hugh said, continuing down the list.

'What about this one?' Cecelia tapped her finger on another name. 'James Vandergraff.'

Hugh's brows furrowed. 'I know that name from somewhere.'

The Baron nodded. 'Herr Vandergraff owns –'

'Vandergraff Industries,' the two men chorused.

'I saw him last week in St Moritz,' Hugh said, slapping his forehead. 'He was staying at Fanger's Palace. We had a chat about organic farming.'

The Baron shrugged. 'Perhaps he just wanted a change of scenery this year.'

There was a knock on the door and Valerie poked her head inside. 'Excuse me, I thought you could all do with some refreshments,' she said, pushing the door open with her body. She walked into the room carrying a tray of tea and biscuits.

'Thank you, Valerie. That's very thoughtful of you,' the Baron said as she placed the tray on the sideboard. 'Hugh, Cee, what would you like?'

'White tea, thank you,' Cecelia replied gratefully.

'Same for me,' Hugh said with a grin.

'Are you making any progress with your investigations?' Valerie asked, picking up the teapot.

'Perhaps, but I think we need to make some telephone calls,' the Baron replied.

'May I be of any help?' the young woman asked. She smiled and brought him his cup of tea.

'I think you have enough to do,' the Baroness said gently. 'Are the housekeeping rosters completed?'

Valerie turned around and placed the Baroness's tea in front of her. 'Almost,' she replied. She then poured Cecelia's tea and set the cup down too. 'Would you like me to bring you a list of numbers?'

'That won't be necessary. I've got them here,' the Baron said.

'Oh, did you print that from the computer?' the girl asked as she went to place Hugh's tea on the table.

Florian shook his head. 'You know how dreadful I am with the technology. We found an older one among the registers from the past couple of years – it should do fine.'

Valerie turned to put the Baron's teacup down when, suddenly, she began to wheeze.

'Are you all right?' the Baron asked. As he leapt up to help her, the teacup went flying. Its milky contents spilled all over the table, soaking the documents.

'I'm so sorry, sir,' Valerie said, gasping for breath. 'I need my inhaler.'

Cecelia jumped up and ran into the office next door. She spotted a large black handbag on the floor beside one of the desks and dived into it, searching for the puffer. She found it in the side pocket and was about to run back with it when she noticed the girl's phone light up. The ringer was on silent but the caller ID was clear: Aunt Delphine.

For a fleeting second Cecelia wondered if it could possibly be Delphine Doerflinger, then she shook the thought from her mind and raced back into the room. Valerie was now sitting in a chair with the Baroness hovering nearby, concern etched into her features.

Cecelia handed the device to Valerie, who tore off the lid and inhaled deeply. 'Thank you,' she breathed. 'That's much better.'

'You must go home and rest, my dear,' Giselle said.

'I am fine. It happens all the time,' Valerie replied, standing up. She looked at the tea-soaked papers. 'I've caused such a terrible mess.'

'Never mind about that,' the Baron replied.

While the others were attending to the girl, Hugh dashed out to the kitchenette to get some paper towels. He returned and picked up the sodden pages, attempting to delicately prise them apart.

'Just put them in the bin,' the Baron said, scooping up a small receptacle from the end of the room.

'I will print you off a new copy right away,' Valerie said.

'Please do not fuss,' the Baroness insisted.

'No, really, I am fine. These attacks go as quickly as they come.' Valerie excused herself and walked to the adjacent office. She sat down at her desk and pulled her phone out of her handbag. There were six missed calls.

Valerie put the phone down and wriggled the mouse beside her computer. That had been far too close. She resolved to be more careful from now on, and for the moment Aunt Delphine would have to wait. She had a list to print.

Chapter 29

Lights twinkled in the village and on the mountain-side as dusk fell. Alice-Miranda stomped up the front steps of the Grand Hotel Von Zwicky. An old man with a bright smile greeted her at the door. 'Good afternoon, young lady,' he said.

'Herr Schlappi!' Alice-Miranda beamed. 'It's lovely to see you again.'

The man dipped his top hat, now flecked with snow. 'It is lovely to see you too.'

'Have you seen Mummy and Daddy?' she asked.

'They have been in the boardroom with the Baron and Baroness for most of the day,' the doorman replied. 'Would you like me to get them?'

'If you wouldn't mind,' the child said. 'I really need to talk to Mummy, and I shouldn't walk through the hotel in my ski boots.'

The man nodded and disappeared through the doors. He promptly returned with Cecelia, who had an anxious look on her face.

'Is everything all right, darling?' she asked.

'Yes, we had the most wonderful day. The snow is beautiful and Michaela took us on lots of secret trails. We found big jumps and we had a race and Nina won,' the child prattled on excitedly. 'Oh, and we found Caprice by herself near the top of the mountain. Is it all right if she stays with us?'

'Caprice?' Cecelia looked out at the children, who were standing together a little way off. She counted the heads and saw that there were indeed eight children instead of seven.

Michaela waved and skated over to join Cecelia and Alice-Miranda.

Cecelia smiled at the woman. 'I hope the children weren't any trouble.'

'No, not at all,' Michaela replied. 'But I do have an extra one for you. I am afraid the cable car had closed and I wasn't able to take her back over to Cervinia to her parents.'

'Oh, goodness, they'll be beside themselves,' Cecelia gasped. 'I'll call her mother right away.'

Cecelia whipped out her phone and scrolled through her list of contacts. She quickly found Venetia Baldini's number and dialled, hoping that she wasn't out of range.

'Hello Venetia, it's Cecelia Highton-Smith,' she began. 'Before you say anything I've got Caprice here with us in Zermatt and she's fine.'

Michaela and Alice-Miranda heard a high-pitched squeak on the other end of the line, and winced.

'It's all right,' Cecelia said, trying to calm the distraught woman. 'She can stay with us tonight and we can meet you somewhere tomorrow. Don't worry another minute. Let's talk in the morning, shall we?' The women spoke for another couple of minutes before Cecelia said goodbye and hung up. 'Thank you, Michaela. I suspect you've earned your keep today.'

Michaela's mouth turned up at one side. 'It's okay. She's not the worst I've ever come across.'

Cecelia grimaced. 'Really?'

'Well, she's close,' Michaela conceded with a chuckle.

'Right, let's go and get everyone sorted,' Cecelia said, walking out onto the snow. 'Hello Caprice. This is a surprise.'

'Hi Cee,' the girl replied sweetly.

'I've just spoken with your mother and everything's fine. We'll get you some spare pyjamas and you can stay here tonight. Actually, do you want to talk to her? I can call her back.'

'No,' Caprice snapped. She paused and took a deep breath. 'I mean, no thank you.'

'I had better get moving,' Michaela said. 'I'll meet you all at the ski school in the morning.' She gave them a wave and skated off into the fading light.

'Bye,' the children chorused.

'I should go too,' Nina piped up.

'Can you ski with us again tomorrow?' Alice-Miranda asked. She turned to the others. 'I wish you could all see Nina's grandfather's museum. He is so clever. I promise you won't have seen anything like it before.'

'Perhaps you can come later,' Nina suggested, although she knew her father would disapprove of her playing any of the instruments. He had caught her a couple of days ago, when he returned from work a little early, and was not at all pleased. He worried that she would break something, not realising that her grandfather had taught her well.

'Nina!' her father called as he trudged along the roadway towards the house.

'Hello Papa,' she said.

'Herr Ebersold,' Cecelia said, stepping forward to shake the man's hand. 'I am so sorry to hear about your wife,' she added quietly.

'Thank you,' Sebastien replied. He put his arm around his daughter's shoulders and gave a squeeze. 'Did you have a good day?'

Nina smiled up at him. 'The best.'

'I can't wait to hear all about it, but we should probably rescue Frau Gisler from your grandfather first,' the man joked.

Nina and Sebastien bade farewell to the group and walked across the street.

'So, is anyone hungry?' Cecelia asked.

'Starving,' Lucas replied.

Sep nodded like a jack-in-the-box. 'Me too.'

'I could eat a horse,' Millie said, then thought for a second. 'They don't eat horses in Switzerland, do they?'

'No, only in France and Belgium,' Alice-Miranda replied.

Millie nodded. 'Phew!'

'Come inside,' Cecelia said, ushering them over to the hotel steps. 'I'll order you hot chocolate and cake while you put your skis and boots in the drying room.'

The children headed around to the side of the hotel where there was direct access to the ski shop and storerooms beneath the hotel. As Lucas and the others disappeared inside, an explosive whinny sounded from the stables. Millie nudged Alice-Miranda.

'Look,' she said, pointing to a group of men in black. 'It's those maniacs who nearly ran me over.'

Alice-Miranda looked over and frowned. 'I wonder what they're doing,' she said.

Millie stood her skis up in the rack beside the door. 'Come on, let's see what they're up to.'

Alice-Miranda followed suit, and the two girls trudged through the garden. It was impossible to scurry in ski boots but the soft snow disguised their footfalls.

There was another loud whinny and the sound of a horse stomping its foot. Alice-Miranda and Millie hid behind a hedge, craning their necks to see what was going on. The horses were hitched to the carriage and they could see Marius Roten around the back. One of the men in black was standing in front of Hazel, slapping the horse's nose with a glove. Millie gasped and was about to run over to stop him when Alice-Miranda grabbed her and held her back.

'Would you leave her alone?' Marius shouted.

'Why? She likes my tickles,' the young man retorted.

Marius stalked around to the front of the carriage. 'Stop it, Dante!'

Alice-Miranda glimpsed two men struggling to carry a big white box out of the stables. They lifted it into the trailer that was attached to the back of the carriage. Another two men followed behind them, carrying an identical box.

'Hurry up, this weighs a tonne,' one of the men groaned.

'Do you think it's the boxes of Fanger's Chocolate?' Millie whispered. 'I thought Marius said they were empty, and eating them is like nibbling clouds, anyway.'

Once the second box was loaded, they saw Marius shut the lid of the trailer and secure it with a large padlock. 'Take your backpacks and get out of here,' he barked.

A deep line appeared on the bridge of Alice-Miranda's nose. She wondered why anyone would take such care to lock a trailer filled with empty boxes.

'Are you ready for the big shipment?' one of the men said.

Marius shrugged. 'The contract hasn't been signed yet, so I know as much as you.'

'Well, things had better be in place by the end of the week or there will be hell to pay,' another man said. 'We need somewhere more secure than this for the amount that is coming.'

The two girls looked at each other.

'Millie, Alice-Miranda, are you out here?' Jacinta called into the night.

The men stopped and glanced over. 'What was that?' one of them said.

'Go and look,' Marius ordered, pointing in the girls' direction.

'Come on,' Alice-Miranda whispered, grabbing Millie's arm. The two of them backed away from the hedge, then turned and dashed through the garden.

The man walked through the archway and spotted fresh footprints leading to the side entrance.

'Just kids,' he said, noting the size of the prints.

Marius narrowed his eyes. He had a strong suspicion it was that pesky little brunette and her red-haired friend, who had arrived yesterday. She was the most curious creature he had come across in a while. He made a note to put a stop to her snooping. He had been working too long and too hard for her to come along and ruin things now.

Chapter 30

Caprice sat down on the foldaway bed and frowned. 'This bed is horrible,' she complained.

'Feel free to go and sleep in another room,' Millie said. 'There are plenty of spares.'

Caprice poked out her tongue and stayed put. The girl would never admit it, but she hated the idea of being on her own in unfamiliar surroundings.

'You can have my bed if you want,' Alice-Miranda offered, drawing the curtains.

'No, she can't,' Millie said, outraged by such a proposal. 'She shouldn't even *be* here.'

Caprice glared at the girl.

Millie ignored her and hopped under the covers. 'You still haven't told us why you were so mad with your mother.'

'Who said I was mad with my mother?' Caprice snapped.

'Well, you didn't want to talk to her on the phone and something must have caused your massive tantrum up there,' Millie said.

'You won't care, so why should I tell you?' Caprice muttered, throwing her full weight back onto the bed.

Alice-Miranda propped herself up on her pillows. 'Be fair, Caprice. Millie is one of the most caring people I know.'

'Weren't you supposed to be at home helping your mother film *Sweet Things*?' Millie said, referring to Venetia Baldini's cooking show.

'The filming went faster than Mummy thought, so Daddy decided we'd go skiing for a week,' Caprice said. 'Not that I have to explain myself to either of you.'

Millie folded her hands behind her head and gazed up at the beautifully carved ceiling. 'So, you get to come to Italy and Switzerland on a surprise skiing holiday and you're still in a foul mood?' she asked, incredulous. 'I guess there's no pleasing some people.'

Caprice balled her fists in frustration. 'Stop talking!' she ordered.

'You can't tell me what to do in my own room,' Millie retorted.

'Please don't argue,' Alice-Miranda said, trying to keep the peace. 'Caprice, are your brothers here too?'

The girl rolled over to face the wall. 'Yes, and I hate them all.'

'What on earth did *they* do?' Millie asked. She was beginning to wonder if there was anyone in the world the girl actually liked.

'They said the director thought I was hopeless,' Caprice said, her voice reduced to a whisper.

'I'm sure that's not true,' Alice-Miranda reassured her.

Millie grinned. 'Is it?'

Alice-Miranda looked over and mouthed for Millie to stop her teasing.

'Apparently it is,' Caprice sniffed.

'But you're the best actress I've ever seen,' Millie said, biting her lip to stop herself from laughing.

'That's just the point,' Caprice insisted, her voice wavering. 'The director said I was overplaying my role. They've cut me from the entire episode and Mummy will have to go back early to reshoot some sections.'

'Is that why you had a fight with her?' Alice-Miranda asked.

'She told me we had to go home tomorrow and I said that I didn't want to. Daddy and the boys are staying, so why should I have to go?' Caprice whimpered, pulling the duvet up over her head.

'I'm sure your parents will only do what they think is best,' Alice-Miranda said.

Millie yawned. 'I'm exhausted. Goodnight.'

'Goodnight,' Alice-Miranda replied, switching off the light.

'I'm not talking anymore,' Caprice said, her voice muffled by the covers.

'You just did,' Millie said.

Caprice huffed loudly. 'Well, I won't do it again.'

Millie and Alice-Miranda giggled softly, and not five minutes later all three girls were fast asleep.

Chapter 31

Outside, the snow was falling heavily and the village was shrouded in a thick blanket of fog.

'Looks like you won't be going up the mountain this morning, kids,' Hugh said, sitting down at the breakfast table. 'It's blowing about a hundred miles an hour up there and all the lifts are closed.'

Sep wrinkled his nose. 'That's a bummer.'

'Caprice, I'm afraid that means we can't get you back to your parents just yet,' Cecelia added. 'I've called your mother and we'll reassess later today, though it's not looking good.'

The girl smiled and flicked her long copper-coloured hair over her shoulder. 'I don't mind,' she said pleasantly.

Millie could have cried into her bowl of porridge.

'What does everyone feel like doing today?' Hamish asked. 'Pippa and I are planning to check out the Matterhorn Museum and then wander around the village.'

'Sounds good,' Jacinta said.

'Boring,' Sloane quipped. 'No offence, Hamish. Could we go ice-skating?'

Cecelia nodded. 'Yes, of course. There's a fantastic rink back along the river.'

'I'd love to see if Nina can show us around their museum,' Alice-Miranda said. 'I know you don't like museums very much, Sloane, but it's seriously amazing. What are your plans?' she asked her parents.

'We were hoping to continue our work and then meet you all for lunch,' Cecelia said.

At that moment Baron von Zwicky walked into the room. 'Good morning, good morning,' he greeted them. 'I trust everyone slept well.'

There were nods all round.

The Baron sat down at the end of the table, and the group chatted away while two waiters brought them drinks and food.

Alice-Miranda leaned in close to the man, who was sitting beside her. 'Uncle Florian, do you know much about the Black Diamonds?' she asked quietly.

'Not much at all,' the Baron replied, shaking his head. 'They're one of a number of new ski schools on the mountain. I preferred it when we only had the Reds, who have been here since the very beginning and, as far as I am concerned, they are the best. Why do you ask, my dear?'

'Well, apart from the fact that they almost mowed Millie down on the mountain yesterday, Millie and I saw them out the back with Herr Roten last night,' Alice-Miranda reported.

The man's brow furrowed. 'Really? What were they doing?'

'One of them was slapping Hazel on the nose with his glove,' Millie said indignantly.

The Baron gasped.

'Don't worry, Herr Roten made the man stop,' Alice-Miranda added.

'Which was just as well because I was about to rip that glove out of the man's hand and slap *him* with it,' Millie said, shovelling another spoonful of porridge into her mouth.

'I think it might have happened before,' Alice-Miranda said. 'When we arrived the other afternoon, Hazel and Harry both got upset when Millie and I went to pat them.'

'Good heavens, I must speak with Marius immediately,' the Baron muttered.

'That's not all,' Millie said.

Alice-Miranda nodded. 'They were loading the boxes of Fanger's Chocolate into the back of the carriage and seemed to be struggling under the weight of them, which is odd considering they were supposedly empty. Don't you agree, Uncle Florian?'

A waiter placed an espresso in front of the man. The Baron looked up and smiled before turning back to the two girls. 'I wonder what they are up to,' he said. 'That reminds me – Frau Doerflinger is staying in the hotel at the moment.'

'Really?' Alice-Miranda frowned. 'She didn't mention it when I told her that we were going to see you and Aunt Giselle.'

The Baron shrugged. 'I imagine Frau Doerflinger

is a very busy woman. Her chocolate business seems most successful. But I will ask Marius what was going on yesterday. Thank you for telling me, girls.'

The conversation turned to lighter things as the children regaled the adults with tales of their exploits on the mountain. The Baron hooted with laughter when Millie and Lucas described their attempts at snowboarding and told him how they'd had a pile-up on the magic carpet on one of the beginner slopes.

The group finished their breakfast and made plans to go their separate ways until midday, when they would meet back at the hotel for lunch. It turned out that the Baroness had accumulated the most amazing collection of lost property over the years, much of it near new, so Caprice was kitted out in a jiffy. Although the girl wasn't best pleased at the thought of wearing anything second-hand, she realised that she didn't exactly have a choice. And after the debacle with the identical gowns at the Queen's Jubilee Ball, Cecelia was loathe to ask either Jacinta or Sloane, who were about the same size as Caprice, to lend the girl any of their things.

The children donned their hats and jackets in the foyer. Millie caught Caprice admiring her reflection in the giant mirror.

'You look perfect,' she said.

'I know,' Caprice retorted.

Millie rolled her eyes and Sloane giggled.

'Ready?' Alice-Miranda asked everyone.

'As ever,' Millie replied, jamming her beanie onto her head and following Alice-Miranda out into the blustery cold.

Chapter 32

'Good morning, Herr Schlappi,' Alice-Miranda greeted the doorman, who was rugged up extra-tight against the bitter chill.

The old man smiled and held the door open for the children. 'How are you today, young lady?'

She smiled at him as the group traipsed out onto the hotel driveway. 'Very well, thank you. I'm going to see if Nina's home,' she said, then raced across the road and knocked on the green door. A minute later, Nina poked her head outside.

'Hello,' said the girl. 'I'm sorry I cannot come with you today. I have to stay with Opa.'

Alice-Miranda shook her head. 'We're not going up, either. The lifts are closed, so we're staying in the village.'

'I knew it was windy but I didn't think it was that bad.' Nina's stomach twinged. She always worried about her father when the weather was extreme.

'I was wondering if you might be able to show everyone the museum,' Alice-Miranda said.

Nina's eyes lit up. 'I would love to! I just have to get the key.' The girl took off upstairs, returning a minute later.

Alice-Miranda turned around and beckoned for the others to join her. The children scrambled inside and stood in a large entrance hall.

Millie gasped and pointed at the handpainted ceiling. 'That's so beautiful,' she breathed.

'Welcome to Lars Dettwiller's Mechanical Musical Cabinet Museum,' Nina said with a bow.

'What's a mechanical musical instrument?' Sloane asked.

'Be patient and you will see,' Nina replied as she held back a red velvet curtain and motioned for everyone to walk through. On the other side, she unlocked a wide timber door and the group followed her into a dimly lit room.

'What's that?' Millie pointed to a long cabinet that looked like a Middle Eastern palace. It had three figurines right in the centre of the stage. There was a colourfully dressed man with a turban in the middle and two women with veiled faces and sparkling clothes on either side of him. At both ends were two large drums suspended on their sides like gongs. 'It looks like something from an old-fashioned carnival.'

'That's exactly where it came from,' Nina said proudly. She walked to the side of the cabinet and flicked a switch. Organ music, the kind one hears on a carousel, blared. The male figurine began to move his arms as if he were singing, while the women swung their hips from side to side like belly dancers. Every few beats the gongs would clash.

'Cool,' Lucas said above the din.

'It's just the start,' Nina promised with a smile. She led them through another doorway and into a room filled with unusual contraptions.

'That's a gramophone,' Jacinta said, spotting a turntable with a large trumpet on top. 'My granny used to have one of those and it sounded terrible.'

Nina took a vinyl record from a sleeve and put it on the turntable. She cranked a handle and gently placed the needle in the groove. There was a crackle then the music began.

'Frank Sinatra,' Sep said, recognising the man's voice.

'May I have this dance?' Lucas asked, holding a hand out to Jacinta. He smiled and the girl felt her heart skip a beat.

'Why, sir, of course,' she replied with a curtsy.

He took Jacinta in his arms and spun her around the floor while the other children giggled and swayed in time with the music.

Sep stepped forward and held his hand out to Alice-Miranda, and the two of them waltzed around the room, quickly followed by Millie and Sloane.

Caprice rolled her eyes, her gaze falling on what appeared to be a large piano with two cylindrical cabinets on top of it. 'What's that?' she asked.

'It's a violina,' Nina answered, lifting the needle off the record. 'I'll show you.' She walked over to the instrument and opened the keyboard lid.

'Wait until you see what those are,' Alice-Miranda said to the others, her eyes sparkling.

Nina parted the doors on the left cylinder to reveal three violins, then did the same on the right.

Millie moved closer to inspect the unusual instrument. 'What is that thing?' she asked.

What came next was a complete surprise as Nina switched on the contraption. The piano keys came to life, as if they were being struck by a ghost. The violins rotated, their tune in perfect harmony.

Jacinta marvelled at the machine as it played a famous composition by Wolfgang Amadeus Mozart. 'That's the most bizarre thing I've ever seen.'

'I love *Eine kleine Nachtmusik*,' Alice-Miranda said wistfully. She looked around the room at her friends, smiling to herself.

'Why don't we have instruments like this anymore?' Lucas said.

'I'm not really sure, except that they are very hard to maintain,' Nina answered. 'Opa has been restoring them for years and they need regular attention.' She turned a switch and the tune immediately slowed before stopping completely. 'Now for my favourite.'

Sloane's eyes bulged. 'There's more? Who knew museums could actually be interesting?' she said, following Nina into the next room, where a huge cabinet took up the length of one wall.

'It's so pretty,' Jacinta gushed. 'Look at those ballerinas! Do they dance?'

Nina nodded, smiling.

The children spread out in front of the glass box, pointing and commenting on the funny little figurines. Nina pulled the handle on the side of the instrument and the players sprang to life.

Millie leapt into the air. 'I wasn't expecting that,' she said, giggling at herself.

An old man entered the room, his white hair sticking up all over the place. 'What is going on in here?' he asked in bewilderment.

Nina froze. This is what she had been hoping for more than anything – she just hadn't expected her grandfather to come now. 'I . . . I was just showing my friends the museum, Opa,' she said hesitantly.

Alice-Miranda bit her lip, wondering if Nina was going to get into trouble.

Herr Dettwiller stood there staring at the cabinet, entranced by the music. For several minutes nobody said a word. When the tune came to an end, the old man turned to the children. 'So, did you like it?' he asked, his stern face fracturing into a smile.

Millie grinned. 'It's amazing!'

'Brilliant,' Lucas said, nodding.

The other children weighed in with their words of praise, all except Caprice, who said nothing.

Herr Dettwiller looked at the girl. 'And you? What did you think?'

'It's clever,' she conceded.

Nina placed a hand on her grandfather's arm. 'How are you feeling, Opa?'

The old man gazed around the room. It felt as if he were visiting a long-lost friend. 'Better than I have in a long time,' he replied.

Nina looked into the old man's green eyes. 'You're not cross?'

'Whatever for?' Opa said in surprise.

'For playing the instruments,' Nina replied.

Her grandfather shook his head sadly. 'They are meant to be played. And, thanks to you, something inside me has woken up. I have been numb for such a long time.'

'Shall we show my friends the rest of the museum, Opa?' the girl asked, taking his hand.

'Why not?' he said with a wink.

Alice-Miranda blinked back tears of happiness.

'How much more is there to see?' Millie asked.

Nina's eyes twinkled. 'This is just the beginning. There is something Opa has been working on for years. No one has ever seen it – not even you, Alice-Miranda.'

'Really?' The girl smiled. 'That sounds intriguing,'

The children looked at one another, eager for the unveiling.

'Well, there is no time like the present,' the old man said. He shuffled across the room to a huge bolted doorway. The children held their breaths as they watched Herr Dettwiller pull out a small brass key from his pocket and turn it in the lock.

Chapter 33

The children followed Nina and her grandfather through the door and onto a large landing. Herr Dettwiller flicked a switch, revealing a wide staircase with an ornate cast-iron balustrade. Though the paint on it was flaking, the marble stair treads hinted at the grandeur that lay beneath.

'Are we going to the cellar?' Millie asked, noting the damp air.

'Those are the fanciest cellar stairs I've ever seen,' Jacinta said as she glanced around at the shiny tiles that covered the walls and ceiling.

'What's down there?' Sloane asked.

'Wait and see,' Nina replied mysteriously.

The children followed Nina and her grandfather into the unknown. When the old man neared the bottom, he reached for another switch. This time the entire chamber lit up.

'Whoa! What is this place?' Lucas gasped, his voice bouncing around the walls.

The children spilled onto a platform beneath a dome ceiling lined with glossy cream and sage-green tiles. There was a pile of paint tins and a ladder propped up against the wall beside stacks of tiles and some other tools. Running through the centre of the chamber was a train track that stopped abruptly at the rocky wall to their right. Behind them, printed in the tiles, were the words 'Monta Rosa'.

'Where are we?' Sep whispered.

'It's a secret,' Nina said. 'Opa has been restoring the old railway station. We were going to put some of the instruments down here because the acoustics are amazing.'

Millie frowned. 'Why is there a railway station beneath your house?'

Herr Dettwiller shuffled to the edge of the platform. 'This building wasn't always a house,' he told the children. 'Back in the early nineteenth century, it was the first hotel in Zermatt – the Monta Rosa.'

'Why did the hotel close?' Alice-Miranda asked.

'It was during the war,' the old man said.

'But Switzerland wasn't in the war,' Caprice piped up.

'No, but we are in the centre of Europe and it was impossible for the tourists to come. My parents were young back then. Papa had inherited the hotel from his father, though his heart was never in it. We moved away to Basel and this place was locked up tight. It was my wife who wanted to come back here,' the old man explained. 'But, alas, I was a watchmaker, not a hotelier. Although we raised our daughter in Zermatt, the hotel was never reopened. I had a clock shop and we rattled around for a long time until I started the museum.'

'There would have been steam trains back then,' Sep said. 'Were they able to come down here?'

Herr Dettwiller nodded, his face lighting up. 'Clever boy! That was precisely the conundrum. The guests complained of getting covered in soot, so after a couple of years the trains stopped at the main station instead. They used handcars to take passengers and their luggage to their hotels. Eventually, the horse-drawn carriages became the favoured mode of transport, while the tunnel was only used for the transfer of luggage and goods.'

'Hotels?' Sep asked.

'See the platform on the other side?' the old man said, pointing ahead of them. Sep and the children nodded. 'Although it is covered up now, there was an entrance to the Grand Hotel Von Zwicky too, but it has been sealed tight for many, many years,' Herr Dettwiller explained.

'Where does the tunnel lead?' Lucas asked.

'To the railway station in Zermatt, but it is boarded over now too. You wouldn't even know it was there,' the old man replied.

Sep and Lucas leapt down onto the tracks. At the end of the line was a large handcar with a seesawing handle.

'Does this still work?' Sep asked, jumping onto it.

Nina's grandfather nodded. 'Be careful not to go too far. It is dark down there.'

'This place is incredible. You have to reopen the museum and finish it,' Alice-Miranda said. 'People should see this.'

Lucas and Sep stood opposite one another, pumping the handle up and down as the old carriage wheels grated on the metal, making the most hideous screech. Everyone cringed at the noise. The two boys soon disappeared out of sight, and the noise with them.

'Come back!' Jacinta called into the darkness.

For a few moments there was nothing but silence.

'Stop messing around,' Millie shouted, her voice echoing back to her.

'Perhaps they don't know how to make the handcar go in the other direction,' Nina's grandfather said. 'You have to pull the lever the other way, boys,' he shouted into the tunnel.

There was a clattering sound as the handcar came back into view.

'Thanks for the tip, Herr Dettwiller,' Lucas said as the contraption slowed to a stop. 'We thought we were going to have to push it back.'

'Can we all go for a ride?' Millie asked.

With a nod from her grandfather, Nina turned to the others with a wide grin. 'All aboard the Monta Rosa Express!'

The children returned from their adventure just after midday, bubbling with excitement. As the weather hadn't improved, they were going to have lunch with their parents at a traditional Swiss cafe on the main street, not far from the hotel. The children gathered in the foyer to meet the adults when Alice-Miranda realised she'd left her earmuffs in her room.

She ran upstairs to collect them. When the girl reached the first-floor landing, she spotted a familiar figure. 'Frau Doerflinger?' she called.

The woman at the end of the hallway hesitated before slowly turning around. 'Oh, you,' she said flatly.

Alice-Miranda smiled. 'Hello. Uncle Florian mentioned you were here.'

'I leave tomorrow,' Delphine replied.

'We've just had the most amazing morning,' Alice-Miranda began, her eyes widening. 'My friend Nina gave us a guided tour of Herr Dettwiller's Mechanical Musical Cabinet Museum. We got to see the most incredible thing!'

The old woman nodded and began to turn away.

'You won't believe it, but there's an old railway station *underneath* the museum. Well, it's actually under the road between the museum and the hotel.

Nina's grandfather told us that trains used to bring passengers all the way up here back in the early nineteenth century.'

Frau Doerflinger turned back and stared at the child. 'It can't be . . .'

'I told you you wouldn't believe it,' Alice-Miranda said with a grin.

'Did you *see* it for yourself?' the old woman asked.

'Only half of it,' the child answered happily. 'The other side of the train track was boarded up, but Herr Dettwiller says there is another platform underneath this hotel – beneath our very feet! I can't think where the stairs leading to it would be. Maybe Uncle Florian or Aunt Giselle will know.'

'Really?' Delphine said, arching an eyebrow. 'That *is* amazing.'

Alice-Miranda nodded. 'We thought so too. Anyway, I'd better go or Mummy and Daddy will be wondering where I've got to. We're going for lunch. Goodbye, Frau Doerflinger!'

With that, Alice-Miranda skipped away to her room.

Frau Doerflinger stood there, stunned. She still had to find the entrance but at least she now knew there was access via the museum across the road. Perhaps someone could find it from there. 'I might as well employ that child,' she muttered to herself. 'She would do a much better job than the idiots who work for me.'

Chapter 34

Valerie Wiederman rubbed her eyes and pinched the top of her nose. She'd spent all morning on the telephone – or at least pretending to be – going through the list of past guests and writing down their reasons for not returning this season. There had been knee replacements and elderly parents, children who'd had accidents and businesses gone bust. She scratched her head and wondered what to put next. Creative writing had never been her forte.

The telephone on her desk buzzed and she picked it up. Valerie listened intently, then, without saying a word, she replaced the handset and stood up.

'Herr Schlappi,' she called.

The man was standing just inside the door, polishing its brass frame. He stopped and looked up at her. 'Yes?'

'Could you listen out for the telephone?' she asked, smiling sweetly. 'I have to make an inventory of the housekeeping cupboard upstairs. I won't be long.'

The man nodded and returned to his polishing.

Valerie rode the lift to the third floor, walked to the end of the hall and rang the bell. The door opened and she walked inside. The young woman smiled and went to kiss her aunt's cheek, but the older woman ignored her and turned on her heel.

'Aunt Delphine, is something the matter?' Valerie asked. She had barely seen her aunt since the woman had arrived, as Delphine had a habit of disappearing for hours on end.

'Of course something is the matter,' the old woman snapped. 'You know very well the deal I had hoped to close last week is now in ruins.'

Valerie gulped. 'I did everything you asked. There are no guests . . . I have told so many lies.'

'And you will tell many more before we are done.' Frau Doerflinger sighed and rubbed her temples. 'Stop being so nice to everyone too. I heard you going gaga over those brats.'

'I like children,' Valerie swallowed.

'You will learn,' Delphine scoffed.

Valerie wrung her hands together. 'I promise, Aunt Delphine, I will be the best manager the Grand Hotel Fanger has ever seen.'

The old woman's eyes flickered up at her niece. 'The Grand Hotel Fanger,' Delphine repeated, enjoying the way it rolled off the tongue. 'I hadn't even thought of changing the name, but of course we will. Fanger's is a much more reputable brand. Valerie, if you want to be the manager anytime soon, you must find the hotel blueprints.'

Valerie bit her lip. 'I have never seen them. If I were to hazard a guess, I would say the Baron most likely keeps them in the safe in his apartment.'

'Then I need the key too, unless you happen to know where the entrance to the phantom railway station under the hotel is.'

'Actually, I do,' Valerie said, her eyes lighting up.

'What?!' A wave of crimson crept up Delphine's neck. 'Why haven't you told me before now?'

'You never asked,' Valerie said, fidgeting nervously. Her mind raced. As far as she knew, the old station had been boarded up for decades. The woman wondered what it could possibly have to do with her aunt's acquisition of the hotel but she knew better than to ask. 'It's in the basement. There's a door at the back of the boot room, but I don't think it has been opened in years.'

'How do you know all this?' her aunt demanded.

'The Baron told me,' Valerie replied with a shrug. 'He said he planned to reopen it one day, to entice guests back to the hotel. I was worried that he might do it, so I took the key and hid it.'

Her aunt grabbed her by the arms and shook her. 'Do you still have the key?' she asked, her eyes were wild. 'Tell me you have the key!'

Valerie nodded frantically. 'Y-yes. It's old and I knew that he would never be able to find another like it. He seems to have forgotten about it, anyway.'

'You are a genius, my dear girl. A genius!' Delphine kissed the girl's cheek and hugged Valerie so hard she almost squeezed the life out of her. 'Bring it to me. Bring it to me now!'

Chapter 35

The children entertained the adults with tales of Lars Dettwiller's museum over schnitzel and strudel. But it was the story of the secret beneath the building that had them completely entranced.

'That's incredible,' Hamish said, shaking his head. 'Why doesn't the Baron renovate his side too? It would make for a terrific attraction.'

Hugh scraped the last of his dessert onto his spoon. 'My thoughts exactly. I wonder why he's never mentioned it.'

'I think Herr Dettwiller has been working on it for years, Daddy. It would cost a lot of money to fix it all properly,' Alice-Miranda said.

'Well, the Matterhorn Museum was fascinating too,' Hamish said. 'I think all of you kids should take a look before we go home. There are artefacts from the first successful ascent of the mountain and parts of the rope that broke on their way down.'

'Did they all die, Daddy?' Millie asked.

'No, but four of the party did. It's no wonder, given their rope was only a bit thicker than twine. I can't imagine what they were thinking,' Hamish said, shaking his head.

'I'll go,' Sloane said.

The others stared at her in astonishment.

'You hate museums,' Sep said.

Sloane shrugged. 'Isn't a girl allowed to change her mind?'

'Of course,' Cecelia said. She noticed Caprice fidgeting with her napkin. 'Now, Caprice, I've spoken to your mother again and she has to head home for some urgent work. I know that you were supposed to be going with her but she can't wait another day. I'm sorry to disappoint you but, until the weather clears and we can meet your father and the boys, you're going to have to stay with us.'

Millie almost choked on a mouthful of strudel.

'Oh, I'm not disappointed,' Caprice replied cheerfully. 'That's the best news I've heard all week.'

Sloane and Jacinta exchanged horrified glances.

'I knew we were going to end up with her,' Millie whispered to Alice-Miranda.

'She's been fine today,' Alice-Miranda pointed out.

Millie gave her a look. 'Leopards don't change their spots.'

'What does everyone want to do after lunch?' Cecelia asked the table.

'Ice-skating!' Sloane said.

There were nods all round.

'We'll come too,' Pippa said, glancing at her husband.

'I hope I don't fall over,' Millie said. 'You should see the bruise on my bottom – it's so gross. First it was purple but now it's yellow *and* green. I'll show you.' The girl began to lift up her top.

'Millie!' her mother exclaimed.

'Eww.' Sloane wrinkled her nose. 'You can keep your pants on, thanks.'

Millie grinned. 'I was just being cheeky.'

'We love you, Millie, but seriously we don't need to see your cheeks,' Lucas teased.

Sloane rolled her eyes and groaned. 'Have you been taking comedy lessons from Sep?'

'I think we might come skating too,' Cecelia said, changing the subject.

Hugh nodded. 'Florian and Giselle have gone down the mountain for the rest of the day, so I think we can take the afternoon off.'

The group finished their desserts and headed down through the village to the skating rink on the edge of the river. The wind whipped huge flat flakes into their faces.

'It's like having a floating slurpee.' Millie stuck out her tongue and caught a snowflake. 'Just without the flavouring.'

The other kids laughed and everyone started doing it – even Hugh and Hamish.

'Stop it,' Cecelia chided. 'You all look as if you haven't been fed.'

The rink was almost deserted as the group changed into their skates and hit the ice.

'Do you think the weather will clear up tomorrow, Daddy?' Alice-Miranda asked, the pair skating hand in hand.

Hugh nodded. 'I hope so. Your mother and I would love to get up there for a bit too.'

'Will the Baron and Baroness be all right?'

Hugh looked at his daughter. 'It's hard to say. There has to be some logical explanation for what's going on. People don't just stop coming to one of the most beautiful hotels in the village for no reason.'

Cecelia skated up to them and took Alice-Miranda's other hand in hers.

'Perhaps there's a saboteur in their midst,' Alice-Miranda said, thinking aloud. 'There are lots of new staff members since we were here last time.'

Hugh and Cecelia looked at one another over the top of their daughter's head. 'Stranger things have happened,' Cecelia admitted.

'I hope for their sakes you're wrong, darling,' Hugh said, a grim look on his face.

But Alice-Miranda had a strange feeling. It was nothing she could put her finger on exactly, but she couldn't help wondering if foul play was to blame.

The afternoon passed in the blink of an eye. Before they knew it, the bells on the town clock were striking four. Hamish and Millie skated over to the edge of the rink to join the others and hit the barrier with a *thunk*.

'I don't know about the rest of you, but I'm going to head back and have a nap before dinner,' Hamish said between breaths.

Hugh nodded. 'I'm with you.'

'Look at you old guys,' Lucas teased. 'I hope I'm not having grandpa naps at your age.'

'Can we stay a little while longer?' Millie pleaded. Jacinta had been teaching her to pirouette and she was just beginning to get the hang of it.

Despite the cold, the entire group had enjoyed their time on the outdoor skating rink. Caprice had especially appreciated the chance to show off her skills. Everyone had admired her leaps and twirls until a younger girl arrived and began to jump and spin like a gold medallist. Caprice had stormed off in a huff, saying that she'd twisted her ankle. She'd made a big show of heaping snow on her foot and elevating it on the bench, but when everyone's concern began to wane, she made a miraculous recovery and put her skates back on.

'All right, then, who wants to stay?' Pippa asked.

Millie, Alice-Miranda, Sloane and Jacinta raised their arms as high as they could, wiggling their fingers.

'I think I'd like to go back and have a swim,' Lucas said.

Sep nodded. 'Me too, and then I might have a nap.'

Caprice rolled her eyes. 'I suppose I'll stay here with you lot. At least it's better than hanging out with my brothers. They don't even speak to me.'

'Who could blame them?' Millie said, much louder than she'd intended to.

Caprice's jaw dropped.

'Stop that, Millie, or you can come with me,' Pippa scolded.

'Sorry, that was mean and I shouldn't have said it,' Millie apologised. She hated that Caprice brought out the worst in her.

Cecelia and Pippa decided to have a wander around the shops and instructed the children to meet them back at the hotel by half past five at the latest.

'I wish I could do that,' Millie said as she watched Jacinta gracefully skate in a circle on one leg.

'I could show you,' Caprice offered.

Millie looked at the girl warily. 'Are you going to make me crash or something?'

'Well, as much as I'd like to, I probably won't,' Caprice replied.

'You'll be fine,' Alice-Miranda reassured her friend, hoping that was the truth.

In the past half-hour the lights in the village had come on and the clouds had completely enveloped the surrounding mountains. Alice-Miranda was skating on her own, trying to master a camel spin, with one leg outstretched behind her, when a figure on the other side of the rink caught her eye. She glided past Millie and Caprice, who actually seemed to be getting on for once.

Alice-Miranda squinted at the woman dressed in a thick black coat, furry hat and sunglasses. Her suspicions were correct – it *was* Frau Doerflinger and she was entering one of the cafes that overlooked the rink. The child was about to call out to say hello when she spotted Marius Roten heading to the same place. It could have just been a coincidence except that Andreas, the engine driver on the Glacier Express, appeared seconds later. Alice-Miranda watched as the two men shook hands before walking into the cafe together.

The girl's brows knotted as she replayed the conversation she'd had with Herr Roten. The man had told her that he didn't know anyone on the train, but that clearly wasn't the truth at all. More importantly, Alice-Miranda thought, why would Marius Roten lie?

Chapter 36

Alice-Miranda pulled back the curtains, flooding the bedroom with light.

'What does it look like out there?' Millie asked, yawning and stretching her arms up above her head.

Alice-Miranda turned around and smiled. 'Acres of blue sky,' she announced.

'Yes!' Millie exclaimed, pumping her fists.

Caprice threw herself back on her pillow. 'Argh! I'll have to go back to Daddy now,' she moaned.

'Oh well, all good things must come to an end,' Millie said brightly.

'I suppose you'll have a much better time without me, anyway,' Caprice sulked.

'Stop doing that,' Millie groaned. She knelt on her bed and looked down at the girl, who was lying there with her eyes scrunched tight.

Caprice sat up to face Millie. 'Stop what?' she retorted.

'I know you're just trying to make us feel guilty so you get invited to stay,' Millie said.

Caprice eyeballed the girl. 'I guess you're not as stupid as you look.'

'That was a horrible thing to say, Caprice,' Alice-Miranda chided as she ran a brush through her unruly curls. 'Why don't you want to go back now? Your mother has already left to go home, so you'll get to stay and ski anyway. Isn't that what you wanted?'

Caprice's eyes began to well up.

Alice-Miranda shook her head. 'Stop that, Caprice. No tears and no tantrums,' she said firmly. 'Just tell the truth.'

Caprice brushed her eyes and sat up. 'Well . . . I *was* mad with Mummy about the stupid show and I didn't want to go back home with her, but when you found me I wasn't angry about that. My instructor told me I wasn't trying hard enough. And I was!' she said, scrunching her duvet cover between her fingers. 'But she wouldn't let up and told me I couldn't enter the Ski School Cup competition if I didn't do better. I told her that was stupid because I won a race last year. So I took off and left her and skied over to Zermatt.'

'She must have been so worried,' Alice-Miranda said.

'I doubt it. She didn't even come after me, which made me even madder,' Caprice huffed. 'I know Daddy will make me apologise to her and I don't want to. She's a big bully.'

Millie rolled her eyes. 'Takes one to know one,' she muttered.

'I'm sure you can sort it out,' Alice-Miranda said.

'But I don't want to go back,' Caprice whined.

There was a knock, and Cecelia Highton-Smith poked her head around the door. 'Good morning, girls,' she said, walking into the room. 'Did you all sleep well?'

'Heavenly,' Alice-Miranda replied, giving her mother a hug.

'I was so tired after ice-skating I fell asleep as soon as my head hit the pillow,' Millie added.

Cecelia smiled and turned to Caprice. 'I'm afraid I've come to deliver *more* bad news for you, sweetheart,' she said gently. 'Your brother Toby slipped on a patch of ice yesterday and has ended up with a badly broken arm.'

Caprice's face paled. 'Is he going to be all right?' she asked.

Cecelia walked over and sat on the edge of the foldaway bed, placing an arm around the girl's shoulders. 'Your father has had to drive the boys to Turin. He's asked if we can take you home with us at the end of the week,' she said, rubbing the girl's back. 'Would you like to call him?'

Caprice nodded. 'Yes, please.'

Cecelia handed the girl her phone and Caprice dialled the number.

'Hello Daddy,' she said. 'Is Toby going to be all right?'

The others watched and listened as Caprice spoke to her father for several minutes.

'How is he?' Alice-Miranda asked when Caprice hung up.

'Daddy says he'll be fine but he's in a lot of pain.'

'I'm sure he'll be okay. Kids break their arms all the time,' Cecelia said, giving Caprice a gentle hug.

'You sound really worried,' Millie said to the girl, feeling a bit sorry for her.

'Of course I am. He's my brother,' Caprice said with a frown. 'Wouldn't you be worried if your brother was in hospital?'

Millie nodded. She supposed she couldn't argue with that.

Thursday morning whizzed by as Millie and Lucas continued their snowboarding lessons while the rest of the children, including Nina, hit the slopes with Michaela. They were all thrilled to hear that Nina's grandfather had been out of bed early that morning, looking better and brighter than he had in a very long time. Frau Gisler had been called upon to stay with the old man but Herr Dettwiller shooed her away only an hour later, assuring her that he would stay in the house tinkering with his contraptions.

At lunchtime Michaela collected Millie and Lucas and, together with the other children, they met up with Hugh, Cecelia, Hamish and Pippa at a restaurant halfway up the mountain. Millie unclipped her bindings and stood her snowboard in one of the racks outside the tiny dark timber hut, which stood high on its stone foundations. She and Lucas had both decided they would keep boarding in the afternoon so long as Michaela didn't take them anywhere too challenging. 'How cute is this place?' she said, looking around.

'This is one of the original buildings on the mountain,' Michaela said. 'One hundred years ago a whole family and their animals would have lived and worked here.'

'It's just like some of those cute houses in the old part of the village,' Alice-Miranda said.

Michaela nodded. 'Yes, exactly.'

Inside, the children were surprised to find that the hut wasn't tiny at all.

Cecelia waved from a long table on the sunny balcony that overlooked the village and had a stunning view of the Matterhorn. 'Hi kids. How was it this morning?' she asked.

'Amazing,' Alice-Miranda fizzed.

'How are you getting on with the board, Millie?' Hamish asked.

Millie rubbed her bottom. 'The cheek-o-meter says that I haven't had too many falls today.'

'So, no more colours for that bruise?' her mother asked with a smile.

Millie shook her head. 'I don't think so, but Lucas is going to have a good one.'

'What happened to you?' Hugh asked the lad as the children and Michaela sat around the table and Cecelia ordered some hot snacks and drinks.

'I stacked it getting off the chairlift and took out a whole row of Japanese tourists,' the boy replied.

'Oh dear.' Pippa grimaced. 'Bet you were popular.'

'He sure was,' Millie said, playfully thumping the boy on the arm.

Plates of rösti arrived and the group were soon swapping stories of their heroics on the mountain.

'Michaela took us up to a double slalom course, Mummy, where we could race each other,' Alice-Miranda said, grinning from ear to ear. 'It was so much fun.'

Hugh looked up from his plate. 'Who won?'

'Well, it was close,' Michaela said. 'I was very impressed with Caprice. That girl can certainly ski,' she said, winking at the child.

Caprice beamed back at her. 'Nina was the winner,' she added, without so much as a hint of jealousy.

Millie couldn't believe what she was hearing. 'Did she hit her head or something?' she whispered to Alice-Miranda.

'Though, Nina should be able to beat me,' Caprice continued, flicking her copper-coloured locks behind her. 'She lives here and can ski every day. Imagine how good *I* would be if I lived here too.'

'And she's back,' Millie mumbled.

'Hey, there are those guys that almost steam-rolled you the other day, Millie,' Lucas said. He pointed at the trail of black skiers tearing down the mountainside.

Michaela shook her head. 'I don't know how that school survives. They never seem to take any lessons.'

'There's a lot more of them today,' Millie said, squinting.

As the group drew closer to the restaurant, the last skier appeared to be struggling to keep his balance. He was up on one ski then the other before he lost control and tumbled down the mountain-side, his arms and legs flailing. He came to a stop just below the restaurant deck and didn't move.

Hugh and Hamish ran over to him. 'Are you all right?' Hugh called.

The fallen man moaned, then rolled over and pushed himself up gingerly.

'Take my hand,' Hamish offered.

The man suddenly sat up and felt over his shoulder. He looked around, his eyes darting back up the mountain. 'My backpack! Where is my backpack?' he yelled before charging off, up the slope.

'It's okay, I'm sure we'll find it,' Hamish said.

'He looks pretty freaked out,' Millie observed as the rest of the group watched on.

'We should help him,' Alice-Miranda said. She and the rest of the children stood up and raced off the veranda and into the snow to search for the man's lost bag.

Several minutes later it was Sep who came up trumps. 'Here it is,' he called, struggling under its weight. 'Geez, what have you got in there?'

The man lunged at the boy and snatched the bag from his hand. 'Give it to me,' he said, quickly pulling the straps over his shoulders and settling the heavy pack onto his back.

'You're welcome,' Sep said, raising an eyebrow.

'I am sorry,' the man replied, nodding his head. Beads of perspiration dripped from his temples despite the cold. 'Thank you.'

With that, he pushed off and disappeared in a cloud of powder.

'What was all that about?' Millie asked.

Sep shrugged. 'It's no wonder he lost his balance. His backpack felt like it was full of bricks.'

The family and friends headed back onto the balcony to resume their lunch.

'Gosh the mountains are spectacular.' Pippa pushed her chair out, soaking up the warmth of the sun on her face. 'It's a shame we have to go home.'

'Yes, it's an early start tomorrow, I'm afraid,' Hugh said.

Millie inhaled sharply. 'Tomorrow! I thought we were leaving on Saturday.'

'Sorry, kids, but it's all Cee's fault,' Hugh said.

'My fault?' the woman protested with a laugh.

Hugh grinned. 'Maybe not.'

'Why do we have to go, Daddy?' Alice-Miranda asked.

'Your father and Dolly have been invited to speak at a United Nations symposium on World Hunger,' Cecelia explained.

'They mustn't be very organised if they've just asked you now,' Millie said.

'Actually, we were told about it some time ago but there was never any confirmation. Then, out of the blue, a message came through last night,' Hugh said with a shrug. 'Dolly and Shilly are meeting us back in St Moritz tomorrow evening. Cyril is now fit to fly, so we can leave as soon as we get in.'

'And my locum has come down sick and is barely hanging on until we get back,' Pippa piped up. 'So it's my fault too.'

'That's okay.' Alice-Miranda smiled. 'We didn't expect to have this time at all and it's been so lovely to see Nina and Uncle Florian and Aunt Giselle.'

'Speaking of which, I'd better get down the mountain. I said I'd meet Florian at two,' Hugh said, pushing back his chair and standing up.

'I'll come with you, darling,' Cecelia said. 'We'll see you all at dinner.'

Hugh and Cecelia kissed Alice-Miranda and headed inside while the rest of the group worked out where they were going to ski for the remainder of the afternoon.

Chapter 37

Florian von Zwicky sat at the head of the board-room table, deep in thought.

'Hello darling,' Giselle said, walking in carrying two steaming cups of tea. 'What are you doing in here all by yourself?'

He glanced up and smiled. 'Just thinking, my dear.'

'What were you thinking about?' she asked, setting the tea down in front of him.

Florian sighed. 'I ran into Frau Doerflinger this morning as she was leaving the hotel.'

Giselle sat down beside him. 'And?'

'She asked when we were planning to retire,' he said, staring into his teacup.

'I suppose we can't do this forever, can we?' Giselle said softly, placing her hand on his. 'It's not as if we have heirs to pass this place onto.'

Florian nodded, almost to himself. He and the Baroness had longed for children of their own, but sadly it was not to be. Having the hotel had in its own way filled that void. With so many people coming and going, there had never been much time to be lonely, and over the years they had come to accept that their lives could still be full of children – those who passed through with their mess and havoc, laughter and tears, only to leave at the end of their holidays.

'There was something else,' Florian said. 'Frau Doerflinger mentioned that she would be very interested if we ever consider selling the hotel. She runs a good business and has an excellent reputation. Perhaps we should think about it . . .'

In the room beside them, Valerie's mouth twitched into a smile. The Baroness had left the door open and she could hear every word. She had to call her Aunt Delphine at once. It seemed the dream of the Grand Hotel Fanger was going to come true after all. Valerie wondered why her aunt had only approached the man now. She thought that a deal had been in motion some time ago. Valerie shook the thought from her mind. It was not her place to question how her aunt conducted her business as long as the hotel would soon be in their hands. She couldn't wait to be in charge. There were so many things she wanted to do to bring the hotel into the twenty-first century.

'If we can't turn things around soon, I suppose we will have no choice,' Giselle said.

The Baron squeezed her hand. 'I don't want Hugh and Cecelia to invest money that we might not be able to repay. I shall call Frau Doerflinger and commence negotiations.'

Giselle stood up and kissed her husband's forehead. 'Whatever happens, my darling, we will always have each other.'

Nina walked through the front door to the sound of a violina playing. She paused for a moment to soak it in, then quickly removed her ski boots and hung up her coat.

'Opa!' she called, running to the back room.

'Slow down, my Nina Bear,' her grandfather chuckled. 'Have you had a good day?'

Nina nodded, grinning. 'It was the best, but it is not over yet, Opa. It is Alice-Miranda's last night in Zermatt and she has invited me to stay for dinner and a sleepover. Is Papa home yet?'

The old man shook his head. 'Your father will be late. There are some urgent repairs on the mountain from yesterday's storm.'

Nina's face fell. 'I should stay with you, then.'

'Nonsense,' the old man replied. 'Go and have fun. I am happy tinkering away here and I have soup for my dinner. Frau Gisler has dropped by three times now and I promise you I will not wander off anywhere.'

Nina looked into her grandfather's eyes. 'It is so good to have you back, Opa,' she said, hugging him tightly.

'It is good to be back,' he whispered, gently tugging one of her plaits.

Nina giggled. 'Opa, you haven't done that for ages. Now I know you are well and truly home.'

Her grandfather kissed the top of her head. 'Do not forget to pack your nightdress. I will tell your papa where you are. It is good to see you smiling too.'

'I love you, Opa.' Nina gave him a final squeeze before running back into the foyer and up the stairs.

Her grandfather brushed a tear from the corner of his eye. 'I love you too, my Nina Bear.'

'Here's to good friends!' the Baron said, raising his glass.

'Good friends,' the adults and children echoed, clinking their glasses.

Seated at a long table in the centre of the dining room, the family and friends were enjoying a sumptuous meal of roast beef and vegetables, to be followed by a chocolate gateau.

'It has been so lovely to have you all here,' the Baron said with a smile. 'It is all the more special because this will be somewhat of a last supper.'

'What do you mean, Uncle Florian?' Alice-Miranda asked.

'Giselle and I have reached a decision. We are, as you all know, approaching an age where this –' the old man swept an arm across the room – 'is all too much for us. We cannot fathom what has happened differently these past months but, for some reason, people do not come like they once did.' He looked at his wife, who was sitting at the other end of the long table. 'Hugh, Cecelia, we value your help and support, and even more than that, we value your friendship. We do not want to muddy that water with any loans or arrangements, so we have decided to sell.'

Alice-Miranda's eyes widened. 'But Uncle Florian, the hotel is your life.'

The looks on the faces of her fellow diners showed that they were similarly surprised, except for Hugh and Cecelia, who had already been told of their decision.

The Baron nodded and smiled at the girl. 'It is the beginning of a new chapter.'

'What will happen to the Grand Hotel Von Zwicky?' Millie said, buttering her bread roll.

'Actually, I have already negotiated the sale this afternoon,' the Baron replied.

'Who's the lucky buyer?' Hamish asked.

'It is Delphine Doerflinger and her husband, Otto Fanger,' the Baron said.

Millie recoiled. 'Not that witch! She's mean.'

Jacinta gave her friend a swift kick under the table.

'Ow!' Millie yelped.

Pippa eyeballed her daughter. 'Millie, where are your manners? Apologise at once.'

Millie flushed red with shame.

'It is all right, dear,' the Baroness said. 'Frau Doerflinger certainly is a formidable business-woman. Everyone knows that she is the reason her husband is so successful.'

The children exchanged glances.

'Millie's right,' Lucas whispered to Sep, who was sitting beside him. 'She is mean and weird and she definitely hates kids.'

Sep nodded.

Dinner was served and the room was soon filled with chatter. Try as she might, however, Alice-Miranda could not shake the feeling that something was awry. There was something about Delphine Doerflinger that had her worried. It was strange how the woman had neglected to mention that she was heading to exactly the same place as them. And was it just a coincidence that Uncle Florian had met those frauds in her hotel? Not to mention that Alice-Miranda had seen the woman with Marius and Andreas. There were so many things that just didn't add up.

Chapter 38

Lars Dettwiller had spent the afternoon checking each of the instruments, switching them on and listening to their tunes, cringing at the state of some. But for the first time since that terrible day, he felt alive again. Frau Gisler had checked in on him three times and had brought over a huge pot of soup for his dinner. He'd just eaten a bowl of it and was pleased with himself for not burning the house down – unlike his last attempt at cooking, when his son-in-law had arrived home to billowing smoke and a chargrilled lump of beef.

Lars looked at his watch. There was something he was curious about downstairs. He had begun to wonder whether, if he put his mind to it, he could finish restoring the station and reopen the museum. If only he could summon the energy he knew would be required. He had no idea when Sebastien would be home and he didn't want his son-in-law to worry if he returned home to an empty house.

Unable to resist, Lars decided to have a quick look. He unlocked the door and closed it behind him, putting the key in the lock so he wouldn't lose it. Then he flicked the switch on the top of the stairs and carefully made his way down into the subterranean cavern. As he reached the bottom, he felt around for the second light switch when something caught his eye. Was it just his imagination or were there torch-lights on the other side of the tracks? He took his hand away from the switch and peered into the pitch black.

'Hurry up,' a voice hissed.

'It would help if it wasn't so dark,' another voice grumbled.

'The others are coming with the lanterns, so stop your whining.'

Lars could feel his heart pounding inside his chest. His breath quickened.

'How did you find it, Marius?' the first voice asked.

The old man strained his eyes, peering into the darkness. He could hear things being shifted about.

'What does it matter?' Marius replied. 'We have access now.'

'Just as well you did,' the first man said gruffly. 'This shipment is far too big to have gone through the village, and now we will be able to handle so much more.'

'Dante, are you there?' another voice called.

As more torches lit up the space, Lars could make out several silhouettes. There seemed to be seven or eight of them, loading boxes onto one of the handcars. His mind raced. He had heard stories of smugglers using the route over the mountains, from Cervinia to Zermatt, during the war. They had supposedly hidden millions of dollars' worth of jewels and cash in Swiss bank vaults. But that was years ago and he had never really believed it.

Lars felt a tickle in his throat. He clamped a hand over his mouth and turned to go back upstairs before it was too late. As he placed his foot on the first step, Lars sputtered then coughed. Suddenly, one of the torches swivelled to train a beam of light directly at him.

'You!' someone yelled. 'What are you doing down here?'

Two men rushed across the tracks and leapt up onto the platform. They grabbed Lars, covering his mouth while dragging him down into the cavern. Lars tried to resist but it was no use.

Someone noticed the beam of light coming from the stairwell. 'He must be the old man from the museum,' he said.

'I thought he had died,' said another. 'The museum has been closed for a year.'

'No, someone found him on the mountainside last week – they said he was trying to fly. The old boy has lost his marbles,' Dante said. 'That's not all he is going to lose, either.'

Lars gulped. He knew exactly what that meant.

One of the men ran up the stairs. 'Hey, there's a door up here. It must go into the museum,' he called back. 'There's a key.'

Dante leaned towards Lars. 'Who else knows you're down here?' he hissed.

Lars shook his head. 'N-no one.'

Dante nodded, then turned to yell up the stairs. 'Lock that door and bring me the key!'

Chapter 39

All of the children had gathered in Alice-Miranda and Millie's room for the slumber party. To make space, Hugh and Hamish had pushed the beds back against the walls and Caprice's foldaway had been removed. Everyone was dressed in their pyjamas, sitting in a circle on the floor, on top of a mountain of fluffy duvets and pillows.

'Seriously, I can't believe the Baron is selling the hotel to Grouchy Doerflinger,' Millie said, shaking her head. She took a sip from her mug of hot chocolate.

'Me either,' Alice-Miranda said.

'Who is this woman?' Caprice asked, exasperated. 'Everyone keeps saying bad stuff about her, but what did she ever do to you?'

'She's . . . tricky,' Lucas said diplomatically.

'Her nose is too skinny,' Sloane said, wrinkling her own.

'Really?' Sep stared at his sister. '*That's* what you think is wrong with her?'

'Well, it is,' Sloane said, sticking her tongue out at her brother. 'It's so sharp she could probably cut cheese with it.'

'What does she look like?' Nina asked.

'She walks around like this,' Sloane said, getting up and stalking around the room. 'She's pointed and skinny, unlike her husband who's really, really –'

'Sloane, you don't have to be unkind,' Alice-Miranda chided. 'Herr Fanger is very sweet.'

'I don't know what he sees in her,' Jacinta said.

'Hang on, I think I have a photo of her presenting the trophies at White Turf.' Millie picked up her camera from the bedside table and switched it on. She walked over to show Caprice and Nina. 'That's her, there,' she said, pointing at the screen.

Caprice made a face. 'Sloane's right. She's ugly.'

Nina peered at the picture and frowned. 'I've seen her before.'

'Yes, she was staying here this week,' Alice-Miranda said. 'She went home this morning.'

Nina shook her head slowly. 'No, not just here at the hotel. I've seen her visiting Valerie. She lives in the flat next door to my piano teacher.'

Millie and Alice-Miranda's eyes widened. 'Aunt Delphine!' they exclaimed in unison, then quickly relayed their encounter with Valerie in the powder room.

'How long has Valerie worked here?' Sloane asked.

'She wasn't here last time we came and that was probably about a year and a bit ago,' Alice-Miranda said.

'And when did the hotel start losing business?' Millie asked pointedly.

Alice-Miranda nodded. 'I was just thinking the same thing. I should talk to Mummy and Daddy.'

'Am I missing something?' Lucas asked.

Sep slapped his forehead. 'Do you think Valerie has something to do with there being no guests?'

'Well, Frau Doerflinger is going to buy the hotel . . .' Alice-Miranda said, her thoughts racing a million miles a minute.

Chapter 40

Giselle von Zwicky kissed Alice-Miranda's cheeks and gave the child a hug. 'Thank you for raising your concerns about Valerie,' she whispered before drawing back. When Cecelia had said goodnight to the children, Alice-Miranda had quietly told her what Nina had said about seeing Delphine Doerflinger at Valerie's apartment and her own suspicions about the timing of the woman's employment. 'Your mother and I telephoned some of our past guests last night. Everything Valerie had written down about their reasons for not staying this year turned out to be true, but I will ask her when she comes in this morning about her aunt.' Giselle shrugged. 'She is a very private person, so who knows? Families can be complicated.'

Alice-Miranda smiled up at the woman. She wanted to believe it but she still had her doubts, and that niggling feeling simply refused to go away. 'Will you and Uncle Florian come and visit us when you've sold the hotel?' she asked.

The Baroness nodded. 'We would love to, my darling.'

'Nina!' Sebastien Ebersold called from the other side of the street.

'Papa!' the child called back as the man hurried across the snow-covered roadway to join them.

'You look tired, Herr Ebersold,' Alice-Miranda remarked.

'I worked around the clock,' he said. 'We had problems with the funicular, but fingers crossed all will be well today.'

Nina glanced over at their house. 'I hope Opa is okay. I had a sleepover with Alice-Miranda.'

Sebastien's brow furrowed. 'Your grandfather has been on his own all night?'

Nina nodded. 'But Frau Gisler made soup and he was having that for his supper. He is so much better, Papa. Yesterday he worked in the museum all day.'

Sebastien's face softened. 'That is good news indeed, but we should get home and make sure that he is all right.'

Nina and Alice-Miranda hugged tightly. 'It has been so good to see you,' Nina said, grinning.

Alice-Miranda smiled and squeezed her friend's hand. 'I'll write to you when I get back to school.'

Marius packed the last of the bags into the trailer and climbed into the driver's seat. 'We must get going,' he said tersely.

The group of family and friends finished their goodbyes and piled inside. With a flick of the reins, the carriage moved off. Alice-Miranda leaned out of the window, waving to the Baron and Baroness until they turned the corner. Seeing them standing there in front of that beautiful building, she simply couldn't imagine them anywhere else.

While the rest of the group boarded the train, Alice-Miranda and her mother dashed off to the nearby convenience store to buy some snacks for the journey.

'I'm glad that I was wrong about Valerie,' Alice-Miranda said, as the pair walked down the platform with their shopping bags, 'but I still don't understand why she would deny the fact that Delphine Doerflinger is her aunt.'

Cecelia sighed. 'People have their reasons and it's not for us to interfere.'

Just as they were about to step onto the train, someone called out Alice-Miranda's name. They both turned to see Nina running towards them. Alice-Miranda frowned, wondering what she had forgotten.

Nina reached the pair, puffing. Her face was red and she could barely get the words out.

'What's the matter?' Alice-Miranda asked, putting down the grocery bags and clasping her friend's hands.

'Opa,' the girl sputtered, struggling to catch her breath. 'Opa is missing.'

Alice-Miranda's stomach twisted. 'Perhaps he's gone for a walk,' she suggested, trying to comfort her friend.

Tears welled in Nina's eyes. 'It's my fault. I should have stayed with him last night,' she sobbed.

'It's not your fault, Nina,' Alice-Miranda said, shaking her head.

Cecelia hurried onto the train to deposit the bags and speak with Hugh, who emerged onto the platform just a minute later.

'Nina, has your father called the authorities?' Hugh asked gently.

The girl nodded, sniffling.

'So the ski patrol and the police will be out looking for him,' the man said.

Nina nodded again just as the whistle for the train blew.

'Mummy, what can we do?' Alice-Miranda asked. She felt completely helpless leaving her friend at a moment like this.

'You must go,' Nina said, her voice wobbling. 'I shouldn't have worried you. I just hoped that maybe he was somewhere in the village and then I saw you on the platform.'

'Of course you should have told us,' Alice-Miranda said.

'I'll telephone the Baron,' Hugh said. 'I'll ask if he can help to organise the search.'

Nina wiped away her tears. 'I thought Opa was getting better.'

Alice-Miranda's eyes widened. 'Could he be downstairs?' she asked.

Her friend shook her head. 'The door was locked when I checked and Opa has the only key.'

'All aboard!' the train conductor called, then blew his whistle again.

'You'll find him,' Alice-Miranda said. The girls embraced one last time. 'I'll call you when we arrive in St Moritz.'

Cecelia bent down and gave Nina a hug. 'Be brave, darling.'

Nina nodded and stepped back. As the last few passengers clambered on board, she turned and fled down the platform. Nobody saw the man racing for the engine at the end of the train. He leapt onto the step and hurled himself through the door as the train pulled out of the station.

Chapter 41

Alice-Miranda made her way down the aisle to her friends, her face ashen.

'What's the matter?' Sloane asked as the girl took her seat. 'You look as miserable as Caprice.'

'I heard that,' Caprice snapped, swivelling around to face them.

'Nina's grandfather has gone missing,' Alice-Miranda said. She shook her head, still digesting the news. 'We just saw her on the platform.'

Millie looked up from her guidebook. 'Hasn't he wandered off before?' she asked.

Alice-Miranda bit her lip and nodded.

'He's probably just gone to the shops or bingo or something,' Millie said reassuringly, though she wasn't sure whether bingo was a favoured pastime of Swiss senior citizens.

'I hope they find him soon,' Sloane said. 'Imagine being lost in the snow up there. It would be so scary, especially at night. I mean, he could easily fall down a ravine and –'

'We get the picture, Sloane,' Millie interjected.

Alice-Miranda stared out the window, thinking about Nina and her father. Surely they had suffered enough tragedy in their lives. She hopped up and walked over to her parents, who were sitting with Pippa and Hamish.

'Did you get hold of the Baron?' she asked her mother.

Cecelia nodded. 'He's mustered up a search party among their friends and the hotel staff to scour the village while the ski patrol and Sebastien's work crews are on the mountain. Don't worry, darling, there are a lot of people looking for Nina's grandfather.' Cecelia touched her daughter's cheek. 'I'm afraid there's nothing more we can do, but I'll let you know the minute I hear anything.'

As the train chugged through the mountains, the children entertained themselves playing cards and I-spy.

'Is the train moving a lot slower than when we came over?' Sep asked the group.

Jacinta shrugged. 'I can't remember. I was too busy looking at the scenery.'

A young conductor walked into the carriage. 'Hello again,' he said, smiling at the children.

'Herr Anton!' Alice-Miranda smiled at the man. 'Are you always on this train?'

'A lot of the time,' the man replied with a grin. The children handed him their tickets, which he examined before using a little holepuncher to mark each one. 'Did you enjoy your time in Zermatt?'

Alice-Miranda nodded. 'It was wonderful. We had a great time skiing.'

'And snowboarding,' Lucas added.

'How many carriages are there today?' Sep asked.

'It's a long train,' Anton replied. 'Seven cars plus the two engines.'

'Seems slow,' Sep said.

'I thought so too,' the man agreed. 'We had better find a way to get up more speed. The Glacier Express might be the slowest express train in the world but we are always on time. Enjoy the rest of your journey.' The conductor gave them a friendly wave, then moved on to the next group of passengers.

✶

'What are we going to do with him?' Andreas said, gesturing to the old man.

'We should have left him where we found him,' Marius replied, shaking his head. 'No one would have questioned a heart attack at his age.'

'Well, you had better come up with something – he cannot be here when we reach our destination.'

'I know that,' Marius snapped.

'This train is too slow,' Andreas said. 'We cannot be late or there will be questions.'

Marius rolled his eyes. 'What do you propose we do about it?'

'We should split the train. I have already spoken with Franz and he agreed. He knows we cannot risk any officials checking the weights.'

'Where will you do it?' Marius asked.

'Disentis. We will split the engine and the two goods cars here at the back, then the train will continue on its way,' Andreas explained.

'And what about him?' Marius pointed at the old man, who was bound and gagged.

Andreas grinned. 'I have an idea.'

Lars Dettwiller gulped and made a silent prayer.

Chapter 42

The train pulled into the snow-covered town of Disentis, with its pretty gable-roofed houses and majestic Disentis Abbey, now home to the Fanger's Chocolate factory. The children grabbed their coats, hats and gloves and exited the carriage, after promising to return five minutes before the train was due to depart.

'I wish we could visit the chocolate factory,' Millie said, glancing at the clock above the station.

'We don't have time,' Alice-Miranda replied, knowing they were due to leave again in half an hour. The children walked along the platform to the front of the train, past Anton, who gave them a wave. Then they turned around and walked back again.

'So there are four passenger cars, split by a dining car in the middle then two goods cars,' Sep said, counting them off.

Sloane rolled her eyes. 'Seriously, are you becoming one of those dorky trainspotters?'

'What if I am?' Sep replied. 'Everyone has hobbies.'

'Boring!' his sister quipped, and everyone laughed.

'I wonder if Nina's grandfather has been found yet,' Alice-Miranda said as she watched an elderly couple helping each other along the platform.

Millie caught sight of a man exiting the engine at the back end of the train. 'Hey, isn't that the cranky driver we met on the way over?'

'Andreas?' Alice-Miranda said, craning her neck to spot him among the crowd.

Millie nodded. 'The one who looked like Rotten Marius.'

The children turned to walk away but Alice-Miranda couldn't take her eyes off Andreas. The man had his coat collar pulled up around his neck and was wearing dark glasses and a hat. She watched as he hurried past the goods carriages and slipped in between them and the first passenger car.

Alice-Miranda scurried along the platform, making sure to keep her distance. As he turned around, it suddenly hit her. It wasn't Andreas at all. It was Herr Roten and there was no doubt in her mind that he was up to no good.

'What do you mean it's Rotten Marius?' Millie exclaimed after Alice-Miranda rushed over to tell her friends what she had just witnessed.

'What's he doing on the train?' Jacinta asked.

Millie frowned. 'Are you sure it was him? He and that Andreas guy look a lot alike.'

'I *saw* him – it wasn't Andreas,' Alice-Miranda insisted. 'I think he was unhitching the goods wagons from the rest of the train.'

'Maybe they do that all the time,' Millie said. 'I mean, they could be loading Fanger's Chocolate for all we know.'

Alice-Miranda bit her lip, unconvinced. 'He was acting like he didn't want anyone to see what he was doing,' she said, almost to herself.

'Let's go and look,' Sep suggested. 'It does sound suspicious.'

The children turned around and made their way back across the chilly platform. There was no sign of Marius but there were lots of passengers from the train milling about and taking in the fresh air.

Sep peered at the end of the first goods carriage. 'It's unhitched,' he confirmed.

Sloane jumped at a thumping sound close by. 'What was *that*?'

'It's coming from in there,' Alice-Miranda said, pointing to the goods carriage. It sounded as if someone was kicking the wall from the inside.

'Let's check it out,' Lucas said.

The only way to get there was through the passenger car, so the children piled back onto the train. As she hopped on board, Millie spotted her parents walking along the platform and gave them a wave.

The children moved through the carriage and the gangway connection, then came to a door. In the distance, they could hear the conductor blow his whistle to indicate that the train was about to leave.

'Can you get through?' Millie asked.

'I'm not sure,' Alice-Miranda said. She turned the handle but it wouldn't budge.

Sep pressed his ear against the door. 'There's someone in there,' he said, his eyes widening. 'I think they're shouting for help.'

He pushed the handle, harder this time, and the door flew open. Inside, the car was filled with stacks of the Fanger's Chocolate containers.

'Wow – that's a lot of boxes,' Millie said, licking her lips.

'Herr Dettwiller!' Alice-Miranda gasped. The other children gasped too. Alice-Miranda ran over to the old man, who was writhing around in the far corner of the carriage. She whipped off his gag while Lucas and Millie untied the ropes around his arms and legs.

'Oh, my dear children, you are a sight for sore eyes,' the man breathed. 'But we cannot tarry. We must get to the front of the train.'

The floor beneath their feet jerked suddenly. Everyone grabbed onto each other to keep their balance. Alice-Miranda and Lucas helped Herr Dettwiller to his feet and they shuffled towards the carriage door.

'It's splitting apart!' Caprice shouted from the entrance.

'Jump then,' Millie called.

Caprice watched as the Glacier Express surged away. 'It's too far.'

The children came up behind her and peered out through the gangway connection. Their train was fast becoming a speck in the distance.

'It's gone,' Sep said. 'They've split the train apart. There's just us, two goods carriages and the engine.'

'And Rotten Marius,' Millie said glumly.

'There is another man too – Andreas,' Herr Dettwiller said, his voice hoarse from yelling.

'What are they up to?' Caprice demanded. 'Surely chocolate is not that valuable – especially in Switzerland.'

Lucas unclasped the lid on one of the Fanger's Chocolate boxes. It was full of chocolate bars the same as the one he had seen in the loading dock at Fanger's Palace. 'At least we've got something to eat,' he said, trying to lighten the mood.

He picked one up and was astonished at the weight. He quickly unwrapped the block and held it up for everyone to see.

'Gold!' Caprice exclaimed.

There was a loud crunch followed by another jolt.

'What was that?' Millie said, holding onto Herr Dettwiller.

'I think they have moved the engine so that we can keep going in the same direction as the other part of the train,' Herr Dettwiller surmised.

'But why? I don't understand any of this,' Caprice huffed. She was beginning to wish she had stayed in Cervinia.

The door between the engine and the goods carriage opened. Marius stepped inside and stopped dead in his tracks. 'What are you lot doing here?' he barked, looking set to explode.

'What is going on back there?' someone yelled from behind him.

Marius sucked in a deep breath and was about to say something when Andreas appeared next to him.

'How did they get in here?' he roared. 'This door was supposed to be locked.'

'I unlocked it so that we could get through once the train was turned around,' Marius hissed.

'Imbecile! I have a key.' Andreas glared at his colleague.

Having had enough of listening to the two crooks, Millie drew herself up to her full height. 'We know what you're up to and as soon as we get off this train, we're going straight to the police,' she said.

Andreas narrowed his eyes at her. They were the colour of coals. 'As soon as you get off this train, my dear,' he said menacingly, 'you are going to spend days in the wilderness trying to find your way home. By then we will be long gone.'

Jacinta shuddered and tears welled in Caprice's eyes.

'Our parents will realise we're missing any minute now and then you're done for,' Alice-Miranda said with her hands on her hips.

Millie shook her head. 'I don't think that's going to happen for a while,' she whispered.

'Why not?' Caprice sniffed.

'Mummy and Daddy saw us getting onto the train,' Millie replied.

'They'll know we're not in our seats,' Jacinta said.

Alice-Miranda gulped. 'Mummy said that the adults were all going for a late lunch in the dining car, so they won't realise for a while.'

'And by then, *you* will be long gone,' Andreas threatened.

'Hadn't you better get back and drive?' Marius said. 'The last thing we need is a crash.'

'Fine. Stay here and make sure they don't try anything,' Andreas spat, then stormed off.

Marius pulled the door shut. 'All of you, on the floor now!' he shouted.

The train was gathering speed, rollicking along the tracks. Millie slipped and fell, landing on her bottom with a thud.

'Ow!' she yelped, grimacing. 'Not another bruise.'

'I think that's the least of our worries,' Jacinta whispered, lowering herself onto the ground.

The rest of the children and Herr Dettwiller sank to the floor as the train bumped and swayed.

Marius Roten took a step closer and reached into his coat.

'Please don't shoot us,' Jacinta whimpered. She grabbed hold of Lucas, who shielded the girl's face. But Marius did not pull out a gun. It was a badge.

Alice-Miranda leaned closer to read the words. 'Interpol.'

Caprice's face lit up. 'Yes! We're saved.'

'You're an awesome actor,' Millie blurted. 'But what about your twin? How come he's a bad guy?'

'Andreas is not my twin. It's just an unfortunate coincidence that we look so much alike,' the man's words spilled quickly.

'Is Roten *really* your name?' Millie asked, thinking it had to be a cover.

'Yes, it is,' Marius said, narrowing his eyes.

Millie flinched. 'Sorry, it just sounded made . . . Never mind.'

'Shush! You must be quiet!' The man held up his hands to quell the children, who were firing questions over the top of one another. If Andreas realised what was going on, they were all done for. He could derail the train at any time, and Marius knew the man was capable of exactly such a thing.

'Is it all gold?' Alice-Miranda asked, gesturing to the stacks of Fanger's Chocolate boxes.

Marius nodded. 'Stolen in Italy and smuggled over the border into Switzerland,' he whispered.

Alice-Miranda's eyes widened with the dawning of a realisation. 'The Black Diamonds!' she gasped. 'They've been moving the gold, haven't they?'

'No wonder that guy was so worried about his backpack,' Sep said.

'But why haven't you arrested anyone?' Millie asked.

'We have been biding our time to catch Signor Grande, the man responsible for all this,' Marius explained. 'My associates and I have received intel that he will be present at the delivery of the shipment tonight.'

'Why did you and Andreas meet Frau Doerflinger at the restaurant near the ice rink?' Alice-Miranda asked. 'Is she part of this too?'

Marius looked at her in surprise, then shook his head. 'She is a mere pawn in this criminal operation – a greedy woman who made a deal with some very bad people.' Marius handed Herr Dettwiller a bottle of water. 'I am sorry that you have been caught up in all of this, sir.'

The old man took a sip. 'Thank you,' he said gratefully.

'What about Herr Fanger?' Alice-Miranda asked. She couldn't imagine the man as a crook.

'No, from what I can tell, he knows nothing of his wife's dealings,' Marius replied.

Alice-Miranda stared at the ground then suddenly looked up. 'I know where I saw Andreas before. He was the man making the delivery when we were in the docks at Fanger's Palace,' she said, pleased to have finally remembered.

Marius nodded.

Millie reached into her pocket and pulled out the little gold disc she'd found at Fanger's Palace. She fidgeted with it, turning it over in her fingers.

'What is that?' Marius asked.

Millie handed it to him. 'I found it on the floor at Fanger's Palace.'

He examined it closely, relief washing over his face. 'It's a key to the Fanger's vault,' he laughed, unable to believe his luck. 'We have been trying to get one for ages. As far as we know there are only two in existence. Frau Doerflinger keeps one on her at all times and the spare is in the safe in her office, for which only she knows the combination.'

'What?' Millie screwed up her nose. 'I tried to hand it in, but the concierge said that it wasn't worth anything.'

'It is worth *everything*,' Marius replied. 'May I keep this?'

Millie nodded.

'What do we do now?' Alice-Miranda asked.

'Andreas had planned to leave Herr Dettwiller behind in the second goods carriage, in a siding high in the mountains off the main line,' Marius replied. 'There are some empty Fanger's boxes in the second car – I want you to find them and bring them here. When the time comes, you will hide inside those until I let you out again.'

Caprice's bottom lip trembled. She imagined all the things that could go wrong – Marius tricking them, their becoming stranded and freezing to death or being eaten by bears. She tried to remember if there were any bears in Switzerland.

'Can we breathe in those boxes?' Millie asked doubtfully.

'They are climate-controlled and well ventilated. You will be fine,' Marius assured her. 'And I will get word to Anton to notify your parents that you are safe.'

'Is he an Interpol agent as well?' Sep asked. 'Because he's a really convincing train conductor.'

Marius nodded. 'Trains are his hobby. This was the perfect assignment for him.'

Sep raised his eyebrows. 'Whoa, I want to be an agent when I grow up – imagine getting to catch bad guys and ride the Glacier Express for months on end.'

'Seriously, we're in mortal danger and that's all you can think about?' Sloane shook her head in disgust.

'Now, make sure you cry out every so often, otherwise Andreas will become suspicious. Listen for my directions.' Marius closed the door, and the children heard a key turn in the lock.

Chapter 43

The train pushed on through the mountains for hours. When Marius returned to their carriage, the children and Herr Dettwiller did exactly as they were asked, curling themselves into the empty Fanger's boxes. It was lucky the old man was quite small and that the boxes were so large. Just as Marius had told them, the train stopped in the mountain siding and he unhitched the second wagon, leaving behind nothing but fruit and vegetables which had been bound for some Alpine restaurants.

As the train came to a halt at St Moritz station, an army of workers began to unload the cargo. A dozen men heaved the boxes into the back of two waiting vans that were headed directly to Fanger's Palace Hotel to be deposited into the vault. Remarkably, the children kept as quiet as church mice. Not so much as a whimper escaped their lips.

The vans travelled the short distance to the hotel and soon the familiar beeping of a reversing vehicle signalled their arrival at their destination.

'Good evening, Frau Doerflinger,' Andreas said, jumping out of the first van.

Marius got out of the other van, which contained the children and Nina's grandfather.

'You have the entire shipment?' the woman asked stiffly. 'No thanks to your investigative skills, Roten. I can't believe in all this time you couldn't locate the entrance to that underground station and yet my niece knew it all along.'

Marius grunted in response and began to unload the boxes onto several large trolleys.

'Ouch,' Millie yelped as her bottom was bumped.

The rest of the children and Herr Dettwiller winced, hoping the smugglers wouldn't notice. Caprice was about to tell the girl off for making a noise when she realised doing so would give them all away. She clamped her hand over her mouth just in time.

'What was that?' Delphine barked.

Marius held up a finger. 'Jammed it between the boxes.'

The woman rolled her eyes. 'Hurry up. My associates are waiting to receive their goods.'

Millie, who had been holding her breath, exhaled with relief.

Delphine followed Andreas to the lift with the first trolley of boxes. 'We will be back soon. No slacking off,' she ordered, glaring at Marius.

As the lift doors closed Marius heaved the top box back to the ground and unsnapped the locks.

Alice-Miranda looked up at him. 'What do you want me to do?' she asked.

'We need to get everyone out,' Marius instructed. 'Quickly!'

Alice-Miranda clambered onto the side of the trolley and released the locks on the box that contained Millie. Marius staggered under the weight of another, which he placed gently on the floor. Sloane almost leapt out of hers like a jack-in-the-box. A minute later all of the children and Herr Dettwiller were free.

'What do we do now?' Millie asked, her green eyes darting all over the storeroom.

'I have to get to the vault. Anton is coordinating backup around the hotel,' Marius said, leading them all to the lifts. 'Do you know the way upstairs?'

Alice-Miranda nodded. 'We accidentally came down here the other day. You should go. I assume the vault is in the basement.'

'Yes,' Marius said, checking his watch.

He reached out to press the button for the lift just as the bell dinged and the doors slid open. Andreas stood there facing them.

For a moment no one said a word.

'What is this?! Liar!' Andreas screamed, charging at Marius's middle. The two men went flying into a pile of green linen sacks. A struggle ensued, with Andreas throwing punches and mostly missing his target.

'Alice-Miranda, Millie, get downstairs and lock them in before it's too late,' Marius shouted. He threw the token to Alice-Miranda while fending off Andreas with his other hand. 'Use the key to scramble the code!'

Alice-Miranda nodded and ran into the lift, with Millie by her side. She pressed the button and the doors closed.

Meanwhile, Sep had spotted a net among the bric-a-brac in the corner of the storeroom. He pointed at it and called to his sister. Sloane and Caprice raced to get it while Lucas and Jacinta launched themselves at Andreas, who had pinned Marius to the ground.

'Get off him!' Lucas yelled, wrestling Andreas to the floor.

Jacinta catapulted herself backwards out of harm's way as Marius rolled out from underneath the scuffle and leapt to his feet. Lucas jumped up too just as Sep and the girls threw the net over Andreas.

'Let me out of here!' the man demanded.

Andreas struggled and kicked, landing a blow against one of the trolleys with its tower of Fanger's Chocolate boxes. They wobbled and swayed.

'Look out!' Herr Dettwiller shouted as the boxes toppled. One smashed open and a stray bar of gold flew through the air, striking Andreas on the head and knocking him out cold.

Without so much as a whisper, the elevator doors slid open to reveal a room with a steel ceiling and walls. A couple of metres in front of Millie and

Alice-Miranda was a giant round door, at least fifty centimetres thick. It was wide open, and the girls could see that Delphine Doerflinger was standing inside it next to a man and woman.

'It's the couple from the ski lift,' Millie whispered.

The man's head snapped in their direction. 'Who is there?' he called.

The two girls scurried behind the door.

'Marius?' Delphine stalked over to the entrance. 'Where is that stupid good-for-nothing –'

'Vincenzo, how much longer do we have to stay down here? Gold is so boring unless I can wear it,' Sancia whined.

Alice-Miranda nodded to Millie. 'That's her, all right.'

Delphine walked back to resume her conversation with the man, discussing weights and quantities.

'Where is the rest of it?' he demanded.

Deciding that the coast was clear, Alice-Miranda and Millie leaned against the door. They pushed and shoved with all their might but it refused to budge. Just as Millie gave one last heave, she lost her footing and skidded across the marble floor.

Vincenzo looked up again and this time he locked eyes with her.

Millie froze. 'Oops.'

'Get her!' the man shouted, running to the vault door.

Delphine's head swivelled around to face the girl, who was sprawled in front of them. 'What! How did she get in here?' she squawked, charging after Vincenzo.

'Not so fast, you two!' Sancia somersaulted past Delphine and, with one swift kick, knocked the old woman back inside the vault.

Alice-Miranda pulled Millie out of reach as the woman grabbed Vincenzo's arm and launched him backwards.

'Who is she?' Millie gasped.

'I don't know but I think she's on our side,' Alice-Miranda said, her eyes the size of dinner plates.

'Sancia, what are you doing?' Vincenzo shouted.

'Quickly, girls, help me,' Sancia ordered, the characteristic whine gone from her voice. She put her back against the vault door and began to push. Slowly, it started to move.

'Don't do this! You know who I am!' Vincenzo's voice echoed through the vault as the door clanged shut. Alice-Miranda grabbed the token from her pocket and pressed it into the coin-sized slot on the keypad, then pushed every button. Delphine's face appeared close up on the video monitor beside it. 'You cannot lock us in. I have the key.'

Alice-Miranda pressed the intercom button. 'So do we.'

'That's not possible,' Delphine screamed. A volley of words unfit for children's ears spewed from her lips.

Millie plucked the token from the keypad and held it up for the woman to see. 'Is too!'

Delphine fainted on the spot.

'You will pay for this, Sancia!' Vincenzo threatened.

The woman curled her lip and whined like a three-year-old. 'No, Vincenzo, that's the price *you* pay for not giving Sancia everything she wants.' She winked at the girls before pressing the button to make him disappear.

Alice-Miranda looked at the woman. 'Who *are* you?'

'Italian Secret Service,' the woman replied.

'You were amazing,' Millie gushed. The woman had leapt and twirled all over the place in three-inch heels. 'So, all that whining was just an act?'

'Yes, and I can't tell you how glad I am that it is over,' the woman said, dusting her hands.

The lift doors slid open, and Marius and the children spilled out.

'Frau Doerflinger and Vincenzo are locked inside,' Alice-Miranda told them excitedly, jigging on the spot.

Marius eyeballed Sancia. 'What is she doing out here?'

'Her name is Sancia,' Alice-Miranda began.

'She's Italian Secret Service,' Millie said proudly, 'and boy, can she kick it.'

The woman pulled out a badge and held it up for Marius to see. 'I am sorry. I had no idea until today that you were on Vincenzo's trail as well. We should have been working together,' she apologised.

The lift doors opened again and this time Anton appeared with Alice-Miranda's and Millie's parents as well as Herr Fanger.

'Darlings, are you all right?' Cecelia rushed over and hugged her daughter, then proceeded to hug every one of the children.

Hamish and Pippa raced to embrace Millie too.

'Your children are very brave,' Marius said. 'They have helped us to bring down Signor Grande, the world's most brazen gold smuggler.'

'What about Frau Doerflinger?' Hugh asked.

'Yes, what has my Delphine got to do with all this?' Otto Fanger asked, clutching Gertie to his chest.

'Herr Fanger, your wife has been a rather unfortunate player in this whole business. From what we have discovered, she borrowed a large sum of money from Signor Grande to cover the costs of running the hotel. Of course, she did not realise the potential consequences of doing so. We know that she has tried to free herself from the deal, but Signor Grande is a persuasive man. He threatened to harm you and your dog if she did not do as he wished.'

'Oh my goodness,' Otto said, shielding Gertie's ears.

'If Frau Doerflinger is borrowing money to run this hotel, how can she afford to buy Uncle Florian's?' Alice-Miranda asked.

'Vincenzo wanted the railway station beneath the Grand Hotel Von Zwicky for his smuggling operation,' Sancia said. 'He would have been able to move far greater amounts of gold right under everyone's noses, so to speak. Frau Doerflinger was obliged to follow, and she had her niece run down the Baron's business to force his hand to sell. As part of her payment she would get the hotel, paid for with his dirty money.'

'Alice-Miranda, you were right all along,' Cecelia said, shaking her head.

'Will my Delphine go to prison?' Otto sniffed.

'We can strike a deal if your wife is willing to testify against Signor Grande,' Marius said solemnly.

'My poor Delphine,' the man wailed.

'Poor Delphine?' Sloane wrinkled her lip. 'Poor Herr Fanger for being married to her.'

'Where is Herr Dettwiller?' Millie asked, looking around the room.

'The police have taken him upstairs to speak to his son-in-law and granddaughter,' Anton said. 'They are over the moon that he has been found, thanks to you children.'

'Well, if it's all right with the police, I think it's time we got going to the airport,' Hugh suggested.

'I'm glad I stayed with you guys,' Caprice said. 'You have way more exciting holidays than my family.'

Millie arched her eyebrow at the girl. 'That's not what you were saying a couple of hours ago.'

Hugh shook his head. 'I don't know if we can cope with this much excitement again.'

The group turned to leave.

'Millie, aren't you forgetting something?' Alice-Miranda said, but her friend looked at her blankly. 'I think Herr Roten might need the key.'

'Oh, that.' Millie reached into her pocket and pulled out the token. 'I wasn't going to take it with me, promise.'

Alice-Miranda grinned. 'It really did turn out to be your lucky charm, didn't it?'

'Not just mine,' Millie agreed.

'If we're in the business of returning things, I think you might like to have these back, Herr Fanger.' The Italian Secret Service agent pulled two sparkling diamond hairclips from her pocket.

'Look, Gertie, you will be Papa's beautiful girl once more,' Otto trilled. Gertie's tongue shot out and licked him on the nose.

Sloane grimaced. 'Still gross.'

A chortle of laughter rang out around the room.

'I can't believe I thought the Cresta Run was going to be the most dangerous thing we saw on this trip,' Lucas said, as they all walked towards the lift.

'I thought it would be my sister's skiing,' Sep teased.

Sloane glared at her brother and poked out her tongue.

'One thing's for sure, when Mrs Oliver and Shilly find out about all this, I don't think they'll ever let us out of their sights again,' Alice-Miranda said.

Cecelia laughed. 'I suspect you're right about that, darling.'

'Absolutely,' Hugh agreed. 'Come on, everyone, let's go home.'

And just in case you're wondering . . .

Vincenzo Luciano, otherwise known as Signor Grande, was the head of Italy's largest gang of organised criminals. The man had created an empire worth hundreds of millions of dollars. He had stolen gold from all over Europe, which was then melted into bars and transported to various vaults throughout Switzerland. By catching him, the authorities also nabbed hundreds of smaller crooks who were part of his shady network.

The Black Diamonds Ski School was just a front for the gang of young skiers who transported the gold across the border. Upon hearing of their boss's demise the young men fled from Zermatt and Cervinia. Several of them were caught and charged. Vincenzo himself was sentenced to a maximum term of twenty years in prison. Interpol and the Italian Secret Service still have outstanding cases against him and expect that he will be incarcerated for much longer once they have finished with him.

Delphine Doerflinger was given a two-year home detention order in exchange for testifying against Vincenzo and his gang. She would never forgive herself for allowing greed and ambition to cloud her judgement so badly. After St Moritz had endured a couple of poor snow seasons, she had overextended the hotel finances. She should have told her husband and worked out some other way of getting back on top of things, but when Vincenzo approached her to use the vault with the promise of a huge payday, she thought it was the answer to all her problems. It didn't take her long to realise that she had made a very bad decision indeed.

While Otto was devastated that his wife had deceived him in such a way, he was quick to forgive. He couldn't bear seeing Delphine wearing such an ugly tracking device on her ankle, so he had it covered in diamantes to match Gertie's new collar (although Gertie's was made of real diamonds, of course). Delphine's confinement within the boundaries of their apartment meant that she and Gertie spent a lot more time together. Otto was thrilled that his girls were finally getting closer – though, never more than three feet – as they sat at opposite ends of the lounge each afternoon to watch their favourite game show, *Winners Are Grinners*.

Otto developed a much greater interest in the hotel's financial affairs and took Hugh up on his generous offer to advance a loan until they could get themselves back on their feet. Hugh and Dolly were interested in the Fanger's chocolate-box technology and decided to buy a small stake in the company. Millie thought this was the best news ever and hoped that meant there would be a lifetime supply of Fanger's Chocolate on hand at Alice-Miranda's place.

Valerie confessed all to the Baron and Baroness von Zwicky, having no idea that her aunt was in cahoots with the most notorious criminal in Italy. The woman resigned immediately, ashamed of her deviousness and misguided ambition. She had evaded their initial suspicions because the first page of the telephone contact list Valerie had compiled had been cleverly engineered to reflect the truth, while anything after that contained false phone numbers and lies. Cecelia and the Baroness had only called former guests on the first page, so they had no cause to suspect her of any wrongdoing.

The Von Zwickys were hugely disappointed but reasoned that, if Valerie was so good at manipulating guests to stay away, she should be equally good at enticing them back again. They were both thrilled at the prospect of keeping the hotel and determined to restore it to its former glory and have enrolled in a computer course too. Valerie is working extra-hard, on half her previous wage, to make up for her diabolical activities.

Shilly and Dolly had indeed been shocked to hear of all the drama that embroiled the family during their few days away. As Alice-Miranda predicted, they both vowed never to leave the family to their own devices again.

With help from Sebastien and Nina and some of the townsfolk, Lars Dettwiller finished the renovations to the station. The following summer his museum reopened to great fanfare. His health continues to improve and Nina and her father are thrilled to have him back. Nina's most treasured possession is her silver music box with the tiny fluttering bird.

Alice-Miranda and Nina have been writing regularly, keeping up with each other's news. They can't wait to see each other again next ski season.

Cast of characters

The Highton-Smith-Kennington-Jones household

Alice-Miranda Highton-
  Smith-Kennington-Jones

Cecelia Highton-Smith	Alice-Miranda's adoring mother
Hugh Kennington-Jones	Alice-Miranda's adoring father
Dolly Oliver	Family cook, part-time inventor
Mrs Shillingsworth	Head housekeeper
Cyril	Pilot

Friends of the Highton-Smith-Kennington-Jones family

Millicent Jane McLoughlin-McTavish-McNoughton-McGill	Alice-Miranda's best friend and room mate
Jacinta Headlington-Bear	Alice-Miranda's friend
Sloane Sykes	Alice-Miranda's friend

Sep Sykes	Lucas's best friend and brother of Sloane
Lucas Nixon	Alice-Miranda's cousin
Pippa McLoughlin-McTavish	Millie's mother
Hamish McNoughton-McGill	Millie's father
Nina Ebersold	Alice-Miranda's friend
Sebastien Ebersold	Nina's father
Lars Dettwiller	Nina's grandfather

Fanger's Palace Hotel

Otto Fanger	Owner
Delphine Doerflinger	Otto's wife
Gertie	Otto's beloved Maltese terrier
Brigitte	Receptionist

Grand Hotel Von Zwicky

Florian von Zwicky	Owner and friend of the Highton-Smith-Kennington-Jones family
Giselle von Zwicky	Florian's wife and friend of the Highton-Smith-Kennington-Jones family
Valerie Wiederman	Receptionist
Marius Roten	Driver
Herr Schlappi	Doorman

Others

Caprice Radford	Student at Winchesterfield-Downsfordvale
Anton	Glacier Express train conductor
Andreas	Glacier Express engine driver
Michaela	Zermatt ski instructor
Gunter	St Moritz ski instructor

Sancia	Whiny skier
Vincenzo	Sancia's boyfriend (among other things!)
Klaus Gerber	White Turf chaperone
Johan Heffelfinger	White Turf horse trainer
Christiane Birchler	Receptionist of a St Moritz guesthouse

Glossary of German terms and phrases

Auf Wiedersehen	goodbye
Dummkopf	idiot
Faulpelz	lazybones
Frau	Mrs
Groß	big
Herr	Mr
Ja	yes
Opa	grandpa
Schnüffler	snoop
Wer ist da?	Who's there?
Wo ist die blöde Kuh?	Where is the stupid cow?

About the Author

Jacqueline Harvey taught for many years in girls' boarding schools. She is the author of the bestselling Alice-Miranda series and the Clementine Rose series, and was awarded Honour Book in the 2006 Australian CBC Awards for her picture book *The Sound of the Sea*. She now writes full-time and is working on more Alice-Miranda and Clementine Rose adventures.

www.jacquelineharvey.com.au

Jacqueline Supports

Jacqueline Harvey is a passionate educator who enjoys sharing her love of reading and writing with children and adults alike. She is an ambassador for Dymocks Children's Charities and Room to Read. Find out more at www.dcc.gofundraise.com.au and www.roomtoread.org/australia.

Want to know how it all began?
Read on for a sample of
Alice-Miranda at School

Chapter 1

Alice-Miranda Highton-Smith-Kennington-Jones waved goodbye to her parents at the gate.

'Goodbye, Mummy. Please try to be brave.' Her mother sobbed loudly in reply. 'Enjoy your golf, Daddy. I'll see you at the end of term.' Her father sniffled into his handkerchief.

Before they had time to wave her goodbye, Alice-Miranda skipped back down the hedge-lined path into her new home.

Winchesterfield-Downsfordvale Academy for

Proper Young Ladies had a tradition dating back two and a half centuries. Alice-Miranda's mother, aunt, grandmother, great-grandmother and so on had all gone there. But none had been so young or so willing.

It had come as quite a shock to Alice-Miranda's parents to learn that she had telephoned the school to see if she could start early – she was, after all, only seven and one-quarter years old, and not due to start for another year. But after two years at her current school, Ellery Prep, she felt ready for bigger things. Besides, Alice-Miranda had always been different from other children. She loved her parents dearly and they loved her, but boarding school appealed to her sense of adventure.

'It's much better this way,' Alice-Miranda had smiled. 'You both work so hard and you have far more important things to do than run after me. This way I can do all my activities at school. Imagine, Mummy – no more waiting around while I'm at ballet or piano or riding lessons.'

'But darling, I don't mind a bit,' her mother protested.

'I know you don't,' Alice-Miranda had agreed, 'but you should think about my being away as a holiday. And then at the end there's all the excitement of coming home, except that it's me coming home to you.' She'd hugged her mother and stroked her father's brow as she handed them a gigantic box of tissues. Although they didn't want her to go, they knew there was no point arguing. Once Alice-Miranda made up her mind there was no turning back.

Her teacher, Miss Critchley, hadn't seemed the least surprised by Alice-Miranda's plans.

'Of course, we'll all miss her terribly,' Miss Critchley had explained to her parents. 'But that daughter of yours is more than up to it. I can't imagine there's any reason to stop her.'

And so Alice-Miranda went.

Winchesterfield-Downsfordvale sat upon three thousand emerald-coloured acres. A tapestry of Georgian buildings dotted the campus, with Winchesterfield Manor the jewel in the crown. Along its labyrinth of corridors hung huge portraits of past headmistresses, with serious stares and old-fashioned clothes. The trophy cabinets glittered with treasure and the foyer was lined with priceless antiques. There was not a thing out of place. But from the moment Alice-Miranda entered the grounds she had a strange feeling that something was missing – and she was usually right about her strange feelings.

The headmistress, Miss Grimm, had not come out of her study to meet her. The school's secretary, Miss Higgins, had met Alice-Miranda and her parents at the gate, looking rather surprised to see them.

'I'm terribly sorry, Mr and Mrs Highton-Smith-Kennington-Jones,' Miss Higgins had explained. 'There must have been a mix-up with the dates – Alice-Miranda is a day early.'

Her parents had said that it was no bother and they would come back again tomorrow. But Miss Higgins was appalled to cause such inconvenience and offered to take care of Alice-Miranda until the house mistress arrived.

It was Miss Higgins who had interviewed Alice-Miranda some weeks ago, when she first contacted the school. At that meeting, Alice-Miranda had thought her quite lovely, with her kindly eyes and pretty smile. But today she couldn't help but notice that Miss Higgins seemed a little flustered and talked as though she was in a race.

Miss Higgins showed Alice-Miranda to her room and suggested she take a stroll around the school. 'I'll come and find you and take you to see Cook about some lunch in a little while.'

Alice-Miranda unpacked her case, folded her clothes and put them neatly away into one of the tall chests of drawers. The room contained two single beds on opposite walls, matching chests and bedside tables. In a tidy alcove, two timber desks, each with a black swivel chair, stood side by side. The furniture was what her mother might have called functional. Not beautiful, but all very useful. The room's only hint of elegance came from the fourteen-foot ceiling with ornate cornices and the polished timber floor.

Alice-Miranda was delighted to find an envelope addressed to 'Miss Alice-Miranda Highton-Smith-Kennington-Jones' propped against her pillow.

'How lovely – my own special letter,' Alice-Miranda said out loud. She looked at the slightly tatty brown bear in her open suitcase. 'Isn't that sweet, Brummel?'

She slid her finger under the opening and pulled out a very grand-looking note on official school paper. It read:

Winchesterfield-Downsfordvale Academy for Proper Young Ladies

📖

Dear Miss Highton-Smith-Kennington-Jones,

Welcome to Winchesterfield-Downsfordvale Academy for Proper Young Ladies. It is expected that you will work extremely hard at all times and strive to achieve your very best. You must obey without question all of the school rules, of which there is a copy attached to this letter. Furthermore you must ensure that your behaviour is such that it always brings credit to you, your family and this establishment.

Yours sincerely,
Miss Ophelia Grimm
Headmistress

Winchesterfield-Downsfordvale Academy for Proper Young Ladies School Rules

1. Hair ribbons in regulation colours and a width of $3/4$ of an inch will be tied with double overhand bows.
2. Shoes will be polished twice a day with boot polish and brushes.
3. Shoelaces will be washed each week by hand.
4. Head lice are banned.
5. All times tables to 20 must be learned by heart by the age of 9.
6. Bareback horseriding in the quadrangle is not permitted.
7. All girls will learn to play golf, croquet and bridge.
8. Liquorice will not be consumed after 5 pm.
9. Unless invited by the Headmistress, parents will not enter school buildings.
10. Homesickness will not be tolerated.

Alice-Miranda put the letter down and cuddled the little bear. 'Oh, Brummel, I can't wait to meet Miss Grimm – she sounds like she's very interested in her students.'

Alice-Miranda folded the letter and placed it in the top drawer. She would memorise the school rules later. She popped her favourite photos of Mummy and Daddy on her bedside table and positioned the bear carefully on her bed.

'You be a brave boy, Brummel.' She ruffled his furry head. 'I'm off to explore and when I get back I'll tell you all about it.'